UB

BLADEN COLE:
THE FIRE OF GREED

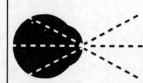

This Large Print Book carries the
Seal of Approval of N.A.V.H.

A BLADEN COLE WESTERN

BLADEN COLE: THE FIRE OF GREED

BILL YENNE

THORNDIKE PRESS
A part of Gale, Cengage Learning

Farmington Hills, Mich • San Francisco • New York • Waterville, Maine
Meriden, Conn • Mason, Ohio • Chicago

GALE
CENGAGE Learning·

LIBRARY OF CONGRESS CATALOGING-IN-PUBLICATION DATA

Yenne, Bill, 1949–
    Bladen Cole: The fire of greed : a Bladen Cole western / by Bill Yenne. — Large Print edition.
        pages cm. — (Thorndike Press Large Print Western)
    ISBN-13: 978-1-4104-6596-2 (hardcover)
    ISBN-10: 1-4104-6596-9 (hardcover)
    1. Large type books. I. Title.
PS3625.E46F57 2014
813'.6—dc23   2013043274

Published in 2014 by arrangement with The Berkley Publishing Group, a member of Penguin Group (USA) LLC, a Penguin Random House Company

Printed in the United States of America
1 2 3 4 5 6 7 18 17 16 15 14

BLADEN COLE:
THE FIRE OF GREED

PROLOGUE

Two horses, a buckskin and a gray, were tied to the hitchrail in front of the low, pale ochre adobe building crouched at the edge of a cluster of cottonwoods. These trees, in and of themselves, constituted evidence of a spring, the presence of which explained the presence of the adobe building, across which was lettered the words ARROYO BLANCO GEN'L MERCHANDISE.

Half general store and half cantina, Arroyo Blanco Gen'l Merchandise was one of those oases of refreshment and sustenance that dotted the lonely wagon roads that crisscrossed the West. Situated in remote and forlorn places, usually near springs, they welcomed travelers as a place where a man could water his horse and usually find something a little stronger to satisfy his own thirst. They were places where a sojourner might buy provisions, graze stock, and find a relatively safe place to camp for the night.

The roan snorted with a sort of muttering half whinny as if to tell his rider that he smelled water — *and* he was very thirsty, *and* very ready to have himself some of that cool wetness dampening his parched throat, *and* he was envious of the two horses at the hitchrail who *had* partaken of that cool wetness.

Bladen Cole patted the roan's neck as if to say that he too could smell the water, and that he too yearned for his face to be submerged in a pool of icy rejuvenation. A slight tug of the reins told the roan that it would all be coming, but *only* in due time.

The roan coughed out another impatient, muttering half whinny as Cole took in the scene in the shallow valley below.

As much as Cole welcomed the sight of Arroyo Blanco Gen'l Merchandise for the promise of the coolness of refreshment, most of all he welcomed it for the sight of the two horses. The bounty hunter had been on this dusty, lightly traveled wagon road leading south from Durango, Colorado, for four days, and the sight of these two horses told him that this was the end of *his* road — or at least it was the climax of four days of boredom mixed with the apprehension that always comes as an integral part of a lonely pursuit.

He had seen those same two horses two days ago, tied to another hitchrail up in Pagosa Springs, Colorado. Then, the cinches on the saddles had been tight, a clear sign of tense and edgy riders, who entertained the likelihood that there would be a need for a quick getaway.

Of course, few things will make a man more tense and high-strung than the knowledge that he is wanted by authorities who plan to string him high upon a gallows.

These two riders had good reason to be nervous, having left four men dead — two at the scene, and two more who died of their wounds the following day — in a botched robbery in Durango.

A warrant had been issued: WANTED, DEAD OR ALIVE.

There had been a great buzzing of angry bluster in Durango that night, but when it came to takers in the enterprise of bringing the perpetrators back "dead or alive," the voices of the loudest blusterers faded like shadows into the night.

Shortly before that night lightened into the following dawn, there had been one taker, and he was on the trail.

Two days had brought the murderers to Pagosa Springs, still anxious that the law was on their tail.

Two more days had brought them to Arroyo Blanco Gen'l Merchandise, increasingly confident that they had gotten away clean. There was no telegraph line to Arroyo Blanco Gen'l Merchandise from Durango — or from anywhere.

Given that he had a choice, Cole had decided that he'd rather accost these riders in a place other than a crowded saloon in a crowded town like Pagosa Springs. He chose to wait patiently until the riders were no longer so wide-eyed in their vigilance as to be at the edge of careless jumpiness. Somebody could get hurt, and Cole was just selfish enough to not want it to be him.

It was obvious that after four days on the trail with no perceived hint of a posse in pursuit, the two men had relaxed. Cole could see this in the loosened cinches that allowed the hard-ridden horses some respite and a chance to relax as well.

Durango was four days behind them, and nothing lay ahead of these men but the 150-million-acre labyrinth of mountains and canyons that stretched from West Texas to the deadly Mojave of California. Out here, lawlessness was a way of life. Across the length and breadth of the territories of New Mexico and Arizona, civilization by the standards of the East, or even of Denver, existed only in a scattering of islands set in a turbulent sea.

Lincoln County, which comprised most of southeastern New Mexico, was the case in point that was often discussed as the "way things are out here."

The county had been little more than a running gunfight for about the past two years, as cattleman John Chisum and his cowboys rose up in insurrection against the Murphy-Dolan gang that had been running the place like a private kingdom. Both factions defied all efforts at the importation of law and order from any quarter. As the bodies piled up on each side, the best that Lew Wallace, the former general and now the territorial governor, could do, was declare a general amnesty in a desperate attempt to halt the Lincoln County War.

Yet Lincoln County, with its cattle industry, was the essence of civilization by comparison to the wild mountainous wilderness *west* of the Rio Grande, where Geronimo and the Chiricahua Apache were the only form of civilization, and where outsiders, even if well armed, treaded only at their peril.

If a man was so inclined, he could lose himself forever in these 150 million acres which the legal system had timidly ignored, or linger long enough to reinvent himself and move on to the new horizons of California. These two men, who had departed Durango under a tempestuous cloud, were men who were so inclined.

Cole circled along the rimrock above the adobe building to its southern approach, so as to advance toward it from its blind side. Keeping an eye on the human watering hole, he watered the roan in the stream that flowed downhill from the spring, loosened the saddle cinch, and tethered his mount in the shade of some cottonwoods.

He spun the cylinder of his Colt, more out of habit than useful purpose, and began walking up the slight incline toward Arroyo Blanco Gen'l Merchandise.

The bounty hunter was about fifty feet from the front door, approaching from the side, when he heard the enormous ruckus of a sudden argument. He was thirty feet from the door with his gun drawn when two disheveled murderers and a Mexican girl exploded through the door, each one shouting and screaming.

Cole leveled his sidearm and demanded, "Hands behind your necks . . . drop to your knees."

There were whiskey-stained expressions

12

of stunned disbelief, and one of the men impulsively went for his gun.

CHAPTER 1

"Fine day, señor doctor," the young man in the virtually spotless white shirt said with a smile, as he entered the low-ceilinged adobe building a short distance from the Plaza in the center of Santa Fe.

"That it is, lad," said the older man with his boots resting comfortably on his desk. "That it is. I 'spect we'll be getting a bit of heat this afternoon, though."

"*Sí,* señor doctor, I 'spect you are right."

"Let me compliment you on your rapidly expanding English skills," the older man said.

"*Muchas gracias* . . . um . . . Thank you very much, señor doctor."

As the teenager took out a broom and began sweeping the office of the coroner of New Mexico's territorial capital, Amos Richardson turned his attention back to the pages of the *Santa Fe New Mexican,* the newspaper that rightfully boasted of being

15

the oldest English-language daily between the Mississippi River and the Pacific coast.

Today, as for most days the past year, the news was dominated by the coming of the Atchison, Topeka & Santa Fe Railroad. Building westward from Atchison, Kansas, the road had put "Santa Fe" in its name as a goal, but it had taken a dozen years and a full-blown war of intrigue, chicanery, and bloodshed against the rival Denver & Rio Grande Western up in Colorado in order for it finally to come close to its namesake.

It was 1880, and the great tide of civilization was stretching its tendrils far into the West, and these were the steel tendrils of the railroads. By now, the westward spread of that tide had more or less tamed places such as Denver and Cheyenne, linking them to Chicago or Omaha by a matter of days, rather than weeks or months.

Now it was the turn of Santa Fe to be joined to the nation by these arteries of steel. When Richardson had first come to New Mexico Territory on the Santa Fe Trail, it took around two months for a wagon train to get out here from Kansas City. With the railroad, the same trip could be completed in a few days.

Ironically, for reasons best understood by the civil engineers who surveyed the route, the railroad didn't actually pass through Santa Fe, but through the town of Lamy, a dozen miles south. However, even as the branch line into the city was still being built, Santa Fe was starting to feel the full effect of its connection to the rest of the country.

"Domingo, the railroad will change everything," the coroner said with a burst of civic pride.

"*Sí,* doctor." The boy smiled. The blank look in his cheerful eyes revealed that he had no idea what Richardson meant. In all his life, he had not been farther than a day's ride from where he now stood. Nor had he ever seen a railroad or a locomotive, except as a line illustration in the pages of the *Santa Fe New Mexican.* Nevertheless, he knew that the railroad was something that pleased his boss, so it was something that pleased him as well.

Amos Richardson took pride in his adopted city. He had long been one of Santa Fe's prominent men, a far cry from the refugee he had been when he arrived after the war. A military man who had served in a losing army, he had left a place where he knew he had no future to seek a fresh future in the ambiguous West, a place whose vastness promised much, but *almost always* delivered on the promise of a fresh start.

Richardson had found his own fresh start here in this long-established island of civilization at the intersection of the Santa Fe Trail and the old Spanish trail coming north from Mexico. Santa Fe was already the capital of Nuevo Mexico when the Pilgrims were still struggling in the wilderness in what was not yet Massachusetts. By its nature as a crossroads with a history stretching back for a quarter of a millennium, Santa Fe had always been a city of immigrants and drifters. Some came as wanderers and continued their wandering. Some came as wanderers and stayed on. Dr. Amos Richardson came, and he stayed.

The turnover in doctors provided opportunities, but irregular income. The turnover in coroners provided a *dependable* income, and a place of prominence in the political hierarchy of the city and the territory. The onetime refugee physician was now the sort of prominent citizen who could honestly welcome a connection to the nation that had defeated his own nation in the war.

He was no stranger to the inner circle, and occasionally the poker table, of Governor Lew Wallace, who had worn general's stars and a blue uniform at the same time that Richardson was wearing gray. Such was the nature of the melting pot of dissolved past affiliations that was Santa Fe.

"Dr. Richardson, señor." Domingo interrupted, stepping into his boss's office. "There's a gringo . . . umm . . . a man who wants to see you."

Richardson glanced out the window. He could make out a rider on horseback. He made a mental note to have Domingo fetch a pail of water and wash the windows.

He rose from his chair and stepped out onto the street.

"You must be the coroner," the stranger asserted.

"You would be correct in that assumption, sir," Richardson replied, both refreshed and taken aback by the man's directness. This man's eyes were alert and piercing, but otherwise, his appearance was that of a disheveled vagabond who had seen neither razor nor bathwater in a week.

"I've got a couple of customers for you," the man explained, nodding to the two horses he led. The clouds of flies that swarmed about the bundle tied to each of the saddles told the coroner that the contents of the canvas-wrapped parcels had once been animate.

"Domingo, could you lend a hand?" Richardson said, stepping close to inspect

19

the stranger's cargo.

The man dismounted, secured the horses to the nearest hitchrail, and helped Richardson and his assistant carry the bodies inside to the coroner's workroom.

"Domingo, you'd better go for some ice," Richardson said as he directed the stranger to help him place one of the parcels on a specialized table that had obviously been the interim resting place for innumerable such objects before.

Richardson gave a cursory glance at the bullet wound to the chest, and probed it with a long, shiny metal tool.

"Won't need an autopsy to determine cause of death," the coroner said casually. "How did you come to be in possession of Mr. Doe here?"

"His name is Griffith," the stranger said, handing Richardson a folded piece of paper.

"So I see," Richardson said, comparing the picture and description on the wanted poster to the man lying on his table. "Healed scar in the shape of a V on the left cheek . . . receding hairline. Yes, this is Mr. Griffith."

"I've got papers on the other one too," the stranger confirmed.

"I have no doubt you do." Richardson nodded. "You still haven't told me how you came by these gentlemen, although by my observation of that weapon on your hip, I could venture a guess."

"I have papers on that as well," the stranger said.

"Of that I have no doubt." The coroner chuckled as the man handed him a warrant. He needed only to glance at the papers to see that they authorized one Bladen Cole to apprehend the two men and return them to Durango, Colorado — dead or alive.

"This warrant's been issued up in Colorado," Richardson said, handing the warrant back to Cole. "Why did you bring them here?"

"Would you want to be spending four days on the trail in this heat with this rotten cargo?" Cole asked, obviously stifling a grin. "A signed and notarized death certificate is the next best thing. And it saves the authorities up in Durango the cost and aggravation of putting 'em in the ground."

"You know the law, Mr. Cole," Richardson said, kneeling to take a look at the face of the second man and to compare his observations to the picture on the second wanted poster. The missing front teeth and the long-healed scar tissue left no doubt.

"Used to wear a badge," Cole said, in reply to the coroner's observation.

"And now you ply the trade of a bounty

hunter."

"Don't like being too long in one place."

"What was her name?" Richardson asked with a smile.

"Sally Lovelace," Cole answered with a startled expression. "How'd you know about . . . ?"

"Been around a bit, sir. Lots of men wander and some settle down. When a man who's settled . . . in a lawman's job for instance . . . starts wandering again, nine times out of ten, there's a woman involved."

By now, Domingo had returned with a wheelbarrow full of ice, and he helped Richardson slide the two corpses through a trapdoor and down a wooden slide which led to a cool subterranean cellar. The younger man then disappeared with the wheelbarrow through a door at the end of the room. Cole could hear the sounds far below of ice being dumped into a metal tub as Richardson slammed the trapdoor.

"Miss Lovelace is none of my business," Richardson said as he pumped some water into a large metal sink and rinsed his hands. Without asking, he filled a metal cup with water and handed it to Cole. There was no need to ask.

Nor was there need for Cole to ask as he handed the cup back to the coroner for a refill.

When Domingo reappeared, Richardson sent him to fetch the justice of the peace, and invited Cole into his office.

"Have a seat while I fill out the death forms on these two," he said as he rustled in a desk drawer. "We'll get the J.P. over here to view the deceased and sign off, and you'll have what you need to go over yonder to the county clerk to get your death certificates."

"Feels good to sit down in something other than a saddle," Cole said, removing his hat and wiping his brow with his bandanna.

"I can't help but detect a trace of the Old Dominion in your accent, Mr. Cole," Richardson said, glancing up from his paperwork.

"I had you pegged for a Virginian yourself, Doc," Cole replied.

"Fauquier County," the coroner nodded.

"Caroline County."

"Were you in the war?" Richardson asked.

"Too young, really," Cole explained. At the time, he had longed to be old enough to wear gray and fight for Virginia, but over time, his perspective had changed, as it might be expected to change the more one meets men who are making do with one arm, one leg, or other battle damage. "I rode in a couple of raids, but not until it was almost over. I didn't turn seventeen till '65. My brother enlisted in '64. I rode with him a few times, but I was never in uniform. What about you?"

"Yes, I was." The older man nodded. "I was a doctor at the time, practicing in Warrenton. Virginia needed doctors. I volunteered. Served as the surgeon with the 7th Virginia Cavalry. Company A, the Fauquier Mountain Rangers. Served under Turner Ashby."

"That's a well-known name." Cole nodded, recognizing the celebrated Virginia cavalry commander.

"I was with him when he died at Harrisonburg," Richardson nodded. "At his side . . . couldn't do anything. He was too far gone."

"Been out West long?" Cole asked.

"Came out in late '65." The coroner nodded. "There just wasn't any future in Virginia."

"What was her name?" Cole smiled.

Richardson looked stunned for a split second, then he too smiled.

"Touché, Mr. Cole," he said, glancing back at the paperwork that he was filling out.

"Did those gentlemen put up much of a fight?" Richardson asked, changing the subject.

"That was their intention," Cole confirmed. "One of 'em drew his gun. The other had hold of a Mexican girl so I had to aim a little more carefully."

"I have to commend you, Mr. Cole."

"How so?"

"Single kill shot to each," Richardson said, nodding in the general direction of his cellar morgue. "You certainly know your trade. As you can imagine, I see a great many gunfight deaths crossing my table. Bloody mess, most of 'em."

"Only takes one shot to kill a man." Cole nodded. "I don't care to do more than is necessary. Truth be told, I wanted to take 'em alive. I caught up to 'em at Pagosa Springs, but figured it would be a helluva shootout, so I let 'em calm down and waited until Arroyo Blanco. Oh well . . . at least nobody else got hurt."

"What about the Mexican girl?"

"She got a fright she won't soon forget." Cole shrugged. "But she had nary a scratch otherwise."

"You work clean," Richardson commented. "Sign of professionalism, I 'spect."

Cole just shrugged.

"I knew a bounty hunter a few years back who favored the use of a shotgun," Richardson continued.

"Reckon that's what you mean by messy."

"Not like what I saw in the war, but often a helluva mess."

"Shotgun's exceptional for intimidation," Cole replied. "It'll scare the bejesus out of somebody. Also good if you aren't a good shot, or if you don't care which innocent parties might catch some stray buckshot. Otherwise the only thing a bird gun is good for is hunting birds."

"As I observed, Mr. Cole," Richardson said as he scratched his signature at the bottom of the various forms that he had been filling out. "You are indeed a professional."

CHAPTER 2

Red chilies.

As Bladen Cole lowered himself into a chair in the small, low-ceilinged Santa Fe cafe called Refugio del Viajero, preparing to have his first store-bought supper in nearly a week, there were strings of dried red chili peppers hanging on the wall near the doorway though which a fire crackled and appetizing aromas wafted.

Long ago, more than a decade back, when Cole was new to the West and herding cattle over around Breckenridge, Texas, he had met someone who told him that the only thing anybody out in New Mexico ate was a mush made out of boiled beans, a kind of flatbread called a "tor-*tee*-ya," and red chilies.

One of the first things he noticed when he finally found himself out in New Mexico those many years ago, was that the fellow had been right. The second thing he noticed was that they ate a lot of other things as well, but that those red chilies, which were about the size of a finger and hotter than the muzzle of a rifle, were everywhere.

Cole had not been in New Mexico for years, and would not have been there now had he not been led by circumstance, and he had forgotten about those small, red peppers.

Cole had been sleeping on the ground and subsisting on salt pork and hardtack for five days, so tonight he was ready for a soft bed and a hot meal. He was even a bit nostalgic for the searing heat of the chilies.

He had two copies of the signed and notarized death certificates in his pocket, and he had sent a wire to Durango, telling them to expect him. He had added that they should have the reward money ready. When the sun rose tomorrow, he would be back on the trail, and back to making his bed on the ground, so tonight he would eat well, and sleep long.

He had gone into this place a few doors off Santa Fe's central plaza on the recommendation of Dr. Amos Richardson, the fellow Virginian who seemed to have taken a liking to him because they *were* fellow Virginians. It was small and dark, but so very cool, which contrasted to the hot, dusty

day that was now fading toward sunset outside.

There were only a handful of patrons in
this place, which looked to have been some
sort of hostelry for about two hundred
years. Nevertheless, the coroner had insisted
that it was a good place for a hot meal, and
this seemed to be confirmed by the fra-
grances that emanated from the kitchen.
Cole's fellow Virginian had even recommended a favorite dish.

Richardson had not, however, prepared
Cole for the sight that was about to greet
his eyes. There was a rustling movement in
the corner of his eye and the hint of a cool
breeze on his cheek. He glanced sideways to
see the flourishing skirts of one of those
colorful dresses that young women in New
Mexico favored.

His eyes, still getting used to the dimness
in the room, roamed upward, past a narrow
waist, a generous bosom, and rested on a
face that would have, had he been intending to say something, left him speechless.

Her lips were the deep crimson of the red
chilies, and her hair was the color of the
night. Her eyes, dark and deep, flickered
with the reflected light of the candle on the
table, and with the animation of her spirit.

"May I help you, señor?" she said and smiled.

Maybe it was the moody dimness, or his not having been in the near proximity of a woman in the better part of a week — and having not seen a truly attractive woman in a month — that utterly disarmed Bladen Cole.

"Dr. Richardson," Cole said after a pause that was a component of his shaking off the initial speechlessness. "He recommends your *carne asada.*"

"Good choice, señor," she replied with a disarming smile.

He watched her glide about the room, efficiently taking orders, topping off wineglasses, and interacting with the patrons with a genuine warmth. She looked very young, barely out of her teens, but she carried herself with a grace and elegance that was beyond her years. He watched as she spoke to another woman who seemed to be in change of the place, a woman who seemed to be an older version of herself, equally graceful in a regal sort of way, a woman whom Cole took to be her mother.

At last the plate arrived, the slices of beef still sizzling, and just enough red chili peppers to keep it interesting. He savored every bite as his thoughts retraced a day that had begun with him tying two dead bodies to their saddles in a snake-infested wilderness, and had ended here.

Things had gone more smoothly and efficiently in Santa Fe than he had anticipated. He was lucky to have found the coroner to be a practical man who didn't insist that he cool his heels a few days for an elaborate autopsy.

He was equally pleased that the justice of the peace was an efficient man. Of course, it didn't hurt that he was authorized to impound the property of the deceased for thirty days or until it was claimed by next of kin. The odds that these two characters had next of kin that were going to make a ten-day round-trip to collect their horses, saddles, and assorted firearms were between slim and none, which would leave the J.P. in possession of these unclaimed items, which could be sold for cash.

"How was your meal, señor?" the young woman asked with a smile as she came to clear the table. They both chuckled as Cole gestured to his empty plate.

"I'm trying to place your accent," he said as she returned to pour him a cup of coffee. "It's not Spanish, is it?"

"You have a good ear, *monsieur,*" she said, looking at him with he dark piecing eyes

31

and smiling with her lips the color of dried red chilies. *"Je suis Français."*

With this, she swirled away, ending what Cole had hoped would be the opening exchange of a conversation.

Bladen Cole relished his next cup of coffee ten hours later, at the cafe in the lobby of his hotel as he finished a plate of eggs and red chilies. He studied the newspaper idly, looking for something of interest other than local news about people he did not know and articles about the arrival in New Mexico of the Atchison, Topeka & Santa Fe Railroad.

"Mr. Cole."

He glanced up at the sound of someone speaking his name.

"Good morning Mr. Cole," Dr. Amos Richardson said as he crossed the room. "I'm glad I caught you before you saddled up for Colorado."

"Sheets felt so good I decided to sleep in," Cole admitted as the big clock across the room began to toll seven times.

"How was your supper last night?"

"Couldn't have been more enjoyable," Cole said, smiling slightly and gesturing for Richardson to join him at his table.

"I take it that you met Nicolette de la

Gravière," Richardson said with a grin as the waiter efficiently poured a second cup of coffee.

"Didn't actually catch her name," Cole admitted. "But she *did* say that she was French. I guess that's her mother who runs the place?"

"That's Therese. She built that place from a seedy cantina into the best place in town for a steak, if you like Mexican-style, and I have learned to like it."

"They come from France, then?"

"They've been around since Nicolette was about ten or so," the coroner began. "They came up from Old Mexico, refugees from the overthrow of the Second Empire. That's why Therese calls the place Refugio del Viajero. They came over from France when Nicolette was just a little bitty kid. They were part of that big French contingent that Louie-Napoléon sent over with Maximilian when he annexed Mexico."

"That adventure didn't work out so well," Cole said, commenting on the ill-fated scheme by Napoléon Bonaparte's nephew to have a New World empire.

"In hindsight, one does see all the flaws," Richardson said with a shrug. "At the time, it seemed like it was going to last forever. The European armies really clobbered the

Mexicans at first. Nicolette's uncle was one of Max's generals. He helped do it. Her daddy was a deputy minister of some kind in Maximilian's government. She sort of grew up in the royal court, but when the whole thing fell apart, everybody had to run for their lives. Her daddy wasn't so lucky. He caught a bullet from the same firing squad that shot old Max."

"Poor kid," Cole said.

"Lots of kids lost daddies on this continent in the sixties," Richardson reminded him.

"So true."

"Let me get to the point of why I interrupted your breakfast," the coroner said, changing the subject. "Something has come up, and I might have a business proposition for you."

"Go on," Cole said, perking up his ears.

"You've no doubt sensed the excitement about the arrival of the Atchison, Topeka & Santa Fe."

"Hard to miss."

"I know that you're anxious to get back to Colorado to claim some reward money," Richardson said as Cole nodded, "but I have a job for you that would add substantially to that nest egg . . . indeed would dwarf it."

"I'm listening."

"Last night, as you were basking in the radiance of Nicolette de la Gravière, there was a robbery," the coroner said, lowering his voice to near a whisper. "The Atchison, Topeka & Santa Fe payroll was taken from a baggage car on a siding about twenty miles east of Lamy. A man was killed."

"How much did they get away with?"

"Something in the neighborhood of nine thousand dollars."

"*Whooee,*" Cole replied. "That's a big one. I didn't hear anyone talking about that this morning."

"You won't. It's being kept quiet. I was told in confidence by a friend who is well connected with the railroad people."

"I take it that the railroad people want me to get the robbers and the dough?" Cole queried.

"I did suggest your services for the task," Richardson said with a nod.

"Why doesn't the sheriff pull together a big posse and go after them?"

"The railroad men would rather keep the whole affair on the quiet side."

"Don't they have hired guns of their own? I seem to recall that they hired a whole army of gunslingers to battle the Denver & Rio Grande last year."

"Yes, they do. That is clearly one option,

but not the *preferable* one in their opinion. They believe that the fewer people involved the better it is for their goal of keeping things quiet. If you are the least bit interested in this, I'd like to introduce you to the Atchison, Topeka & Santa Fe men."

CHAPTER 3

"Your reputation precedes you, Mr. Cole," the tall man with the well-trimmed beard said, standing to shake the bounty hunter's hand. "My name is Ezra Waldron, this is Joseph Ames."

In his denim trousers and scuffed boots, Cole felt a bit out of place opposite the well-dressed gentlemen in the well-appointed offices of the Atchison, Topeka & Santa Fe Railroad. At least he had sent his shirts out for laundering the night before.

Substantially overweight, Ames groaned as he stood to shake Cole's hand.

"Dr. Richardson has proposed you for a job which is of utmost importance to us," Waldron continued.

"That's what he said," Cole said and nodded. "It sounds like you need to have a payroll retrieved."

"That's correct, sir. We need to employ the services of a bounty hunter, and he tells that you, sir, are *the* man for the job."

"I'm impressed with his skill and professionalism," Richardson interjected.

"I'm curious why you don't send out the guns you've already got," Cole said. "I heard tell that you had the likes of Bat Masterson and Doc Holliday on your payroll when you were warring with the Denver & Rio Grande up in Royal Gorge."

"Among others," Waldron said, clearly displeased at being reminded of the fact that his railroad had been defeated by its rival both in court *and* on the battlefield. "But the results were less than desired."

"Discretion is of the utmost importance," Ames explained. "The idea of sending one man is preferable to the notion of sending a dozen."

"Fewer men to tell the tale," Waldron said.

"That's another thing that confuses me," Cole said. "Why is it so damned important that this thing be kept such a big secret?"

"If I may speak candidly," Waldron said. "The lifeblood of our industry is capital, and the source of our capital is investment. This is a critical time for the Atchison, Topeka & Santa Fe. We have barely reached our line into New Mexico, and our need for capital is frankly enormous if we are going to get across this territory and link up with the Pacific coast. Investors are naturally leery of investments in the barbarous West. If the capital markets were to get wind of a robbery of this size occurring within twenty miles of the Santa Fe junction at Lamy, potential investors would just as soon put their money into roads which are located in the East, where such brazen thefts are unlikely."

"Or even worse, they might shift the favors of their wallets to shares of the Denver & Rio Grande," Ames chimed in.

"I see." Cole nodded.

"Why approach the matter with a sledgehammer when it can be addressed with the precision of a surgical scalpel?" Waldron asked rhetorically.

"It this something that interests you?" Ames asked.

Cole nodded.

"Is this something of which you feel yourself capable?" Waldron asked pointedly.

"How many robbers?" Cole asked, bypassing an answer to Waldron's question.

"There were three," Ames explained. "Although they may also have had a lookout."

"They probably did," Cole nodded. "Do you suppose they might have been working for the Denver & Rio Grande?"

"Why?" Waldron asked rhetorically. "Unless they wanted to rub salt into wounds. As you know, the Denver & Rio Grande *won*. They defeated us. *They* won the rights to the route through Royal Gorge. Besides that, these robbers escaped to the *south* not north toward Colorado."

"South? Could they be headed south to Lincoln County?" Richardson asked, referencing the Lincoln County War, which was still raging unabated across lawless southeastern New Mexico.

"I wouldn't rule it out," Waldron agreed, his voice taking on a conspiratorial tone. "I would not rule out the possibility that one or another of the factions down there would undertake a misadventure such as this in an attempt to obtain the resources to finance their spiteful warfare."

"It would be just like those hoodlums in Lincoln County," Ames added. "Especially that homicidal maniac William Bonney, of whom we have read in the papers."

Cole said nothing in the furtherance of this avenue of speculation. He could not imagine a Lincoln County connection. The factions down there were too absorbed in their own affairs and in the endless rounds of feuding and revenge to have an interest in the Atchison, Topeka & Santa Fe. For its

40

distance from the world of Lincoln County, the railroad might as well be on the opposite side of the continent.

"All the more reason to play it quietly and send a lone professional," Ames continued.

"I know that Governor Wallace would not like to see a Santa Fe posse getting mixed up with any of the Lincoln County boys," Richardson interjected.

"Does this sound like something you can handle, Mr. Cole?" Waldron repeated.

"Yes," Cole said after a thoughtful pause.

"Do you think that you can catch them before they reach Lincoln County?" Ames asked.

"Lincoln County is two days' ride," Cole answered. "The city of Lincoln is the better part of five, more or less. That's plenty of time."

Left unsaid was his solid belief that the bandits would not be going to Lincoln County at all.

"So you think you can do it?" Ames asked.

"As I said," Cole repeated. "I can do the job."

"*Will* you?" Ames asked.

"What's in it for me?" It was Cole's turn for pointed questions.

"We'll pay you a thousand dollars," Waldron said.

"Well . . . I don't know . . ." Cole said, finding it hard to be reticent about such a substantial sum.

"Fifteen hundred," Ames said anxiously after a long pause in the conversation.

"What's your price?" Waldron asked impatiently.

"How's two grand?" Cole asked. "As you were saying, this is worth a lot more to you than the cash value of the payroll."

"Conditional on absolute discretion?" Ames asked. "Nobody knows about this? Nothing about the nature of the robbery or the men you seek would be divulged to anyone along the way?"

"My lips would be sealed."

"I'll draw up the papers," Ames said, obviously pleased for the opportunity to lower his considerable bulk back into his chair.

"Can you advance me two hundred to cover provisioning expenses?" Cole asked.

Waldron took out his wallet and handed the money to the bounty hunter.

"In the interest of utmost discretion," Waldron said after shaking the hand of his contractor, "it would not disappoint us if the perpetrators of this crime did not survive. Just knowing that they had been apprehended would be good enough for us . . . if you know what I mean."

Dead or alive, Cole thought to himself, with an emphasis on *dead.*

By noon, Bladen Cole was on the trail.

Ames had been right. A mile south of the siding where the robbery had taken place, three riders had been met by a fourth, who was leading two pack mules. The depth of the tracks made by the mules indicated that the loot contained a substantial amount of gold as well as currency.

They had a twelve-hour lead, but they were carrying a heavy load. Cole figured that he could cut their lead in half by mid-day tomorrow, and probably overtake them the following day.

Cole doubted that this climactic encounter would occur in infamous Lincoln County, but there were no signs on the county lines. Cole wagered the group would eventually turn west, get across the Rio Grande, and into the maze of mountains between the river and the Mogollon Rim.

As he rode, Cole thought about the irony of his being in New Mexico, and heading south, deeper into the territory with every mile he put behind him. He had left New Mexico ten years ago for a reason, and he had once vowed never to return.

Bladen Cole had come here with his

brother Will, just two men at the threshold of their twenties looking for adventure and fortune, as young men often do. When they had left Virginia after the War Between the States, they had spent several seasons herding cattle from Texas up into Kansas, where they picked up a contract hunting buffalo to feed railroad work crews. Gradually, they worked their way farther west, following the promising trail toward the gold and silver strikes in New Mexico Territory.

One night they dropped into a saloon down in Silver City, one of those places where prospectors came down out of the Mogollon Mountains with too much gold dust and not enough sense.

The brothers from Virginia had been drinking far too long for their own good that night, as young men barely into their twenties occasionally do. So too had been another pair of young men barely into their twenties. As often happens in circumstances such as prevailed that night, neither pair of young men walked away, as they should have, from a quarrel that ensued.

Perhaps, if Bladen had tugged at Will's sleeve and insisted that they let the two men go, it never would have happened, but he had not, and it *did*.

What happened next, happened fast. It

happened in such a fog that Bladen never really knew which man drew his gun first, but Bladen knew he was the *last.*

When the dust had settled, two men lay dead, and one was Will. The fourth man, the cowardly one with the narrow face of a rodent who had shot Will, had vanished into the night.

Bladen spent the next several months searching in vain for the rat-faced man who had taken his brother's life. At last, he realized that he was being eaten alive by circumstances that he could never change, so he headed north. He had no particular destination, he rode only to be someplace new, someplace that was not so packed with reminders of Will.

It had been about a year or so after Will's death that Bladen had found himself in a small mining town not far from the bustling metropolis of Cripple Creek, Colorado. Through a series of auspicious events, he played a role in foiling a bank robbery and was asked by the city fathers to consider becoming their sheriff.

It had seemed like the right thing to do at the time, and perhaps it actually was. He had been starting to think that he should be thinking about his future, so he accepted, and decided to settle down.

It was then that he met Sally Lovelace, a young woman with whom there was a mutual attraction and a seriousness that had *almost* led to a wedding. Bladen Cole had always fancied himself as a man who was not meant to be too long in one place, but for a time it seemed that the effects of a steady job, and *mainly* the effects of Sally Lovelace, had changed him.

However, before that could happen, Sally took a fancy to a high roller who swept her off her feet. J. R. Hubbard was one of those men who attracted the attention of good women like a magnet attracts iron filings. Sally had swooned to his charms, and had allowed herself to be seduced by the honey of his sweet talk, and by starry promises that could never have been fulfilled by a man on a sheriff's salary.

Around the same time that Hubbard swept Sally away to San Francisco, Bladen unearthed a festering pool of corruption in the city's government, but he was thwarted politically in his attempts to bring the perpetrators in high places to justice.

Angrily tossing his badge on the mayor's desk, he climbed on his horse and, as he had done after Will had died, just rode away without looking back.

Not long thereafter, in a mining town up

in Wyoming Territory, he began seeing wanted posters of a particular bank-robbing duo, and he decided that the reward money looked good. It also looked like his future.

Several wanted posters, and several successful pursuits later, his remarkable skill with a Colt .45 had found Bladen Cole with a new career — and one that agreed with his innate restlessness.

He drifted up into Wyoming and into Montana Territory, following the trails of malefactors and collecting bounties. Last winter, when the snows were beginning to blow down across the plains from the Arctic, he had chased three criminals north of the Marias River into Blackfeet country.

The farther he roamed, the more he thought he was putting New Mexico behind him.

Now, he was *back.*

Maybe it was the inevitability of fate.

CHAPTER 4

From flattened bottoms the shape and color of anvils, dark purple-gray and menacing, the cumulus clouds billowed upward into downy tops the color and shape of cotton exploding from its bolls. They reminded Bladen Cole of the fields of his boyhood home, so distant in both time and space, in old Virginia.

He took a cautious sip from his canteen and hoped that he and the roan would cross paths with a spring, or even a year-round stream, pretty soon.

Cole took out the gold pocket watch that had once belonged to his father, wound it, and checked the time. He had been on the trail of the four men and their livestock for more than a day now, and the tracks showed no signs of their having slackened their pace. Indeed, they no doubt knew that haste was their only protection from the posse they had every reason to believe was in pursuit.

He scanned the surrounding mesas, shimmering in the dry heat of the mid-afternoon sun. In a landscape in which even the snakes and lizards had sought the shade, his eyes fell upon a cluster of black specks near the southern horizon.

He took out his small brass spyglass to get a closer look. Buzzards were circling the death site of some unlucky creature, probably a black-tailed deer that had been nailed by a cougar overnight. It probably had been killed at a watering hole, which gave Cole hope that he could soon water the roan.

Over the course of the next hour, Cole drew ever closer to the circling, scavenging birds. From time to time, one or two would dive, while others would climb into the sky. They were taking turns picking at the carcass.

At last, he crested a small ridge and gazed down at the clusters of buzzards.

There was no spring, and no deer. The birds were pecking away at two human bodies.

Cole looked around, straining his eyes to see whether there was any additional sign of people in the vicinity.

As he rode wide of the place where the bodies lay, he found the tracks that he had been following, as they continued south from the death scene. There were four sets of horseshoe tracks, and two of mule shoes. His initial supposition that the four men had been ambushed by the Apache was contradicted by the continued orderliness of the trail. An Apache attack would have scattered the horses, and they had not been scattered.

When he returned to examine the scene, he found the scavengers well into their meal.

He approached the first body, which was lying faceup near the charred embers of a fire. He shooed away the buzzards, who complained with raspy voices before reconvening at the second body some distance away.

Cole knelt to examine the remains. The eyes are usually the first to go, and there was little left of the face. It was a grisly sight not for the faint of heart, but Cole had seen worse.

There was a large hole in the forehead, which the buzzards had used to their advantage. Cole kicked the head to one side and saw a bullet hole in the back of skull. The hole in the forehead was the exit wound. The man had been shot in the back of the head at close range, probably while sitting and facing the fire.

He walked to the other body, which lay facedown about thirty yards away. Once again, he interrupted the late lunch of a cluster of angry birds. There was evidence that this man had been shot in the left shoulder and in the back several times. It was hard to tell exactly how many times because of the way that the buzzards had been picking at the body.

Piecing things together, Cole surmised that the man at the campfire had been shot first, probably taken by surprise. The other man had started running and had been hit in the shoulder before suffering a fatal shot.

The bounty hunter rolled him over and started going through his pockets for personal effects that would be useful later in making an identification. He found a letter, handwritten in a woman's hand, which he pocketed without reading and a pass of the kind that were issued to railroad employees. It was from the Denver & Rio Grande Western Railroad. The man also had two silver dollars in his pocket.

A search of the other body yielded another Denver & Rio Grande pass and a pocket watch slightly smaller than the one Cole he himself carried. There was less than a dollar's worth of coins in the man's pocket. Cole left these, but kept the watch and the two passes.

Ezra Waldron had been swift to dismiss any complicity by the rival railroad, yet apparently that railroad, or at least two of its employees, was somehow involved. On one level, Cole was pleased to have seen the cocky Waldron's assumption disproved; on another, he wondered what this meant.

He allowed himself about fifteen minutes of exertion to try to cover the bodies with boulders before he started out again. It was a fool's errand, he thought. Even if the buzzards were deterred, the coyotes could dig under the rocks — if they were feeling ambitious. Still, there was something in his nature that insisted all humans deserved the dignity of at least an *attempt* at a decent burial.

As he carried rocks, Cole wondered about the railroad passes.

Had these thieves really been Denver & Rio Grande men?

Was the railroad itself behind the robbery?

If the latter, why had the men fled south, rather than heading north to the Denver & Rio Grande stronghold in Colorado?

Why had these two been murdered by their accomplices?

Probably it was the oldest reason in the book — nine grand split two ways is worth twice as much as when it's split four ways.

The western sky was turning the color of a butternut squash when he finally came upon a cluster of vegetation that marked the presence of a spring. Smelling the water, his roan practically galloped to the thin trickle. When he dismounted, Cole lay facedown, submerging his face up to his ears as the roan slurped.

After refilling his canteens and resting his horse for a while, Cole pressed on, intending to use all of the daylight that he was offered before camping for the night.

The demise of the two men would improve the odds for Cole when he finally caught up with the survivors, but in the meantime, it gave them each two saddled horses to trade off as mounts.

It grew cooler as the sun waned. A breeze fluttered and crackled through the dry sagebrush. The roan wheezed with what seemed to be a sigh of relief.

Cole studied the horizon with his spyglass. Far in the distance, in generally the same direction as the tracks were leading, he saw a cluster of lights.

He reached the tiny settlement shortly after the sun had set, and darkness began to envelop the land.

"Has visto gringo viajeros pasan por este lugar?" Bladen Cole asked when a kid emerged from one of the buildings. He hoped that he had not butchered the Spanish too badly in asking whether the gringos had come this way. Without speaking, the boy gestured toward the west.

"Cuándo?"

In reply to Cole's wanting to know when, the boy indicated that it had been when the sun was still in the top of the sky.

"Muchas gracias," Cole said, touching a finger to the brim of his hat.

The bandits had now turned toward the Rio Grande, as Cole had expected they would.

Bladen Cole awoke the following morning to the sound of a cactus wren chortling near his head. The sun was not quite up, but the dawn was vast and the view of the purple-hued desert landscape was spectacular.

A moonless night swallows the desert quickly in her black velvet glove, so Cole had suspended his pursuit not long after he passed through the settlement. He had camped on a hillside above the anonymous cluster of homes, near enough to watch it in case any of the bandits doubled back for any reason, but far enough to remain unseen.

He made some cold coffee and ate some hardtack as the roan grazed in a nearby patch of bunchgrass. Cole disliked going without a cook fire, but he had now closed the distance between himself and his prey to half a day, and did not need a column of smoke to mark his location.

At the same time, he scanned the horizon with his telescope, looking for a plume of smoke that would betray *their* location.

There it was. He imagined two men enjoying a *hot* cup of coffee. For their second night on the trail, they had a campfire. They made no attempt to disguise their location, under the apparent assumption that a steady pace and a twelve-hour head start would keep them ahead of any posse.

Despite the fact that their trail made them easy to follow, they were probably right, Cole admitted. Large posses are cumbersome, slow-moving contrivances that waste far more time staying organized than a single horseman like himself.

The cocky assuredness of the bandits gave their hunter an odd sensation. Likewise their predictability. They had done what he had expected them to do, contrary to what

the Atchison, Topeka & Santa Fe men believed.

Cole reminded himself of the old caution-
ary tale which insists that just as you lull
yourself into believing you have figured out
a riddle, you are in for an unexpected twist.

CHAPTER 5

It was noon when Bladen Cole encountered the unexpected twist in the untangling of his riddle.

At sunup, he had picked up the trail of the four horses and the two mules a half mile west of the no-name settlement. The pace of their westward advance, made on this stretch the previous afternoon, was steady, though the distance between the horseshoe and muleshoe impressions was slightly less than it had been during the previous morning. The heat of the day had naturally slowed them, just as he had expected.

He followed them until the midday sun was high in the sky, erasing shadows and forcing even the snakes to seek refuge under rocks. He paused for a sip from his canteen, certain that he was now close to the place from which he had seen the campfire smoke curling up into the sky at dawn. It was here, as he proceeded to crest the ridge above a narrow arroyo, that Cole encountered the unexpected.

Below him was the remnants not of a campfire, but of an enormous bonfire. He saw the charred remains of sticks and scraps of oily creosote brush that had burned like an inferno at some point during the night — and which had smoldered like a campfire at dawn.

Cole cursed himself. He felt like a fool.

They had built the fire in a ravine where flames could not be seen by a potential pursuer at night, but where the residual smoke visible at dawn would look like an average campfire. They had left during the night, deliberately riding out under cover of darkness to add miles to the lead they knew they had.

Did they *know* they were being followed, or had they simply used this ruse just in case?

Cole took some consolation in knowing that their attention was still focused on getting away rather than standing to fight. They were still running anxiously, but they were running *smart.*

If they *had* spotted him and planned an ambush, the ambush would already have taken place. He breathed a sigh of relief, looking up at the rim above the arroyo from which they could easily have turned him into a sitting duck.

Cole nudged the roan and climbed up out of the ravine as quickly as possible. He pulled the small telescope from his saddlebag.

In the distance, but not too far in the distance, a pair of buzzards circled. Cole's mind naturally retraced the events involving buzzards on the previous day and fashioned a scenario under which there had been a second shootout, leaving Cole with only a single man to pursue. If he was lucky, and he supposed that he was *not*, the imagined gunfight would have resulted in both men having been fatally wounded, and the chase would be over.

A half hour later, from a ridge over which the tracks of the bandits led, it was revealed to the bounty hunter that neither of these fancies was true. A single horse stood on the desert floor as the two buzzards circled lazily high above.

Cole cautiously surveyed the scene, looking intently for the other horses and the men.

Was this horse somehow bait for an ambush?

He looked left and right. He looked back

behind him. He studied the scrapings of metal shoes on rocks and gravel, which constituted the trail he followed, for evidence that the men, either or both, had turned and doubled back to outflank him.

Seeing nothing, he returned his attention to the lone horse.

Through the spyglass, Cole watched the horse. He shook his head and mane, and looked around. Cole's roan whinnied, and the horse looked toward them with a forlorn expression. He took a step, and tried to take another. Shuddering with obvious pain, he stumbled, but did not fall.

Cole now knew what the buzzards knew. The horse had gone lame, and had been abandoned. Sooner or later, the horse would grow weak and unable to stand. Sooner or later — sooner in this heat — the horse would topple over and lie helpless. The buzzards would wait. They were, by nature, not in a hurry.

Cole pieced together events that had occurred as the riders crossed the moonless landscape during the night. In the darkness, they had reached the downslope from the ridge, which was invisible and unexpected. As they had clamored down the sudden decline, this horse had twisted an ankle and gone lame, unable to walk.

They should have shot him to put him out of his immediate misery and the inevitable suffering demise, but they could not risk the sound of a gunshot, which would have carried for miles in the nocturnal stillness.

For the sake of the pitiful creature and his painful final moments, Cole knew that he should now do as they had not done, but *he* could not risk the sound of a gunshot, which could carry for miles in the shimmering stillness of the midday heat.

Carefully descending the slope, now clearly visible, the bounty hunter drew the fourteen-inch blade from the scabbard inside his saddlebag.

Bladen Cole's third desert sunset in his pursuit of the Atchison, Topeka & Santa Fe bandits formed the backdrop for several columns of smoke from distant fires in the towns and settlements scattered along the Rio Grande. There had been smoke rising from the cook fires of humans in this broad valley for untold thousands of years, and from fires kindled by European hands for more than three hundred.

The ancientness of the river and of the trails turned to roads that paralleled it, were of neither interest nor concern to Cole. To him, the river marked only a milestone in his quest.

As the sun descended through blood red skies toward the silhouette of the distant western mountains, Cole reached a point where he could look down into the valley of the Rio Grande. The river lay like a snake, reflecting the color of the skies. Along its banks were the pinpricks of yellow light marking the locations, large and small, of human habitation.

The trail that he had followed for the better part of three days had now merged into a larger trail which led into the valley and became blurred by the addition of dozens of other shoe impressions in the dust. From here, he would now have to depend on intuition, rather than physical evidence, to follow his prey.

It had been his supposition that the men would cross the Rio Grande and continue west into the mountains, but he knew that he had been wrong at least once today.

He had also earlier supposed that he would catch, or at least catch *up to,* his prey before they reached the Rio Grande, but their ruse with the fire had cost him this possibility. It had cost *them* a horse, but they still had one to spare.

An alternate possibility that they would be meeting someone in a Rio Grande settlement had crossed his mind, but Cole still clung to his original theory. He was still sure that they planned to get away, far away, and hide themselves until they felt it safe to start spending the money. They had already killed two of their partners, so it was not likely they would rendezvous with *more* partners.

"Evening," Cole said, noticing a man at work in a small corral near the first clump of buildings that he saw as he reached the road paralleling the Rio Grande. The man looked part Indian and part Mexican, but seeing him dressed as an Anglo cowpuncher, Cole took a chance with English rather than his mutilated Spanish.

"Evening," the man repeated, looking up from what he was working on.

"You happen to see a couple of fellows pass this way a few hours ago with two pack mules?"

"Lot of people pass this way with pack stock," the man said, stating the obvious fact that they were practically on top of a major route between cities such as Bernalillo in the north, or Socorro and Mesilla to the south.

"They would have had a spare saddle horse with them," Cole added. "That might have set them apart."

"I've been gone most of the day, but probably wouldn't have noticed if I'd have been here," the man said, nodding at the piles of rope and tack with which he was working.

"Much obliged," Cole said, touching the brim of his hat and reining the roan back toward the road.

"You might want to ask Grandfather," the man said, laying down the rope he was working with and walking toward the perimeter of the corral. "He does nothing but sit and watch the road."

"Where would I find him?"

"Down there. I'll show you," the man said, climbing between the fence rails.

"Down there" turned out to be a small shack about two dozen yards closer to the main wagon road.

As they rounded the corner, an old man seated in a large handmade armchair looked up at them with dark piercing eyes that betrayed no expression. His long hair, which tumbled nearly to his shoulders, but which was cut short in a jagged line across his forehead, was as white as the cumulus. His skin was wrinkled and leathery, making him look like a centenarian, although the sparkle in his eyes made him seem half that age.

Abuelo, the younger man said, addressing the white-haired man as "Grandfather."

64

Cole wasn't sure if he was the man's actual grandfather, or simply someone so old that he was called by that term generally. *"Ves todo, no lo hace usted?"*

Having been asked if he saw *everything,* the old man nodded and turned away peevishly.

The younger man asked him the same question that Cole had previously presented, adding the part about the spare saddle horse.

Grandfather nodded in the affirmative, pointing to the road.

Before Cole could say anything more, the young man asked Grandfather to tell him when they had come by and which way they had been headed.

The old man spoke a few words, chewed some tobacco thoughtfully, and spit into a large pottery spittoon. He wiped his mouth on his sleeve and continued talking, making what seemed to be an elaboration of his earlier comments. His Spanish was heavily accented by a Pueblo dialect, and Cole could make out almost none of his words. He was glad to have a translator.

"Grandfather said that they were here just after he ate his lunch. They came from the same direction as you," the younger man said. "They were in a big hurry, he says.

65

They were in what he calls a 'white man's hurry.' For him that's just about any kind of hurry, because Grandfather is never in a hurry of any kind."

"So I see." Cole nodded, observing that the younger man didn't seem to be in much of a hurry to tell what Grandfather had said about where they were headed.

"He says that they were in a big hurry to get across the Rio Grande," the younger man continued in his own unhurried way. "He sent 'em down to the ford by Sabino."

"About . . . how far is that?" Cole asked, trying to space out his words to distinguish himself from the objects of obvious derision who were in a "white man's hurry."

"Mmmm," the younger man said thoughtfully. "I reckon you'd be able to ride it in about an hour."

Cole looked at the sky. While they had been speaking, the sun had gone down, and the stars were starting to appear.

"I wouldn't try and cross down there in the dark, though," the younger man advised.

Cole nodded. He had seen recent evidence of imprudent nighttime riding by men who were in too much of a "white man's hurry."

Chapter 6

Bladen Cole camped on a hill above the hamlet of Sabino and crossed the ford at first light, observing for himself the rocks, rapids, and sandbar that were the reason for the young man's caution.

He was in the nearest west shore town, a place called Alamillo, before most people there had awakened. A handful of chickens were scuttering about, ignoring an abrasively crowing rooster who was wandering back and forth across the street like a tippling dandy.

The first human inhabitant Cole saw was a middle-aged Anglo shopkeeper who was sweeping the accumulation of trail dust from the boardwalk in front of his wagon-stop general store.

"You're up mighty early," the man said in the warm and friendly way that a good shopkeeper — who treats *everyone* as a potential customer — greets said potential customers.

"Yep," the bounty hunter agreed. "Lost time is not found again."

"That is a maxim by which an efficient and successful man might live his life, sir," the man said and smiled.

"You wouldn't be able to sell a man a cup of hot coffee, would you?" Cole asked.

"Got a pot on at this very moment," he said, putting his broom aside.

Relishing his coffee, Cole reached the point in their interaction where it was time for conversation, and used the moment to make his inquiry about the men and their pack mules.

"Just so happens I *did* see those fellows, yes sirree," the man acknowledged. "Thought it strange that they were trailing a *saddled* horse. Fellows out for a long ride often trail a spare saddle horse, but I don't reckon you often see someone trailing a *saddled* saddle horse."

Cole nodded and took another sip of coffee.

"They friends of yours?"

"More that we have friends in common who want me to convey a message," Cole replied vaguely. "Did you see which way they were headed?"

"Thataway," the man said, pointing north

and west.

"What's out there?"

"That's the Sierra Magdalena Mountains country," he said, using both the Spanish and English word for "mountains," as Anglos often did. "Nothing up there unless they're headed over to the valley over around Luera. People headed up into the Magdalenas usually stop in here for supplies, but by the looks of their mules, I'd say they were pretty well provisioned for a long ride. That's a good thing, because they ain't gonna be able to get much at Santa Rita."

"Where's Santa Rita?"

"Hour or so's ride up yonder and well into the mountains. I reckoned that was probably where they'd be planning to make camp last night. You might be able to catch 'em. You figure that they're headed over by Luera?"

"I believe so." Cole nodded, feigning knowledge of Luera.

"Makes sense they'd be headed that way, otherwise they'd have gone south to Socorro and over that way."

"I couldn't agree more; they would definitely not have gone through Socorro," Cole said with a smile, taking out some coins to pay for his coffee, and for some beans and cornmeal that he figured he would need. "I'm much obliged for your help."

Climbing out of the Rio Grande Valley, with its small cultivated fields of corn and squash, took a traveler back into the same dry, arid desert landscape that existed to the east of the river. The only difference was that the terrain now grew steeper and more rugged. Several days' ride in the distance, deeper into the wilderness, there were taller mountains, wooded with ponderosa like the Rockies of Colorado and Montana, but in the interim, a traveler was still in the desert.

Here and there along the lightly traveled trail, Cole detected the tracks of the two men and their livestock, and he could see that their pace had slowed considerably. Either they had come to feel that they had eluded all potential pursuers and had grown more relaxed, or they were becoming gradually more tired. Probably, Cole reasoned, it was a combination of the two.

Gradually, their urgency and their alertness was waning. Several boring days on the trail does that to a man, whether he realizes it or not. Like the two men whom he had pursued south of Durango, these two had started out edgy, certainly edgy enough to spitefully murder two of their own. Gradually, though, that edge was being worn down.

As he paused to water the roan at a trickle of water coming off the slopes of the Magdalenas, he imagined the bandits looking back, and perhaps seeing him. Unless they had seen him following them over the past few days, he guessed that they would not be unduly wary of a single man on an existing trail. They could catch their breath up there wherever, confident that the imagined posse had been successfully eluded.

As he climbed the trail, Cole took the two Denver & Rio Grande passes out of his pocket and studied them. They were standard issue railroad passes such as he had seen from time to time. All railroads issued them to employees to use for official business and for personal use as part of their compensation. It was clear that either these were the property of the deceased, or they had been left on the bodies deliberately.

Santa Rita was a larger settlement than he had imagined, even boasting a small cantina.

Cole studied the few horses tied at the hitchrails. He had not expected to see three saddle horses tethered near a pair of mules, and he was not disappointed. He was

71

pleased, however, to see no horse at all tied at the cantina, despite its rail being situated in the inviting shade of a cottonwood. This meant that his conversation with the bartender would be uninterrupted.

"Howdy," the proprietor said, greeting Cole from his position in a chair near the bar. "What can we do to brighten your day?"

"A whiskey would work itself a long way down the road of making that happen," Cole said, packing more words into the sentence than was typical of his usual greeting. It was his intention to establish himself as a conversationalist.

The man stood, swatted at a fly, and went behind the bar.

"You're a long way from home," the man said, taking his own turn to establish himself as a conversationalist.

"How'd you guess?" Cole asked.

"Because you ain't from around here," the man said with a crazed chuckle as he poured two fingers of inviting amber liquid into a glass. "And Santa Rita is damned far from *everywhere.*"

Cole could not help but smile as the man laughed boisterously at his own joke. Cole guessed that it was not the first time he had used that line.

"You guessed right," Cole said, savoring

the welcome taste.

"Where you headed?" the man asked.

"West," Cole answered, nodding in that direction. "Thought maybe I'd take a buck and smoke me some venison. Get a jump on winter. California's a long ride."

"They'll be in the high country this time of year," the man said, offering hunting advice.

"Yep," Cole agreed. "It'll be cooler up there."

"What takes you out to California?"

"Woman."

"Either love or money," the bartender proclaimed. "Anybody who tells you there's a third thing that drives a man's intentions, he's either a fool or a liar."

"Ain't *that* for sure." Cole nodded.

"She know you're coming . . . ? Not that it's any of my business."

"She ran off with a gambler," Cole explained, adding an element of fact to his fable. "I've come to figure that she'd be getting tired of him. I was just thinking . . ."

"You want to be there at the right time."

"Yeah, I was just thinking that," Cole said. It was true that he had been unable to push Sally Lovelace out of his mind completely, even though it had been the better part of four years since she had run off to San

Francisco with J. R. Hubbard. It was *not* true that he had entertained any plans of going after her.

"The reason I asked . . . not wanting to pry into your business . . ." the bartender continued, "was that I had been wonderin' if you were with those boys who were headed over to Luera."

"Guess not. What boys?"

"Two boys who was in here last night. They was all loaded up with a couple of mules like they were headed for somewhere."

"They were headed for Luera?"

"Not till they heard about the Dutchman."

"Who's the Dutchman?"

"He's a fellow over in Luera who knows a lot about the old Spanish gold strikes up in these hills round about."

"Do tell," Cole said, nodding to an empty glass as if to say that hearing the fellow's yarn about this Dutchman called for a refill.

"There's stories," the bartender said. "There's stories that he's found a lot of gold, and stories that he hasn't. People see him around Luera, and then he disappears for weeks or a month or so. People have seen him with gold, but he doesn't seem to live beyond his means. There's stories that

74

he takes it over to Socorro or some place and puts it in a bank."

"What made these boys take an interest in the Dutchman?" Cole asked. "Were they going over to Luera to rob the man?"

"No, they were drinking in here last night, and they got to talking with a couple of other fellows who *were* headed over to see him."

"What about?"

"They were gonna try'n get the Dutchman to tell 'em how to find the Lost Dearing Diggings."

"What's that?"

"Fellow name of Dearing came in through here back in the fifties, just before the war I guess it was," the bartender began, relishing his role as storyteller. "He was a cowboy from over in West Texas who had some kind of scrape with the law. Came out here to get away. He rescued this half-breed Mexican kid from a bunch of Apaches. The kid was real thankful as you can picture, so he showed Dearing this place way up in yonder mountains where there was gold nuggets the size of wild turkey eggs just laying around."

"I've heard variations on that story before," Cole said truthfully. The barrooms and backcountry of the Southwest

75

abounded in such tales.

"Dearing showed up in Mesilla with a bandanna full of these nuggets," the cantina owner insisted. "He said he'd go back in there and get more, but that he was scared off by the Apaches. He got some others to go with him."

"They find the place?"

"Yup. They sure did. They caused quite a fuss, too. Went back up there with a mule train to haul the stuff out."

"And . . ."

"Disappeared without a trace. Never seen again."

"What does that have to do with the Dutchman?"

"Word is that he knows where the Dearing Diggings is, but won't take nobody in there on account of he likes to work alone."

"So the fellows that were talking in here last night are gonna try'n get the Dutchman to take 'em there?" Cole asked.

"Get him to *tell* 'em," the bartender clarified. "The story is that he'll *tell* you where to go, but he won't take you. The Dutchman works alone."

"Why you figure those other fellas told all this to the two strangers last night?"

"Apaches," the bartender explained succinctly. "Four's better than two if you're riding into Apache country. The Chiricahua are still up in those mountains. As the story goes, there's more gold at the Dearing Diggings than any two men can carry, so sharing it is a small price for being able to get in and get back out *alive*."

CHAPTER 7

Two men had been escaping the law with a $9,000 payroll, sufficient money to set two men up comfortably for a long time — even in California. *Then,* on the verge of vanishing across the line that could have realistically been expected to keep them safe from the law forever, they had met two men with a story.

Suddenly, the success of their escape was not enough. The $9,000 was not enough. They had been shown the promise of even greater riches and had succumbed to its siren call. It was like the man who wins magnificently at the tables, and pushes it back onto the table, rather than walking away to relish the fortune that is already in hand.

Greed is the fuel that feeds the fire of greed.

Somehow, this is an undeniable aspect of human nature, perhaps not found in all, but certainly not a rare affliction.

However, the hotter the fire burns, the more likely it is to consume the finer qualities of rational thought, and to tip the greedy toward the cauldron of madness.

Bladen Cole reached Luera at nightfall.

It was a forlorn little collection of adobe buildings, with a tiny Spanish mission church at one end of town and the inevitable cantina at the opposite end, as though the two were squaring off in a contest over the souls of men.

If Santa Rita was "damned far from everywhere," Luera was at the very end of the earth.

In Santa Rita, the bartender was a man with a proclivity for talk. In Luera, the bartender was a woman of few words. She was a hard-looking character of indeterminate middle age with a leathery face and her hair tied in a knot at the top of her head.

"Do you for?" she asked.

"A shot from that bottle with the orange label over there would brighten my day," Cole answered. His third in one day when the sun was still up was a record for him, but by the looks of the deep orange light streaming in the cantina's single window, it was close to being *not* up.

She poured his whiskey without a word. She may have looked mean and miserly, but Cole noticed that she was not quite so given to cutting her whiskey with branch water as had been the proprietor in Santa Rita.

"You lookin' for the Dutchman?" she asked.

"Why do you ask?" Cole asked.

"Most strangers who come in here *are* lookin' for the Dutchman," she explained. "Figured I'd get that out of the way. He ain't here, but he may come in later."

"Heard there was some fellas comin' and lookin' for him this morning," Cole said, relishing the closer-to-full-strength whiskey.

"Friends of yours?"

"Friends of friends, sort of."

"Won't ask what that means," she said skeptically. "They're a bunch of fools. Most who come lookin' for the Dutchman are."

Without further elaboration, she left him to savor his whiskey and went about her chores, rattling about with her glassware and moving things in a small pantry.

What passed for a back bar was cluttered with an odd collection of artifacts that had apparently been found in the desert. There were deer antlers, a coyote skull, some old rusty pieces of iron, and a rusted pistol with its handgrip rotted off. And naturally, there were strings of dried chilies.

There were also several dried birds which would have been an embarrassment to any taxidermist, including a raven that seemed to be looking straight at Cole. He guessed that this had been the bartender's intention when she placed it in that spot. At the top, in a place of honor, there was an old brass helmet of the kind the Spanish conquistadors wore hundreds of years ago.

"I see by that sign that you sell suppers," Cole said as he saw her stoking her stove.

"Yep," she said without elaboration.

"What's your specialty?"

"Beans and rice on a tortilla with some chicken thrown in."

"Sounds good."

"You want eggs on top?"

"They fresh?"

"You seen all them chickens runnin' around in the street this afternoon?"

"Yeah, I'll have a couple of eggs."

Maybe it was the aroma of the cooking, and maybe it was their force of habit, but as she began cooking, three other men wandered in, bought whiskey, and asked for supper. It was soon evident that the woman's specialty was her *only.* Everything she cooked was a variation on beans and rice on a tortilla with some chicken, as well as a handful of dried red chilies, thrown in.

Cole studied the newcomers, wondering if one of them might be the Dutchman.

He imagined that none of them looked the part, but then realized that he really didn't know what a Dutchman was *supposed* to look like.

As he ate, Cole thought back to his last store-bought meal, the *carne asada* at the Refugio del Viajero in Santa Fe. His thoughts naturally also went back to Nicolette de la Gravière, with her graceful movements, her long dark hair, and her lips the color of dried red chilies.

Just as Santa Fe and Luera were opposite poles on the scale of civilization in this territory, Nicolette de la Gravière and tonight's hostess were opposite poles on the scale of womanhood. Cole imagined the bartender when she was as young as Nicolette de la Gravière. He imagined Nicolette in twenty or thirty years, and wondered whether those years would be as unkind to her, or if she would retain that sort of timeless, regal beauty that women such as her mother seemed to preserve.

Naturally, being a man, he had imagined himself as part of Nicolette's life. He knew that he could not tire of a face like that, or of a smile like that. He had thought of the similarity of that face to the face of Hannah Ransdell, the woman of about that same age he had met last winter up in Montana Territory. Hannah was quick and perceptive — and she could ride and shoot as well as most men. She was naturally, and almost perfectly, beautiful, but the little threesome of freckles on her nose added a humanizing touch, softening the classical perfection of that beauty.

He often thought about Hannah, and he thought often of Natoya-I-nis'kim, the Blackfeet woman with the long black hair who had saved his life, and he thought about several other women he had met in the years since Sally Lovelace had left him.

It seemed that it all came back to Sally.

She had changed his life by turning a wandering man into a man who could think about settling down. She had changed his life *again* through the revelation that *she too* wished to wander, but *without* Bladen Cole.

It all came back to Sally.

She had not so much cursed his life as she had painfully exposed the curse that had been there all along. Cole was meant to be a man who would not, indeed *could* not, stay long in one place.

"Guess you didn't like your supper,"

Cole's hostess said, clearing his nearly spotless plate and interrupting his thoughts. "If you were lookin' for the Dutchman, you don't need to be waitin' no more."

She nodded toward a place in the corner of the room, and his eyes followed her as she delivered a glass of whiskey to the table.

The Dutchman was a stocky, powerfully built man with close-cropped gray hair and a large gray mustache cut short on the two sides. He had sharp eyes, which instantly picked up on Cole's looking at him.

Cole tossed several coins on the bar and stood. The Dutchman watched as the bounty hunter approached his table.

"Evening, sir," Cole said politely. "I hear that you're the man they call the Dutchman."

"*Ist Deutsch,* not '*Dutch,*' but most people call me the 'Dutchman.' Ist my nickname, as it were," he said without smiling.

"I'm Bladen Cole," he said, extending a hand.

"Otto Geier," the German said, taking Cole's extended hand in his firm grip. "Please sit."

"Thanks. I'm told you may have seen a couple of men I'm looking for."

"You are a bounty hunter," the Dutchman asserted. "You have that look."

84

"What look?"

"The look of a bounty hunter. What men are you seeking?"

"Two men with a pair of pack mules," Cole explained. "They're riding with a couple of others they met over in Santa Rita yesterday."

"What are they wanted for?" Geier asked. Screened through the sieve of a thick German accent, his English words were precise and clearly articulated.

"Robbery . . . and murder," Cole said, deliberately not mentioning the Atchison, Topeka & Santa Fe.

"Where?"

"Up toward Santa Fe."

"Not a few of those who come to Luera are escaping such deeds," the Dutchman said, shaking his head.

"Have you seen 'em?"

"*Ja.* The men you describe were here today. They asked about the Dearing Diggings. They were not the first, and they will not be the last."

"What did you tell them?"

"I told them where to look."

"Where?"

"In the Mogollons," he said, nodding his head toward the southwest. "Across the mountains, into the Sierra Blanca, in the

85

headwaters of the Gila River. Are you looking for the men or the gold? You seek the
men to fulfill your contract, but your imagination ist tempted by the lure of treasure."

"I'd be a liar to deny it," Cole admitted.
He knew that his expression betrayed the
desire that engulfs all men when they are
offered stories of nuggets the size of turkey
eggs.

The Dutchman smiled the wry smile of
someone who knows more than he tells.

"Is it real?" Cole asked. "Do the Dearing
Diggings exist?"

"*Ja.*"

"You're sure?"

"I have with my own eyes seen this gold."

"Why haven't *you* . . .?

"Only two kinds of men imagine that they
will come back from the Dearing as rich
men . . . dead men and fools."

"Apaches?"

"Apaches and terrain," the Dutchman said
soberly. "*Und wolves* . . . angry packs of
wolves which will tear a man apart. I barely
escaped with my life. I will not go back."

"Did you explain this to the four men?"

"*Naturlich.*"

"Guess it didn't stop them."

"They believe that there ist safety in numbers."

"Well, I guess that I'll be needing to ask you for the same directions," Cole said. "I believe I'll take a chance on catching up before they get to the part of the trail that's patrolled by wolves."

"Who was it that was murdered?" Geier asked.

"Just a man who was in the wrong place at the wrong time," Cole explained, again shying away from mention of the railroad. "They had no grudge, didn't even know him. He was unarmed. That happens in robberies. There were originally four robbers. These two killed their partners. One got it in the back of the head at close range. The other was shot in the back as he ran."

He watched the German shake his head in anger.

"Do you have provisions for the mountains?"

"Some," Cole said. "I'll be buying more in the morning."

"I will meet you at the general store at precisely eight o'clock," the Dutchman said. "I will lead you."

"I thought you said you'd never go back."

"*Nein,* never," the Dutchman said emphatically. "Not the *entire* way, but there are many miles between here and there."

CHAPTER 8

"We sure are appreciative that you fellahs let us ride with you," Jasper Gardner said as the four men rode though the New Mexico mountains.

"Like I told you yesterday," Ben Muriday repeated. "There's more than enough to make every man of us rich beyond measure, but it ain't worth a damned nickel if you got an Apache bullet in you. Four men are a better match for the Chiricahua than two."

"Still mighty generous," Gardner added. "You figure that the Dutchman was right in saying that it's a four-day ride?"

"I reckon. He's been there. From what I know about these mountains, four days is pretty much right. Unless we gets ourself turned around and lost up in there."

"What are the odds of that happening?" Gardner asked, trying to conceal a tone of alarm. "I thought you *knew* these mountains."

"Been a lot in these mountains," Muriday replied with confidence. "As long as we keep a south-by-southeast heading, like the Dutchman said, long as we keep an eye out for the Dutchman's landmarks, we don't have nothing to worry about. Only reason that Dearing's find ain't been found again is that it's so far back that nobody's gonna chance onto it. Like the Dutchman hisself says, it ain't *hidden*, it's just in a place where nobody goes."

"Unless he's goin' *to* it," his partner, Simon Lynch, said and nodded, finishing Muriday's thought.

Jasper Gardner fought the premature temptation to visualize the promised mountain ravine filled with nuggets the size of turkey eggs, but it was painful to deny his imagination the opportunity to envision himself presenting a bundle of these at an assay office.

Gardner was one of those men about whom they say that you should count your fingers after shaking his hand. Some people lie to their mothers. Some people steal from their mothers. Then, there is Jasper Gardner. When he was seventeen, he stole the deed to his mother's house and sold it to a carpetbagger. He took the money, headed west, and never looked back.

As time went on, Gardner found a kindred spirit in the equally unscrupulous Gabe Stanton. Recognizing a symbiosis, the two men realized they could accomplish much by joining forces. Over time, they had formed a loose affiliation of men one might describe as a gang. They alternated between petty theft and hiring themselves out as enforcers. They had worked for cattlemen in Kansas and even for a bank down in Oklahoma. They came west during the railroad wars in Colorado and found that there was ready employment for men of their trade.

Gardner and Stanton had eventually decided that there was adventure to be had in Lincoln County. However, as they were heading south into New Mexico with two of their regular followers, an unprecedented opportunity had fallen into their laps.

On the first night after they had exercised this opportunity and had robbed the Atchison, Topeka & Santa Fe baggage car, they made camp and inventoried their spoils. The net of $9,000 was more than any of the four men had ever seen in one place.

One of the two new men, who had joined the Gardner-Stanton gang up in Colorado, calculated that when split four ways, there would be $2,250 for each of them.

Gardner disagreed. He disagreed more with the man's assumptions than with his arithmetic — and put a bullet into the skull of this man who had ridden with him faithfully for two years.

Looking at the expressions on the faces of Gardner and Stanton, the other man ran, sprinting into the darkness. The man may have thought of his having invested two years of his life as part of the Gardner-Stanton gang. He probably thought of the irony of running through the desert dodging bullets fired by men with whom he felt he'd formed a common bond. He certainly felt the .45-caliber slug tear into his shoulder.

Knocked off balance, he dropped to his knee, writhing with searing pain. Despite this, he staggered to his feet and continued running. He may have felt the second bullet strike him, but he did not feel the third.

The Gardner-Stanton gang, its numbers now trimmed merely to its namesakes, broke camp before the bodies were cold and continued their dash toward the Rio Grande, eyes peeled for the expected posse. The cloud of dust they logically anticipated to see boiling up behind two dozen mounted riders never materialized. Nor were they intercepted as they crossed the Rio Grande and the well-traveled wagon roads that ran along its banks.

As they turned to look back at the Rio Grande Valley one last time, Gardner and Stanton finally dared to congratulate each other on having shaken the posse. All they saw, as they looked down from their perch in the Magdalenas was a single lone rider in the far distance, making his way up the trail from Alamillo.

Had they any doubt that Lady Luck was riding sidesaddle on their spare horse, they had only to wait for their chance encounter with Muriday and Lynch in the cantina in Santa Rita. For the second time in a week, an unprecedented opportunity had fallen into their laps.

What does a man do when he has just escaped into secure anonymity with more money than he has ever seen in his life — and he is suddenly offered *further* riches beyond his wildest imagination?

Greed is the fuel that feeds the fire of greed.

Bladen Cole began the fourth full day of his pursuit with a much later start than he would have liked. The Dutchman had arrived at their rendezvous precisely on time, but the shopkeeper from whom the necessary supplies would be purchased was late to arrive at his shop. After all those days, it bothered Cole immensely that the thieves still managed to maintain a half-day lead, and this bother was not relieved by what he considered to be a mid-morning start.

The Dutchman was an ideal traveling companion. He was efficient, knowledge-able, and, like Cole, he was used to riding alone. It was afternoon before any meaning-ful conversation passed between the two men.

"Few white men make it a habit to travel in these mountains," the Dutchman replied when Cole made a comment about the absence of well-used trails. "If you think like an animal, the trails are easy to see."

"Now and then, I can see evidence of our friends having passed this way," Cole said. "But they are harder to track here than they were in the desert."

"See that mountain?" Geier asked, point-ing to a prominent snowcapped mountain in the distance. "I told your friends to fol-low the ridgeline and keep this mountain dead ahead for three days. They will then come to red sandstone cliffs that mark a canyon. They will follow the water in this red rock canyon upstream."

"I reckon you know a lot about where to

find the gold in these parts," Cole observed. "But I'm not going to ask, because I know you'll have nothing to say on that topic."

"Das ist gut," the Dutchman replied. "You are a good judge of men."

"I guess the Spaniards back all those years ago found some, but sure wasted a lot of time looking."

"It was not a waste," the Dutchman observed. "Much was found . . . Mexico . . . Peru . . . even *here.*"

"The Spaniards spent a lot of effort and never found El Dorado, though," Cole observed.

"That's because it was found by a *German,*" the Dutchman said, grinning at his companion. "Have you heard of Philipp von Hutten? He ist the 'Dutchman' who *found* El Dorado."

"What happened to him?"

"Imprisonment by the Spanish. He died before he could be freed and return to El Dorado. Many stories of treasure end that way. *Nein,* I should say that *most* stories about hunters of treasure end this way, or end with the avaricious who go back for more and never return to civilization."

"That's what happened to Dearing," Cole recalled.

"That ist what continues to happen with

his discovery. Many men come to me to help them find the way to the Dearing treasure. I tell them honestly, and bid them farewell. If I ever see them again, they have terror in their eyes, not the glow of satisfied lust."

"How do you know that nobody has found it?"

"Word of *that much* gold going to market would spread far and wide."

"When you gave those men directions to this gold, did you believe that you were sending them to their deaths?" Cole asked.

"It is their choice," the Dutchman said. "They have been told of the risks and the chances of success. There is no difference between you and I. We both possess the power of life and death over men, and the power to offer men the choice of living or dying. You have in your pocket death warrants for two men. They read 'Dead or Alive,' meaning that their lives will be spared if they make the correct choice."

"That's right," Cole agreed. "Most men who operate on the wrong side of the law know they're living a gamble."

"Life ist a matter of choices," Geier said. "A man must never stop weighing the choices that he makes. Some treasure ist not worth having, but it ist up to the man

95

to decide where to stop. I cannot make that choice for them."

"I understand." Cole nodded.

"If all treasure was easy to find and to hold, all men would be rich," the Dutchman said. "Not all men are meant to be wealthy. Fools least of all."

"You strike me as a man who has little use for fools."

"As I said, Herr Cole, you are a good judge of character."

CHAPTER 9

"Bonsoir, monsieur," Nicolette de la Gravière said with smile. She spoke in Spanish to those who she thought spoke it, and English to probable English speakers. She saved her French for her friends.

"Good evening, mademoiselle," Amos Richardson said, returning the smile. "It will be the usual."

"Très bien," Nicolette said as she swirled away toward the kitchen to put in his order.

It was Richardson's custom to dine twice a week at the Refugio del Viajero. There was some variation in the days, but he never varied from a twice-weekly routine.

Therese de la Gravière, the owner of the Refugio, caught his eye from across the room and approached his table with a large bottle.

"New from France, Doctor," she said with a smile. Her smile always reminded Richardson of her daughter's smile, and vice versa.

"Would you care for a glass with my compliments?"

"Absolutely, ma'am."

"The coming of the railroad has changed many things," she said as she uncorked the bottle and poured him a generous portion. "Wine from France was never before possible in Santa Fe . . . at least not at a reasonable price."

In the dim light of Madame de la Gravière's small restaurant, the wine seemed black as night, but where the light of the flickering candles caught it, the hue was that of rubies. She watched his face carefully as he took his first sip.

"Very nice," he pronounced happily.

A broad smile creased the face of Therese de la Gravière.

"A man should not drink a nectar so fine alone," Richardson observed, gesturing to the chair opposite his. "May I buy *you* a glass of this fine produce of your homeland?"

"*Merci,*" she said with a slight bow. "*Pourquoi pas?* It is a slow night . . . not many customers with the legislature out of session."

"To the railroad and the changes for the better," he said, touching her glass.

"To the railroad." She smiled. "There have

been so many things that will now be available to us from the outside world. It is almost as though the world has suddenly grown smaller."

"Do you plan to travel, perhaps to the East, or back to France?"

"Oh no," she said, shaking her head. "My place is here. Nicolette and I have made our lives here. But there I am, speaking for my daughter. She may feel differently. She has never seen the East, and has few memories of France."

"She is certainly an asset to you here."

"The Refugio would not have been possible without her," Therese explained. "She is a wonderful child who works hard and is good with customers."

"Quite true," Richardson agreed.

"But she is of that age," Therese continued. "She is of an age when she should be entertaining suitors."

"That should not be a problem. I see the way the eyes of young men follow her about the room."

"Her attitude is one of diffidence. She makes it a practice not to flirt with them," Therese said. "I agree to an extent. I would not want her flirting with every man who came through the door. She is an affable girl, but at the same time she is quite bash-

99

ful. Sometimes she sees a young man who she likes, but when he is a customer, she feels she cannot . . ."

"I understand," Richardson said in commiseration.

"She was serious about a young man about two years ago, but he left town. There was another woman involved. It hurt her deeply, as such things do for a young girl. There have been others, but nothing serious. Sometimes she sees one she likes, but her shyness gets in the way. There was that cowboy you recommended to us a week or so ago."

"Mr. Cole?"

"Perhaps. Handsome man . . . rough around the edges but very polite?"

"Virginia accent?"

"Yes . . . like yours."

"That would have been Mr. Cole."

"Oh, how Nicolette pined that night," Therese said with the smile of an older person's amused disparagement of youthful passion, but with the sadness in her eyes of a mother who wanted her daughter in a relationship. "For several days, she kept asking 'Mama, will he be coming back tonight? Mama, will he be coming back tonight?' But if he had, she would have merely smiled and kept her conversation to a minimum. He never would have gotten the idea."

"He left town on business," Richardson said. "I don't think he had intended to stay long in Santa Fe."

"C'est la vie," Therese said. "He was not exactly my idea of the ideal man for Nicolette. His kind, with their guns, and their shiftless ways, and their eyes always trained on what lies beyond distant horizons."

"You may not have choice in the matter of who catches Nicolette's eye," Richardson observed.

"She has a mind of her own, that one," Therese said with a wistful sigh. "It will cost her a good husband, paid for with a broken heart. Is my daughter doomed to be an old maid like her mother?"

Looking into her eyes and seeing both sadness and beauty, Richardson was about to say something about how Therese need not feel doomed to perpetual old maidhood, when Nicolette arrived at the table with his *carne asada* and her usual warm smile, and Therese stood to greet some arriving guests.

Amos Richardson was about halfway through his meal when Ezra Waldron entered the room. They made eye contact, and the railroad man approached Richardson's table.

"Good evening, Doctor," he said, extend-

101

ing his hand.

"Pleasure to see you, sir," Richardson replied. "Would you care to join me?"

"Thank you, that's kind of you."

When Nicolette visited the table, Richardson recommended that Waldron try his favorite, and he also ordered a bottle of the wine Therese had offered previously.

"Beautiful girl," Waldron remarked.

"Daughter of the owner," Richardson clarified possessively.

"I see." The railroad man nodded.

"How are things in the railroad business?" Richardson asked, changing the subject.

"Excellent. Freight revenues are up on this division, and eastbound passenger bookings are starting to materialize."

"The war with the Denver & Rio Grande?"

"Behind us, I hope."

"How are things going with that matter for which you employed Mr. Cole?" Richardson asked.

"There has been no word from Mr. Cole. I had hoped that he would have sent some manner of a progress report by now."

"There are no telegraph offices in the wilderness," the coroner reminded him.

"Certainly there are post offices in Lincoln County," Waldron insisted.

"The mail takes a long time. Patience is required."

"I realize that, but the lack of news does not lessen my concern. It is as though all these men have dropped from the face of the earth."

"As I recall, one of your expressed concerns was that no news of this incident be allowed to circulate. In that sense, you may regard the absence of news as a success."

"For the moment, I am pleased by the absence of news, but I fear a surprise that could come at any moment. I'll breathe much easier when Mr. Cole has delivered and I can consider the matter resolved with finality."

CHAPTER 10

"Ain't seen that damned peak in an hour or two," Simon Lynch complained.

"It's just the damned trees," Ben Muriday assured his partner. "We been headed in the same direction all this time. I'm sure of it."

It was the afternoon of their second day out of Luera, and they were impatient to catch sight of the red rock canyon that was the landmark that would take them to the Dutchman's gold. He had said that it would be found on the third day, but they had been in such a starry-eyed hurry that none of them had thought to ask him whether it would be early or late on the third day. Meanwhile, Muriday had more than once advanced the theory that if they picked up their pace, the red sandstone cliffs might be found on the *second* day.

"You still sure we done the right thing with this gold?" Gabe Stanton said to Jasper Gardner in low voice so no one else could hear. "I mean goin' off on this tangent with Muriday's wild-goose chase. We could be sittin' around with our feet up right now . . . or headed to California to spend our *own* gold."

"Why do it halfway? We talked about this. Why settle for ridin' off to California with nine grand when we could have as much as ten times that?"

"You're right," Stanton admitted. "But these woods and these mountains . . . it all gives me the willies."

"Ain't as hot as the desert though," Gardner reminded him.

"Nope. T'ain't so hot no more, but this brush makes for slow going. I sure wish somebody woulda cut a trail through this crap."

"If there was a trail, somebody *else* would already have made off with Dearing's gold by now," Gardner reminded him.

The four men, each driven toward the promise of wealth of fantastic proportions, urged their horses through increasingly difficult terrain where none of them would have gone otherwise. There was no question of picking up their pace. If anything, the pack mules were slowing their progress. The lead ropes on the mules, as well as on the spare saddle horse, which now carried their expedition supplies, were occasionally snagged or tangled in the brush or on the limbs of deadfall. This cost time and tried the patience of Muriday and Lynch.

They had believed Gardner and Stanton when their new partners explained that the cargo on their mules was merely the possessions they were taking with them on their westward migration to California. Naturally, Gardner and Stanton had chosen not to tell them that the packs contained a pilfered payroll, or that their spare saddle horse had belonged to a previous partner who had died from a bullet in the back of his head. Had Muriday and Lynch known the latter, they would not have been so quick to invite Gardner and Stanton to join their expedition.

"You'll find a better use for them damned mules when we get ourself up to Dearing's," Muriday laughed when Gardner and Stanton both had to dismount to extract a mule from an especially difficult entanglement with the brush.

It was at that moment that shots rang out.

Gardner felt the rush of air on his cheek as one round came within inches of hitting his head.

He and Stanton, already dismounted, scrambled to take cover, while Muriday and

Lynch quickly dropped off their horses to crawl behind a nearby log.

More shots came, nicking the log and spattering fragments from the boulders above them.

"Bushwhackers!" Lynch shouted, stating the obvious.

"Apaches!" Stanton replied, advancing a theory with which no one took exception.

"How many?" Gardner asked.

"At least two," Muriday guessed.

"The bastards got us ambushed in a real good spot," Gardner observed.

The attackers had no doubt been shadowing the large, noisy party of treasure hunters for some time, waiting for a favorable spot to spring their trap. They had been dealt an especially fortuitous hand when the pack mule became snarled in a place where the four men were hemmed in by a line of boulders.

In such a place, those springing the ambush from high ground had the advantage, which was always magnified by the proclivity of the startled victim to make rash decisions. If the latter survived the initial moments when he was totally exposed to opposition fire, and got under relatively safe cover, he could gain back a measure of control. The ambusher still had the advantage if he had sufficient force to press the momentum of the initial attack, but he had to do so quickly to prevent a standoff from developing.

Muriday aimed his Model 1860 Colt .44 and squeezed off three rounds in rapid succession.

Gardner was about to admonish him for wasting ammunition, when he realized what the man was doing. His three shots elicited a fusillade of return fire, which resolved the question of how many attackers were in the high ground above them.

"Just two of 'em means they're just a couple of young bucks out to steal horses," Gardner explained. "They were hoping to spook us and grab some stock. I've seen it before. Sometimes, they just break off and run if they don't nail you right off."

"You see 'em?" Stanton asked.

"Yeah, but just barely," Gardner replied.

"You fellas cover Stanton while he grabs his rifle out of his scabbard," Gardner ordered. "He was a sniper in the First Pennsylvania. He can hit anything."

As Muriday reloaded, Lynch crawled to a position as far as possible from Stanton's. On a count of three, they both began firing at the ambushers, while Stanton stood to grab his old army-issue Trapdoor Springfield.

Without hesitation, he aimed at one of the Apache who had shifted his position to fire his Winchester at Lynch.

A high-pitched howl told them that Stanton's .45-caliber, 405-grain slug had found its mark.

The second attacker, now finding himself alone, decided that his position was no longer tenable, and he ran.

A second shot from Stanton's Springfield, fired at a moving and partially obscured target, failed to find its mark.

Jasper Gardner leapt on his horse and urged it to clamor up the hillside in pursuit.

The other three watched as the powerful animal lunged upward and was lost from view in the thick ponderosa. They listened as horse and rider crashed through the brush, imagining that the second Apache would have reached his own horse by now. There was the sound of shouts and then of gunfire. There was the crack of a Winchester, the pop of Gardner's Colt, more shouts, a scream, and then nothing but the afternoon wind in the higher branches of the trees.

The three men held their breath, staring at the unseen place up on that hillside where they had last heard the shouting. A moment later, perhaps half a whole minute, as their ears began to ring, as so often is the case when a cacophony is superseded by deafening silence, they looked at one another.

Next, they looked around as the cool chill of apprehension seized them with the fear of an ambush, which can often materialize out of silence.

From somewhere in the trees, a jay shrieked, and from elsewhere came a return comment in the voice of one of its own.

A moment later, perhaps half a minute, though it seemed like ten, there was a resumption of noise from where the fourth of their foursome had disappeared.

There was a shout as though in triumph, as Jasper Gardner reappeared. High above his head, he held a long, streaming, black thing. None of them immediately recognized what it was.

It was only when he came near that they recognized that he had not one, but two, long, black, bloody scalps.

The bounty hunter and the Dutchman had heard the fusillade in the distance, and each had instinctively gone low in his saddle and touched the stock of the rifle in his scabbard.

"Four miles at least," Geier whispered. "It

sounds closer, but this ist how sounds carry in these mountains."

They counted not the shots, but the clusters of the shots, both knowing to delineate the initial volley from the separate cluster that ended the exchange.

The Dutchman cocked his head as they heard the shouts, but his expression said that he could make nothing of it.

"Apache," Cole commented.

The Dutchman merely nodded, and after a moment to listen for more shots, they both pulled their long guns and continued, as quietly as possible, with eyes peeled at the surrounding high ground.

For about an hour, they followed the path through the brush disturbed by the four men, but as they approached the ambush site, they made for higher ground, not wanting to follow the trail to that exact point. There was still a faint trace of burnt gunpowder in the air. The breeze that toyed with the treetops had not much intruded upon the air at ground level.

They dismounted and continued cautiously. There was no reason to believe that anyone was still about, but they took no chances. They parted company, moving in parallel, separated by about twenty yards, to make themselves two targets, rather than one.

"Ach, du lieber!" Geier exclaimed.

It was the Dutchman who had found the body of the second Apache.

He was studying the deceased when Cole arrived.

"I found another over yonder," Cole said as he approached his companion. "Bullet in the head at some range. Probably a rifle shot."

"This man was hit at closer range . . . two times," the Dutchman replied.

"What would possess these devils to take the time to *scalp* two Apaches?" Geier asked rhetorically.

"The same thing that possessed them to shoot their partners in the back," Cole answered.

"They probably don't know they did themselves a favor," the Dutchman observed after he had inspected the other body.

"How's that?" Cole asked.

"Our friends have mutilated them in the Apache way . . . not the white man way. This will confuse the Chiricahua."

"Not infuriate them?"

"These savages are Mescalero," the Dutchman explained. "They are likely two who wanted to prove themselves as great warriors by riding into Chiricahua country to steal horses. The Chiricahua will not be alarmed by finding dead Mescalero. They will be pleased that the trespassers have been killed and humiliated. But the Chiricahua will come if they heard the shots, so we should move quickly."

CHAPTER 11

In the aftermath of the ambush, the four treasure seekers had continued in silence, united by a concern that more Apache would pounce at any moment. Three of the four rode in the silence of concern, unnerved by Gardner's impulsiveness in lifting the hair of the two ambushers then casually tying the scalps to his saddle as trophies.

Even Stanton, who had killed the first Apache, and who had been Gardner's willing accomplice for all manner of mayhem for years, cast his partner a glance that expressed his opinion that the scalping of two Apaches in the heart of Apache country was unnecessarily provocative.

By late afternoon, the consternation had faded, superseded by renewed optimism as they broke out of the trees into a small meadow and could clearly see the snowcapped peak, straight ahead.

"Told you so," Ben Muriday shouted.

"Lookie there. We been on the right track all the day. Just like I said we was."

"I'll be damned," Stanton said with a smile.

They paused to let the horses graze in the meadow, and to study the terrain in the distance for any hint of red sandstone cliffs.

Stanton noticed Muriday looking askance at the pack animals, and imagined he wanted to complain to Gardner, as he had earlier, about them slowing down their progress. However, even someone like Muriday, not given to politeness, was not going to incur the wrath of the man with two scalps tied to his saddle.

Like those whom they pursued, Cole and Geier guided their course by the snow-capped peak, although after passing the ambush site, they altered their trajectory toward the top of the ridgeline so as to maintain a position on higher ground. Here, they found a deer trail, and made good time following it, while the others continued in a more dense section of the forest below.

"Can't believe it," Cole said with a sigh of relief, handing his brass spyglass to the Dutchman.

"So," Geier said, focusing on a group of riders in a clearing below. They had dismounted and were checking cinches while their stock grazed.

For the first time since he had left the railroad line east of Santa Fe at the beginning of this adventure, Bladen Cole was able to cast his gaze upon the men whom he had been trailing. They seemed to have stayed one step ahead of him for the past five days. Now he had caught up, and it was time to plan his next move.

"You have caught your prey," the Dutchman said and smiled.

"Not quite," Cole said cautiously. "Catching them dismounted *is* how I'd like to do it, but they're a quarter mile away. They'd both see us and hear us coming down this rocky slope. They could start shooting, or mount up and ride out faster than it would take to get down there . . . or both."

"I see." Geier nodded. "You have a bit of a hunter in you."

"That's the job. Now is the time to follow . . . watch . . . wait."

"Until tonight, perhaps."

"Yeah," Cole confirmed. "Probably until after they dismount again to make camp. Probably until they turn in for the night and the only real obstacle is a dozing sentry."

"At their most vulnerable." Geier nodded. "And before they arrive at the red rock canyon."

"I expect that there will be some shooting, and some spilling of blood, tonight," Cole told the Dutchman. "I thank you greatly for taking me this far, but I think I should take it from here."

"Are you dismissing the old Dutchman?" Geier laughed.

"You promised to help me find these men . . . and you did. It's my hide on the line to take them into custody. This will be my fight, not yours."

"I'm offended that you feel my services would not be useful in the next phase of your enterprise, Mr. Cole. Ist not two guns better that one?"

The Dutchman's smile said that the extent of the offense he took was not deep, but there was a trace of disappointment in his voice.

"But . . ."

"The fact that I came with you at all ist due to my huge resentment at the deeds which you told me were done by these men. I would like to remain with you to assure that they *will* be taken into custody. I have invested my time in this venture of yours, and I do not want it to come to naught."

"I don't want to see you taking any chances," Cole said.

"I am not a man who is given to chance," Geier said, the smile fading from his face.

In the distance, the gathering cumulus had now billowed up around the snowcapped peak, obscuring much of it. A long line of steel gray clouds had shouldered their way in from the west. Thunder rumbled across the landscape, and late afternoon lightning crackled within the thunderheads. As with most summer thunderstorms across the Southwest, the threat of rain was an idle threat, but the wind picked up as the two riders made their way down the talus slope to the clearing where their quarry had paused.

Between the wind blowing through the trees and the rolling thunder, the sounds made by the two riders were masked from those whom they followed. Using his telescope to keep an eye on them, Cole matched their progress, as he and the Dutchman stayed to higher ground.

Two hours passed, and then a third. The disturbance within the clouds built to its crescendo and began to slacken as the sun dipped toward the western horizon and fell behind the thunderheads. The lightning flashes were fewer, but more vivid in the gathering darkness.

The four riders kept going, wringing every

possible mile out of the day before it was overpowered by the evening. Cole recognized that he would have done, and often had done, the same, when his progress was ruled by urgency.

"It's starting to get on toward night," Ben Muriday observed, staring into the shadowy forest ahead of them. "We better ought to make camp before we have to do it in the dark."

"And in the rain," Simon Lynch added.

"We had rain clouds all around us for the last three hours," Gabe Stanton reminded him, "and we ain't had a drop of rain."

"It can come up sudden in these parts," Lynch replied. "Don't mind settin' up camp in the rain. Just don't wanna do it in the dark too."

"He's probably right," Jasper Gardner said disgustedly. "If we keep on, we could go past those red cliffs and not even see 'em. Over yonder in that open space would be a good spot. That way there ain't no cover the Apaches can use to sneak up on us in the night."

With that, they chose their campsite, dismounted, and began setting up a picket line for the stock. As he had the night before, Lynch set about building a fire pit as soon as he had unsaddled his horse.

Gardner and Stanton unsaddled their own mounts and began to pull the pack saddles from their mules. The first one came off with practiced efficiency, but the ropes on the second pack saddle had become tangled, and the tangling was hard to see in the quickly gathering darkness. Stanton gave it a hard jerk, the mule bucked violently, and the whole apparatus unraveled suddenly. This sent the pack saddle crashing heavily with a sharp metallic clatter as the bags of gold coins hit the ground.

"What the hell you got in there?" Ben Muriday exclaimed. "Sounds like you're carryin' a whole load of horseshoes."

"Yeah," said Stanton.

"None of your damned business," Gardner said.

They had not anticipated the need to merge their stories about what exactly they carried on their mules.

As Muriday approached, they saw that there had been a tear in the corner of the pack saddle and about two handfuls of twenty-dollar gold eagles had spilled onto the ground.

The fire flared up as the three men stared at the ground, the recently minted coins seeming to be inflamed in the flickering reflected light.

"*Ooooh,* God in heaven, what have we here?" Muriday asked. By now, a curious Simon Lynch had hurried to see what they *did,* indeed, have there.

"Lordy, you have got yourself a king's ransom in there. Where'd you get all that?"

"It's ours . . ." Stanton insisted.

"What'd you do to get paid all that?" Lynch asked.

"You fool," Muriday spat. "They didn't get *paid* all that . . . they *stole* it!"

"Don't recall saying that," Gardner said. "You're jumpin' to conclusions that you ain't got proof for."

"Tell me I'm wrong then," Muriday insisted. "I ain't never seen nobody goes around scalping Indians who's been gettin' paid hundreds . . . thousands of bucks for doing anything."

"What if it did get robbed somewhere?" Stanton interjected. "And I ain't sayin' it *was.* Tell me you ain't stole your share or you wouldn't steal it if you was given a chance."

"So, how much you got there?" Muriday asked.

"More like thousands than hundreds," Gardner admitted.

"Both them all full of gold?" Lynch asked,

pointing to the other packsaddle.

"Some of it's greenbacks," Stanton explained.

"Where *did* you get it?" Lynch asked.

Gardner looked at Stanton. Stanton looked at Gardner, and Gardner shrugged.

"Up around Santa Fe," Stanton said.

"Is somebody lookin' for it?" Muriday asked.

"I s'pose it's more like somebody wished they had it back," Stanton said. "Ain't nobody actually *lookin'* for it. If there was, we lost 'em."

"Tell me this, then," Muriday asked. "If you got all *this,* why in hell you sign on to go with us after the Dearing Diggings?"

"Helluva lot more gold up there than's here," Gardner replied. "This stake we got here's pretty good, but there ain't a man I ever met who has got hisself *too much* gold."

Greed is the fuel that feeds the fire of greed.

CHAPTER 12

Tethering their horses on a ridge some distance away, Bladen Cole and Otto Geier closed in on the encampment of the four who dreamed of riches beyond their imagining.

Their plan was quite straightforward. They would wait until three were snoring and the sentry nodded. They would then wake them up, tie them up, and saddle them up. In this simplicity, there were expansive margins for errors, and untold opportunities for the unexpected, but two Winchesters held by two men were deemed sufficient to equalize any threat presented by four groggy men groping for their weapons in the half-light of the fire.

The thunderheads of afternoon had long since faded away, leaving a clear sky studded with stars and the sliver of a moon. Crickets provided a monotone of background noise, as a succession of sentries began taking turns cocking their heads and straining their ears for sounds of Apache warriors coming to exact revenge for the taking of the two scalps.

One man took the first turn, and he woke another around midnight.

Soon the first man was snoring. The second man relaxed, started to nod off, caught himself, shook his head, and walked a short distance away to take a leak.

Cole and the Dutchman watched as he returned to the fireside, sat down on his saddle, with his rifle across his knees, and yawned. Somewhere high above, an owl moaned, but the man did not seem to notice. He was fading.

Cole looked at the Dutchman, and the Dutchman nodded. It would not be long.

Suddenly, a long-haired man rolled out of his bedroll and stood up holding his rifle.

"Okay, you two," he shouted, kicking rifles and gunbelts away from the two men who were still asleep. "Time to rise and shine. I been having me some thinking."

The two men who had been still asleep now rose to their hands and knees, reaching for weapons that had been kicked away.

"What the hell?"

"I been having some thinking," the long-haired man in the red and white striped shirt, now standing with his back to Cole and the Dutchman, repeated. "You boys done got away from Santa Fe with thousands of somebody else's dollars. I seen the railroad company markings on those bags. I figure those boys had gotta be pretty mad. Right? Mad enough to put a pretty good price on your heads?"

There was some grumbling from the two men, but no audible answer.

"The way I figure it, we could just shoot you right here and take this dough and get the hell out of this wilderness and run off. Me and Lynch, we been looking for a nest egg and a new start, and if we was to take off we'd have the nest egg, but still be lookin' over our shoulders. But if we take you boys *in,* hand you over to the law with all this loot, then we gets us a reward *and* a new start. We'd be heroes and get ourselves reward money, free drinks, and *women.* We'd be heroes. I ain't *never* been a hero. Always wanted to be one."

"How do you know things are gonna work out like that?" one of the other men growled angrily.

"I ain't as dumb as I look," the long-haired man said. "Right, Lynch?"

"No, you ain't," the man called Lynch replied.

"No, I *ain't,*" the long-haired man said firmly. "Now, get some rope, Lynch, and tie up these two. We're goin' back to Santa Fe for payday."

"What about the Dearing Diggings?" asked one of the other men awkwardly, as Lynch pushed him facedown to tie his hands. "I thought we had a deal that we was goin' in there so we'd *all* get rich. There's more money there than any of us can use. You're just throwing that all away."

"Change of plans," the long-haired man replied. "I've been doin' me some thinking."

"If you ain't dumb, and I ain't sure you ain't, you're sure as hell crazy as hell," the other man shouted as Lynch began to bind his hands behind his back. "You're out of your goddamn mind, Muriday. You're out of your goddamn mind for givin' up on the Diggings just as we're almost on top of it. You're out of your mind for plannin' on takin' us back through Indian country with two of us tied to our saddles. You gotta remember that it was Stanton's rifle shot that got the first one of those red savages that we got, and I got the other one."

"It's you who is the crazy one, Gardner," asserted the long-haired man, whom Cole and Geier now knew was called Muriday.

"It was you that scalped them two up there."

"If we go riding back through there with two of us tied up, it's gonna be four white man scalps on some Apache saddle by sundown," Gardner replied, with a fearful undertone to his angry observation.

"You're the one done the scalping," Muriday reminded him. "You're the one got Apache blood on your saddle where those god-awful things been swinging' all afternoon. If we see any damned Apaches, we'll just show 'em that and let 'em have you."

"You're out of your goddamn mind, Muriday," Gardner said in disgust. "What makes you think . . . after yesterday when we done got ambushed . . . what makes you think them savages are gonna come down all nice and ask which one of us to kill? Look . . . I'll make you a deal. We'll split this cash and you can ride off. Me and Stanton will go on our way to California, and you and Lynch can go on up to the Dearing Diggings and get yourself filthy rich and there's no hard feelings. You can go an awful long way on this gold and all *that* gold."

"Yeah, sure, and I got your *word* that you wouldn't double-cross us if we let loose of you?" Muriday said with a laugh.

"My solemn word," Gardner assured him.

"What's it worth . . . the word of a crazy

man who scalps some damned Indians right here in the middle of Indian country?"

"I tell you, let us go and you can have half our haul, and you'll *never* see us again."

"Shut your damned mouth," Muriday said as he pulled a knife, hacked the drying scalps from Gardner's saddle, and threw them into the embers of the fire.

Lynch just shook his head nervously at the sight — and the *smell* — of this.

With the sound of their movements concealed by the ruckus in the camp, Cole and Geier slipped away and returned to their previous perch on the ridge above.

"It seems that circumstances ist changed," the Dutchman said.

"So it seems," Cole said.

"Your prey has been taken by another predator," Geier observed. "What will you do? Will you kill them and take your prisoners?"

"That's not a line that I want to cross," Cole said. "At least not at the moment. They aren't *my* prisoners. I never caught up to 'em. What these men named Lynch and Muriday don't know is that I was hired, not by the law, but by the *railroad.* I'll have to keep following . . . and hope to think of something before they arrive in Santa Fe."

"Because if these men go to the law to collect a reward, they will behold blank stares?"

"Something like that," Cole said and nodded. "*Unless* the railroad men have alerted the law, which they insisted they did not plan to do."

"They might have had a change of mind."

"Anything's possible," Cole said with a nod.

Nobody slept well during what was left of the night.

The sun was not yet up, and a number of stars still hung in the purple sky as the Dutchman woke Cole out of his doze. He nodded to the camp below. The foursome were stirring, and the captors were already saddling horses.

Geier handed Cole a cup of cold coffee, and the two sat quietly, unwrapping hardtack while watching the preparations below.

"I suppose we better saddle up," Cole said at last. "Guess we might as well ride together back as far as Luera."

"I have been thinking," the Dutchman said. "Just as our friend last night had an epiphanous moment of thought, I too have experienced a change of my mind. I don't think I'll go home. I won't go back to

129

Luera . . . for now."

"I think I know what you mean," Cole said with a smile.

The Dutchman pointed into the distance. Far to the south, just a few miles away, the first rays of the morning sun had fallen upon the vivid red sandstone cliffs of a canyon wall.

"You're welcome to join me," Geier said.

"Thanks," Cole said in a tone that said the offer was tempting. "Good luck up there."

"Safe travels, *mein herr,*" the gray-haired man said with a wink as he reined his horse away.

CHAPTER 13

"Twice in one week." Amos Richardson smiled as Ezra Waldron stepped into the candlelit interior of the Refugio del Viajero. "You must have developed a taste for the *carne asada.*"

"Oh . . . hello, doctor," Waldron replied, surprised to see the coroner. "Yes . . . the *carne asada,* it is a memorable dish. I must thank you for introducing me. I had not previously favored the native fare out here in the West. I normally dine at Delmonico's, but old dogs can certainly learn new tricks."

"Would you care to join me?" Richardson asked. "I've ordered, but I could ask Therese to put mine on the back burner."

"Yes, thank you," Waldron said.

"I imagine that you have dined at the original Delmonico's," Richardson said, making conversation after Therese de la Gravière had swooped in to attend to them. While her daughter worked most of the tables, the proprietor always attended personally to her regular patrons, of whom Richardson was among the most loyal.

"But a short distance from my office in New York," Waldron nodded. "And you sir, have you been to Delmonico's?"

"Not the one in New York. I have never, myself, been in the *North.*"

"Yes, I understand," Waldron said, realizing from Richardson's accent that mention of the northern city was treading on the raw nerves of old rivalries. Aiming to alter the course of the conversation, he quickly added, "I had no idea until I came out that enterprising restaurateurs in every town of any size, and some with no size, seem to have appropriated that name for a dining establishment."

"I hope that you've found them living up to the caliber of the original," Richardson said and smiled.

"Most not, as one might expect, but the one here in Santa Fe has not been a disappointment. And now the Refugio. I had not anticipated myself developing a taste for the 'chili pepper' cuisine."

"One rarely sees chili peppers in Richmond either," Richardson laughed, referencing the geographic divide in a lighthearted manner to set the Northerner at ease. "To chilies," he said, holding up a glass.

"To chilies." Waldron smiled, touching Richardson's proffered glass with his own. "To new discoveries and . . . to new friends."

"To friends," Richardson said, smiling.

When Therese had presented two sizzling plates of the house specialty, the two diners dived in, savoring the thinly sliced meat, the thinly sliced onions — and the chilies.

"There is something that I would like to speak with you about," Waldron said as Richardson took a break and reached for his wineglass.

"Is it about the bounty hunter and the robbers? How is that progressing?"

"I have had no word, but it has been less than a week," Waldron replied. "I hope that we will soon have word, and that no harm has come to your friend, the bounty hunter, Mr. Cole."

"More an acquaintance than a friend," Richardson clarified. "But he *is* a fellow Virginian."

Waldron nodded.

"I would expect that you are due for some news soon," Richardson said. "Even with two parties beginning a day apart, I would imagine that it should not take longer than a week for the bounty hunter to return, assuming he has been successful."

"I was thinking the same," Waldron said uncertainly. "Although, I do not know the nature of the wilderness into which they were riding, save the general knowledge that it *is* a wilderness untouched by the niceties with which gentlemen are accustomed."

"A wilderness indeed," Richardson agreed. "And the reputed lair of Geronimo and company if one travels farther south into the Mogollon Rim country."

"A long way indeed from New York . . . *or* Richmond," Waldron observed.

"Or Santa Fe, for that matter," Richardson added.

"What was it that you wanted to ask me before we started talking of fugitives and bounty hunters?" Richardson said.

The table remained quiet for a number of minutes, as the two men savored their dinners.

"May I speak candidly?" Waldron asked at last.

"Of course."

"And in confidence?"

"You have piqued my curiosity, sir." Richardson smiled.

"Miss de la Gravière," the New Yorker said, nodding toward Therese's daughter, who was swirling about a table across the room delivering plates of delicacies.

"Nicolette? Yes?"

"A lovely young lady," Waldron said, blushing slightly.

"Her beauty is that which clearly attracts the eye," Richardson confirmed with a nod. "Her smile can melt ice, and she has an agreeability of disposition which is so often lacking in women of such radiance."

"Do you know whether she has a man who is . . . ?"

"I am unaware of such a man, although I cannot be counted as an authority on her private life. I take it that you harbor aspirations in that direction."

"I do," Waldron said and nodded sheepishly.

"I *do* know that she is only about twenty-three, and I take you for nearly twice that," Richardson said protectively.

"Four years short of double that number, but this is not an *unusual* separation of ages," Waldron insisted.

"That would be none of *my* business," Richardson said. "It would be something for you to take up with her."

"With that in mind, I'd like to ask you for an introduction to her mother so that I might clear the way for doing just that."

"To ask Therese . . . ?"

"Whether I might approach her daughter

with an offer to escort Miss de la Gravière to the theater."

Richardson paused, mulling it over in his mind. At last, he raised his hand, signaling for Therese to approach their table.

"Mama!" Nicolette de la Gravière said in exasperation. "What did you tell him?"

"Only that he might, with my permission, speak to you on the matter," Nicolette's mother explained.

It was early morning, and the two women had just taken the day's delivery from the man who sold them the vegetables for Refugio del Viajero.

"Mama, he is so *old,*" Nicolette insisted, as she sorted and washed a basket of greens.

"May I remind you, Nicolette, that you are not so young yourself. You are nearly twenty-four, an age when a woman should be seriously entertaining suitors. When I was your age . . ."

"Mama, I *know* that you had become engaged to Papa, but you did not wed for two more years."

"At least I was, as the Anglos say, 'spoken for.' "

"John was courting me when I was twenty," Nicolette insisted.

"Where did *that* get you?"

Tears began welling up in Nicolette's eyes.

"I'm sorry, *ma chère fille,* I know that the pain of the wickedness in his breaking of your heart continues to tear at you . . . but, my child, you *must* move on."

"I don't know, Mama," Nicolette choked out. "I'm unsure . . . I'm afraid."

"You must not allow this fear to prevent your happiness now . . . *and* in the future."

"I know . . . My *mind* knows that you are right," Nicolette admitted. "But my heart is stubborn."

"I see the wall you have made between you and the world," Therese continued. "I have seen you with customers . . ."

"I greet them cordially, as I should," Nicolette insisted. "I am never discourteous, never impolite . . ."

"No, I did not mean that . . ."

"Would you have me flirt with customers?"

"No . . ."

"Then what?" Nicolette asked tersely.

"I see your eyes . . . a mother sees . . . I see your eyes when a man you like comes in. There was that cowboy a few days ago. I could tell . . ."

"And . . ."

"You might have allowed yourself a bit of conversation."

"Well, he's gone now," Nicolette said and shrugged. "They come. They go."

"And what of Monsieur Waldron?" Therese asked.

"What *of* Monsieur Waldron?" Nicolette said, rolling her eyes.

"He is a gentleman. He asked me politely whether he could ask you to accompany him to the theater. You *enjoy* the theater."

"I do," Nicolette admitted.

"He is a gentleman, and he is a railway official," Therese explained. "He has money."

"Is it about the money? Is *that* what you want?"

"I want what's best for my daughter," Therese said sternly. "Someday, you will want a man with a reliable income, and it would be nice to have a prominent man. Compare that to a cowboy or a drifter who comes and goes and is never heard from again."

"Is it all . . . ?"

"No. It is *not* all about his money," Therese said, almost scolding. "You deserve better than these cowboys . . ."

"Like John?" Nicolette asked pointedly.

"Like him . . . like that one last week who caused your cheeks to flush, but who was gone the next day, and who is probably in

138

West Texas by now . . . and who has no intention of settling down and making a home. Another rough-edged drifter who could not afford to provide a proper home even if he were convinced that he should or must."

"Not a proper gentleman who would provide a proper home," Nicolette said with disdain and a toss of her head.

"You should allow someone, some *gentleman,* into your world, if not your heart," Therese insisted. "Long enough to give the man a chance to win your heart . . . or at least *try* . . . long enough to give him a chance to put some color into your cheeks."

"Monsieur Waldron?"

"He is a polite man who happens to have a good income. Is it a crime for a mother to want such a man to be interested in his daughter?"

"No, Mama."

"I'm not asking you to *marry* Monsieur Waldron," Therese pleaded. "Just to go to the theater and allow him to treat you as a lady should be treated . . . as a lady who happens to be my daughter should be treated."

"But Mama, he is so old . . ."

"He is not so *old,*" Therese insisted.

"When I was your age . . ."
"Yes, Mama, I *know* how old Papa was."

CHAPTER 14

Pop.

Somewhere in the roughly quarter-mile distance, there was a gunshot.

Pop. Pop.

More gunshots.

Pop-pop-pop-pop-pop.

A fusillade.

Bladen Cole reined the roan to a stop and listened carefully. There had been an explosion of woodpeckers from the tops of the trees, startled by the first sounds of the shots, but they had glided away. The only nearby sounds were the occasional creak of a branch in the wind.

It sounded like there had been an ambush somewhere in the woods up ahead, and Cole was anxious not to be the victim of another one in his location.

Pop.

Another single shot up ahead was followed by the *pop, pop* of a different gun.

The four men whom he was following had been ambushed, probably by vengeful Mescalero, out to repay the man who had lifted the scalps of their comrades.

Should he just let it play out, or should he intervene?

More gunshots.

Pop-pop-pop-pop.

His curiosity got the best of him, so he grabbed his Winchester, tied the roan do a downed snag, and moved forward.

He walked uphill from the sounds of the gunfire, knowing that the attackers would have ambushed from above, and not wanting to sacrifice any high ground only to wind up in the middle of the shootout.

At last, he was close enough to smell burnt powder drifting through the trees, and finally he was close enough to see the bluish puffs that betrayed the positions of the shooters.

Crouching practically on his hands and knees, he crept through the thick stand of ponderosa until he could see what was happening. Around to his left were four men, carefully positioned behind fallen logs. Cole could not tell whether they were Chiricahua or Mescalero. Before them, they had a perfect field of fire on the slope below.

Cole could barely make out the targets of

their ambush, and he saw only two rifle positions, identifiable by the gunsmoke. Whoever was down there was also well hidden and well protected.

The situation had all the appearances of a standoff.

It was unlikely that the course of the stalemate would be altered until the attackers withdrew, or someone did something especially heroic or especially foolish.

Whether what happened next was especially heroic or especially foolish would be open to interpretation.

Suddenly there was a shriek from down below, and a man ran out of hiding, trying to advance uphill through that perfect field of fire.

K'pow-k'pow-k'pow-k'pow-k'pow!

The rifle fire from the attackers was much louder now that he was closer, but as Cole saw, no shot from this burst had been effective.

Now safe behind a tree, the man shouted in defiance.

He looked Apache, but Cole could not tell whether he was Chiricahua or Mescalero.

As the Dutchman had pointed out, the Mescalero liked to show their flag in Chiricahua country, and Chiricahua insisted on dissuading them from this endeavor. The two bands had been rivals, and on c asion deadly antagonists, since anyone could remember. Cole had stumbled into one of those occasions.

Luckily for them, the foursome of white men that he was following had been spared the dilemma of a particularly well-executed ambush that had snared rival Apache. So too, Cole realized, had he — at least so far.

Buoyed by his success in getting twenty feet up the hill without being hit, the man behind the tree decided to try for more.

He ducked out from hiding and ran at top speed.

K'pow! K'pow! K'pow!

His friend covered him as best he could from his hiding place below.

K'pow-k'pow-k'pow-k'pow-k'pow!

The opposing force answered with the bark of four Winchesters.

"Aiio-ooh!"

This time the man had not been so lucky. He was hit in the arm. It was only a flesh wound, but it was obviously quite painful.

K'pow-k'pow-k'pow-k'pow-k'pow!

Sensing that they had drawn blood, and hoping to finish him off, the four men above resumed firing again, but the man was now safe behind a downed tree.

Deciding that he had seen enough of

some one else's fight, Cole started to back away. s.

However, his foot slipped and a small dribble of gravel spilled down the slope.

Hearing this, the four Apache turned abruptly in his direction.

K'pow-k'pow-k'pow-k'pow . . . k'pow!

The splintering of wood just inches from his head told Bladen Cole that this was *no longer* someone else's fight.

Unlike the two Apache who were downslope, Cole had an advantage in that he was slightly uphill from the four shooters.

They may have heard him, but for the moment, he had the advantage of their having not yet seen him.

K'pow!

That shot was tentative, a probing shot, like a man poking the brush, looking for a hiding possum that he knows is in there somewhere, though he is not sure exactly where.

K'pow!

That shot was like a dare, trying to get the unseen ambusher of ambushers to show himself.

Cole held his fire, but mainly because he was not really in firing position and he wanted to wriggle himself around to where he could aim.

145

At last, he was ready.

K'pow!

Another probing shot came his way, missing him by two feet.

K'pow!

He answered and did not miss.

The man who had fired the previous shot toppled over clumsily.

K'pow-k'pow-k'pow-k'pow-k'pow!

Cole's shot was answered by an angry, well-directed wall of lead.

He heard a shout, and watched the surviving trio turn away.

The wounded man from below had resumed his uphill dash when he saw the shooters redirect their attention toward Cole.

K'pow-k'pow-k'pow-k'pow-k'pow!

"Aiiah-aaaaagh!"

It was the scream of death.

This time, the fellow had not made it to uphill cover.

Cole, meanwhile, used this distraction to rise up and take aim.

K'pow!

He was not sure that he had hit the shooter nearest to him, but he aimed at the next man anyhow.

K'pow!

Cole dropped for cover after the second,

carefully aimed shot.

K'pow. K'pow.

Two shots came from the other ambushed man, who was still far down below.

Cole peeked through the brush.

Only two ambushers remained, and one of them was wounded.

At this point it was dawning on them that they had lost half of their attacking force, and that they were taking fire from two directions. In the space of about two minutes, they had gone from being a commanding presence on the battlefield to being one that verged on the untenable.

This was the point when they realized that they should probably withdraw to fight another day, but also that this move was rendered nearly impossible by their being in a crossfire.

K'pow! K'pow! K'pow!

Three shots, no longer probing, but furious in their statement that the shooters planned to execute their only acceptable option — they were going to try to shoot their way out of a situation turned sour.

K'pow!

Cole fired and missed, and thumbed more cartridges into the Winchester as they returned fire.

K'pow! K'pow!

He could see them weaving and dodging, getting ready to make their dash.

K'pow. K'pow.

Two shots from below.

K'pow. K'pow.

Two more.

K'pow!

One of the men had stood, aimed, and fired at Cole.

It was a near miss, too close for comfort.

K'pow! K'pow!

He had aimed carefully, fired, levered, and fired again, as fast as he could. One or the other of his shots found its mark. It did not matter which.

K'pow!

K'pow!

The last surviving ambusher decided to shoot on the run, taking his chances that Bladen Cole was not so good against a moving target.

K'pow!

He had wagered wrong.

Cole took a deep breath, and then another.

He stood up, holding his rifle away from his body with his left hand, with his right hand high, signifying to the man below that he was not a threat.

He had wandered into this shootout allied with no one, only to wind up as *this* man's ally — and possibly his savior.

He saw the last surviving Apache lower his gun.

Cole indicated by sign that his intentions were friendly, and the man responded in kind.

He was young, barely out of his teens, if that, and he was visibly shaken by the experience.

"Speak English?" Cole asked.

The man just shrugged.

"Español?"

This time, he thought for a moment, as though he knew some words of Spanish, but then he just shrugged hesitantly. Up north around the pueblos near the Rio Grande, the people had been speaking some Spanish for centuries, and a little English for decades, but the Apache kept their distance, preferring to have as little to do with the outsiders as possible.

Cole knew almost no Apache words, and those only if reminded. He had come to this place as a man who had never wanted to be in New Mexico again in his life, so he had come unprepared.

The man's gaze flicked upward, and Cole turned. Above, on the hill where the ambushers had been, there were six mounted Apache.

He glanced to the side and saw five more approaching from below. One of them was leading his roan.

He was surrounded.

They approached cautiously and deliberately, carefully eyeing Cole and the young Apache man.

An older man sitting astride a large gray stallion began to berate the ambush survivor as a father would a son.

The young man protested and pointed up the hill.

"*Dii'i*," he said, holding up four fingers and pointing up the hill. "*Ndee*."

Cole heard him use the word *ndee*, which he recognized as the Chiricahua word for people. The Mescalero word was the distinctly different *haasti'*. Cole now realized that he had stumbled in among a heavily armed group from Geronimo's own Apache group.

He swallowed hard, expecting not to see another moonrise.

After considerable talking and bickering, the man on the gray, who seemed to be in charge, gestured to the man who was leading Cole's roan.

In turn, this man tossed the halter rope to Cole.

The man on the gray stallion turned and

stared at Cole as he mounted up.

"Ha'do'aal," he said firmly, pointing to the north, in the direction that Cole had been headed before all of this had started.

"Much obliged," Cole said, touching the brim of his hat as he rode away.

CHAPTER 15

"Full of vexation come I, with complaint against my child, my daughter," the man portraying Egeus, the father of Hermia, explained to the actor cast as Theseus, the Duke of Athens.

"Stand forth, Demetrius. My noble lord, this man hath my consent to marry her. Stand forth, Lysander: and my gracious duke, this man hath bewitch'd the bosom of my child . . . And stolen the impression of her fantasy."

The complaints of Egeus about Lysander were the same complaints as expressed by Therese de la Gravière about the mysterious cowboy who had "bewitch'd the bosom" of *her* child, *her* daughter.

In deference to her mother, Nicolette *had* agreed to speak with Ezra Waldron. She had even admitted to herself a certain excitement at his asking her to the theater. Though she knew in advance that he would, the fact of its happening did bring a smile to her lips, her lips the color of chilies.

In deference to the season, the theater company was performing *A Midsummer Night's Dream,* and Nicolette made a point of pulling that book off the shelf and reading it in advance of the performance. To her surprise, the words of the Bard had served to bewitch Nicolette in a way that was unexpected. She had thought herself finished with thoughts of the unnamed cowboy, until her mother brought him back into her mind.

She had intended to scoot him out at the first opportunity, but with every line of *A Midsummer Night's Dream,* this knave Shakespeare effectively reinstated him.

Now, escorted to the theater on the arm of Mr. Waldron, she found herself watching the play as though she was part of it. She was Hermia, of course, and her mother was Egeus, insistent that she be at the side of someone else, when the "impression of her fantasy" had been stolen by the cowboy, whose name, in the fantasy which she had contrived within her mind, was Lysander.

"I do entreat your grace to pardon me," the actress portraying both Hermia and Nicolette asked the duke. "In such a presence here to plead my thoughts; But I beseech your grace that I may know the worst that may befall me in this case, if I refuse to wed Demetrius."

Of course, in the Athens of Shakespeare's imagination, such a refusal was a capital crime, but Hermia, dramatically, and unrealistically, could not abide being untrue to her heart.

"So will I grow, so live, so die, my lord," the actress into whose persona Nicolette had projected herself said with a shrug. "Ere I will my virgin patent up unto his lordship, whose unwished yoke my soul consents *not* to give sovereignty."

Nicolette was so absorbed that she forgot to blush at the suggestive phrasing.

When Demetrius looked down at Lysander and told him that he, Demetrius, and Egeus were on common ground with respect to the upcoming nuptials, Nicolette scowled visibly.

However, when Lysander told Demetrius that he should, in that case, marry Egeus rather than Hermia, Nicolette burst out laughing. A startled Ezra Waldron glanced askance at his companion, but decided it was a good thing that she liked the play.

When the woodland sprites of the Bard's fantasy got involved, Nicolette knew that both Lysander and Demetrius would fall in love with Helena, instead of Hermia. She waited patiently — and she applauded when Oberon sorted this out and matched Demetrius with anyone *but* Hermia.

When at last Egeus admitted defeat, Nicolette was on the edge of her seat.

"Enough, enough, my lord; you have enough," the routed parent conceded to Lysander. "They would have stolen away; they would, Demetrius, thereby to have defeated you and me, you of your wife and me of my consent, of my consent that she should be your wife."

"You seemed to have enjoyed the performance," Waldron observed with the suggestion of understatement in his tone, as he pulled out a chair for Nicolette in the lounge next to the theater where the patrons gathered to socialize.

"I did, Mr. Waldron." She smiled. "I really did. Thank you *so* much."

"I'm delighted, Miss de la Gravière." He smiled in return. "Brandy?"

"Umm . . ." she replied. It had been so long since she had been to a high-class social event with a gentleman that she was unsure of whether a lady was supposed to drink with him under the circumstances. Glancing around, though, she saw other ladies having brandy, and brandy was, unlike whiskey, an approved beverage for ladies.

"Yes, please."

"Had you seen this play before, Miss de la Gravière?" Waldron asked, removing his gloves.

"No, although I *have* read it." She continued to smile. "I read part of it yesterday in fact. I wanted to get in the mood."

"It unquestionably kept your attention," he said. That was an understatement, and he phrased it as such.

"It is an agreeable escape from day-to-day reality," she said, still smiling.

"That it is."

"Had *you* seen it before, Mr. Waldron?"

"Yes, one time . . . in New York. One has frequent opportunities for the theater in New York."

"I've never been," Nicolette admitted. "Perhaps one day. I have not been far from Santa Fe since I was a little girl."

"You are not from this territory, then?"

"No, I was born in France, but I have few memories of it. I grew up in Mexico during the Empire. My father was in the government."

"Did he . . . ?"

"He lost his life."

"I'm sorry."

"We miss him . . . but it has been a long time," Nicolette said, looking down into her brandy snifter and trying to move her mind along to something else. "Tell me about yourself, Mr. Waldron. What is it like to run a railroad?"

"Well, I don't exactly *run* the Atchison, Topeka & Santa Fe," he said modestly. "I am in finance."

"Does that mean you pay for the railroad?"

"Not exactly," he explained. "The shareholders are the ones who *pay* for the road. My role is in the *arranging* of the financing. I help to make sure that there is money in place to meet the obligations of the road."

"Making sure that you are taking in enough money to pay for your workers and railroad ties?" Nicolette asked.

"Yes, that's right," Waldron replied. "Those things are mainly cash-and-carry, but we are also managing for obligations that we pay on long-term contract, like water and coal."

"I suppose that you have income that is on contract, as well?"

"Certain freight customers are like that," he said. Most women just smiled and nodded, or yawned, when he talked about these things. "We also have to manage our obligations to shareholders, which are long-term, and they require dividends as a reward for providing the ongoing capital for things, such as line extensions, that do not generate short-term revenue . . . Am I boring you with this talk?"

"Why?"

"Most women find finance a rather tedious topic."

"Perhaps most women do not manage businesses," Nicolette said with a smile, taking a sip of her brandy. "The Refugio del Viajero is a much smaller enterprise than the Atchison, Topeka & Santa Fe, Mr. Waldron, but we *do* have two important shareholders and we are very anxious to keep *them* happy."

"Yes, I see," Waldron said.

"As you can imagine, our income is all cash-and-carry, but our outlay is mainly on contract, so we spend a great deal of our time planning ahead. Our reputation depends on fresh ingredients, fresh meat, fresh produce, fresh every day. If what we bring in this morning is not sold today, it is gone forever, and it earns our two shareholders, Mama and myself, no revenue. Some things we are able to stock ahead of time, such as dried beans, corn flour for the tortillas, onions, wine, and the dried chilies . . . but we have to plan very carefully when we buy our meat on contract. I hope that I am not boring *you*, Mr. Waldron."

"Not at all," he replied. "You seem to being doing very well with your management of supplies versus sales."

"Mama is very good with planning," Nicolette said proudly. "And we have built a good reputation for Refugio del Viajero."

"You don't seem to have any real competition."

"Mama keeps her eyes open," Nicolette nodded. "There is Delmonico's, but they serve a much different fare . . . We have loyal customers who also dine there as well. The main thing is maintaining our reputation with customers old and new. I would say that your railroad is lucky not to have any competition in this territory."

"Colorado is a different story, of course," Waldron replied. "And the Denver & Rio Grande is desirous of operations here in New Mexico."

"Your success, I imagine, will hinge upon your reputation, and your service to your customers," Nicolette suggested. "We expect to see big changes here in Santa Fe now that the railroad is coming."

"Santa Fe is only part of it," Waldron

explained. "It is very complicated. While service is certainly important, the success of the Atchison, Topeka & Santa Fe is ultimately dependant upon our continuing to build, quickly and efficiently, across New Mexico and Arizona to the Pacific shore in California. The road must have a transcontinental line linking Chicago with the Pacific . . . and to do so *before* . . . and *instead of* . . . the Denver & Rio Grande."

"Why is that a *must*, Mr. Waldron?" Nicolette asked.

"Because this is what the shareholders expect," he said. "This is the basis on which the financiers who *do* pay for the Atchison, Topeka & Santa Fe have put up substantial sums."

"Will there be a railroad war in New Mexico, as we have seen in Colorado?" she asked.

"It is my job to make sure that this does not happen," Waldron said, his brow furrowing. "But if it does come, it may be fought here, but it will *not* be won or lost in New *Mexico,* but in New *York.*"

CHAPTER 16

The air smelled thickly of the imminence of rain.

The towering thunderheads converged above like great, gray boulders, hewn by giants and assembled by titans into a citadel fit for primordial gods. The immense bulwark grew so high as to cover the sun itself. The stamina-sapping dry heat of mid-afternoon abruptly gave way to chill, as the breeze materialized out of nowhere and noisily rustled through the aspen leaves.

Lightning, trapped in the depths of the thunderheads, flashed as an eerie illumination, rather than as jagged rivulets of white-hot fire. The thunder followed almost immediately, blundering through the angry clouds like the sort of fusillade of cannon fire that had so terrified, yet so intrigued, a thirteen-year-old Bladen Cole as the volleys pounded Fredericksburg.

A skittering flock of birds exploded from

a copse of aspen and recklessly careened through the air, briefly hugging near the earth before ascending into a sky filled with the scent that foretold rain.

Cole pushed his hat down low on his head to preserve its place from the gusts of wind.

Ahead lay the broad, northeasterly trending valley, which lay between the mountain ranges of the Sierra Gallinas and the Sierra Magdalena — which, in turn, paralleled the valley of the Rio Grande to the east.

Ahead rode the same men whom Cole had now followed for a week, together with their pair of recent captors — and their mules, who plodded ever onward, laden with the weight of gold.

Yesterday, a half hour after he parted company with the Dutchman, Cole had turned in his saddle to look back. He could see the location of the place on the ridgeline where they had spent the night, but, naturally, the Dutchman was gone. He was a half hour closer to the distant red rock canyon, and to that almost mythical place where the man named Dearing had passed from mundane reality into the pantheon of the legendary.

Descending from the mountain country, Cole watched the dense ponderosa forest give way to scattered groves of aspen. As he crossed the trail that linked Luera with Santa Rita, his view opened up, and he could see the jagged, blue edges of distant mountains on the far horizon. The chances of ambush had lessened as the vista broadened, and Cole had relaxed, allowing his mind a freer rein to wander. As so often on long rides through the vast openness of the West, he often rambled from thought to thought, conjuring random contemplations to fill the spaces in his consciousness that were opened wide by the openness and emptiness of the landscape itself.

The reflections that he rolled around in his head like pebbles between the fingers of a nervous man included all the motivations he had for *not* going with the Dutchman to Dearing's great treasury. Cole questioned his own decision to turn north, rather than to join the Dutchman in this venture. He questioned his single-minded determination to give up the possibility of riches, and to follow the two men whom he had signed on to capture, despite their having been captured by others.

He *had* given his word to the railroad men that he would see the task through. To fail to live up to his word would cast an impenetrable shadow across his reputation of being a man who did what he promised. The last thing he wanted was for these two men called Lynch and Muriday to have the reputation for being able to finish a job after Bladen Cole *gave up* on it.

Then too was the recollection of the young woman with the long dark hair, whose mother owned the dining place in Santa Fe. It would be nice to see her again, and to enjoy the candlelight sparkle in her eyes, and the smile on those lips the color of chilies.

Finally, there was the reason at the heart of all his reasons for riding north. It was not an immunity to greed for the Dutchman's gold that governed his momentum, but his unarticulated aversion to the ghosts of his past.

His compass took him north because to the south lay Silver City, and the source of memories of that night when the rat-faced man killed his brother Will.

"Damned clouds look like rain," Gabe Stanton observed, noting the obvious as the thunder rumbled across the mesquite-studded hills.

"Ain't you never been rained on before?" Ben Muriday snarled.

"Not with our hands tied to a damned saddle horn," Jasper Gardner interjected.

"You got more to worry about when you get yourself brought to justice," Muriday retorted.

"And you ain't never been on the wrong site of justice yourself?" Gardner taunted him. "When we get face-to-face with the sheriff back up there in Santa Fe, I'm gonna tell him he needs to wire around and look for warrants on your sorry hide."

Oblivious to the lone rider who dogged their steps, the four men plodded ever northward. Despite his apparent cocksure self-confidence, Ben Muriday had been questioning his own sanity for the nearly two days since he had made the decision to make the change of direction in his life from treasure hunter to hand of justice.

Gardner was right, and Muriday questioned making this decision fraught with perils, not the least of which was a three- or four-day ride with two dangerous prisoners who might do anything to get away. He could only hope to get them to Santa Fe, collect the reward money, and get out of town before any of the buzzards of his past came to roost.

The dark sky grew suddenly darker, and the nose-curling smell of rain grew suddenly more pungent. Thunder so loud that it shook them in their saddles struck without the warning of lightning.

The horses whinnied and snorted.

On the dry ground, dark patches the size of thumbprints appeared — first a few, then many.

Wet splashes were felt on hands — first a few, then many.

Sharp splats were felt on hats — first a few, then many.

Suddenly, the trapdoor at the bottom of the thunderhead directly above fell open, and a great ocean dropped from heaven.

The landscape changed in an instant. Raging red torrents appeared in every gully. Visibility condensed from limitless to a few yards.

Simon Lynch, who was handling the three pack animals, lost control as they spooked at the abruptness of the deluge. The mules were tied together in a string, but they got tangled with one another, so he was able to grab a halter rope and recover them. In so doing, he had to dismount and became separated from his own saddle horse.

The two angry, stubborn mules each had an independent idea of which way to go, so Lynch found himself quite literally swimming though the downpour while tugging at these animals. Fortunately, he was able to see his horse, huddling against the base of a cliff not far away, and with great difficulty, he reached her and struggled back into a slippery saddle.

This accomplished, he looked around for the spare saddle horse, which they had packed with their supplies. It was nowhere to be seen — nor were Ben Muriday and the two captives.

When the deluge struck, no one had been quite prepared for its suddenness or its volume. Muriday had tied the horses ridden by Stanton and Gardner together, so they were not separated in the confusion, but he lost sight of them. His master plan, which even *he* had come to question, seemed to dissolve in the rain.

Unsure of what to do or where to go, he spurred his horse forward, in the direction that he thought they had been riding.

Stanton and Gardner had, as he had feared and expected, decided to seize the moment as an opportunity to escape, kicking their horses to run. However, without the use of their hands on the reins to provide unified direction, their two animals, tethered together, had quickly dragged each other from a near-gallop to a staggering near-standstill.

Glimpsing them getting away, but not realizing that they were in this predicament, the reckless Muriday impulsively drew his Colt and fired. The sound of his shot was swallowed into a thunderclap so loud that he thought his gun had misfired.

A moment later, he was close enough to see Stanton's horse rear up, and the man slide from a slippery saddle. As he struck the ground, Muriday was closer still and could see the blood.

"Damn you!" Jasper Gardner screamed angrily above the roar of the storm. "Damn you to *hell* . . . you just shot a defenseless man."

Muriday could see the man, and the violent red stream that swirled around him, but his mind was filled only with the image of his own scheme falling apart.

CHAPTER 17

In the Bible it is told of a time when it rained for forty days and forty nights.

In the desert, forty *minutes* can alter a landscape, creating a vast watershed of dangerous, fast-moving streams which render some trails impassible and others nonexistent.

Overhead, a brilliant sun in a deep blue dome was already drying the desert floor as rivers turned to trickles. Buzzards were already circling, looking for unfortunate vertebrates who had not weathered the brief but intense inundation.

Water still dripped from Simon Lynch's hat brim as he searched the hills and canyons for the missing pack horse. He thought of the supplies that were on that horse, provisions which they would need, provisions such as food. He thought of Muriday's anger if he reported back without those provisions.

Lynch scanned in vain, and in desperation, but the desperation and the scanning yielded no results. He guessed that the better part on an hour had slipped away before he reined his horse around and headed back toward where he had left Muriday and the captives.

At least he still had the pack mules, and all the gold. The irony was not lost on him that he had thousands of dollars in gold eagles, but the only food he had was a wad of hardtack in his saddlebag, which he had been chewing on when they mounted up that morning.

Lynch found the others dismounted near a streambed beneath a steep hillside. He had wondered for a moment whether he had lost them as well as the pack horse, but he had heard them before he saw them. Actually, he had heard Gardner's shouting voice. At first he thought the man was shouting for help, but as he neared, he could make out the surging volleys of violent expletives.

"Your damned partner done shot mine," Jasper Gardner yelled to Lynch as he approached.

"He's gonna live, damn you," Ben Muriday said with a mixture of anger and relief, as he finished tying a bandanna around

Gabe Stanton's arm. "It's just a flesh wound. He's more banged up from falling off his horse."

"Wouldn't never have fell off if you didn't shoot me," Stanton muttered. "You didn't have no call to do that."

"You were tryin' to get away," Muriday pointed out. "You'd have stayed put, you wouldn't have this trouble. Now, let's get saddled up and get to gettin'."

"Where's the damned pack horse?" Gardner asked as he looked at Lynch and the two mules.

"Run off," Lynch explained. "Been lookin' all over."

"That's all our food," Gardner said.

"I know . . . but I been looking for an hour and can't see the damned thing anywhere. Might have got caught in a flash flood and knocked down. May be layin' out there somewhere waiting to die."

"We gotta find our vittles," Muriday said with the exasperation of a man whose plan was unraveling.

"We're only a day out of Bernalillo," Lynch said hopefully. "We can make it until then . . . and we gots us plenty of them twenty-dollar eagles to *buy* us provisions for another day or so to Santa Fe."

"You idiot," Muriday said. "We can't ride

171

into Bernalillo looking like this. We got two men tied down and one of 'em shot up and a load of coins that clanks as the damned mule walks. We can't go in there . . . There's gonna be questions enough in Santa Fe. We gotta stay wide of towns."

"There's buzzards over yonder," Stanton interrupted as he struggled to his feet. "Maybe that's our pack horse."

"Okay, let's go take us a look," Muriday said, staring at the distant birds as he helped Stanton back into the saddle.

The deviation from their intended route took them across a ridge that ran perpendicular to the steep slope near which they had dismounted.

As they came across and looked down at the focus of the scavengers' attention, four faces fell in disappointment. Instead of the body being the pack horse, it was merely a small black-tailed deer.

"This year's fawn by the looks of it," Lynch said.

"Got some meat left on it," Stanton observed.

"Not very damned much," his partner added.

Indeed, by the time they got to the deer, the only viable cut left unscavenged was the hindquarters closest to the ground, and insects were already burrowing into this.

"Crap," Muriday said in disgust, dropping the carcass and wiping his hand on his pants.

"What about *that*?" Lynch asked, pointing up to the hillside.

In a cleft that ran across the face of the cliff, about thirty feet above the point where it rose from the steep hillside, there was a series of buildings.

"Pueblos," Gardner said. "Indian pueblos. Might be something up there. You suppose it's abandoned?"

There were cliff dwellings all across the Southwest — some that people knew about and others that were so far back in the hills that they were still turning up. When the Spaniards first came, there were people living in all of them, but now most of the smaller ones were empty. It was said that some of the people had been killed by the Spanish, or that they died of the fever. Other cliff dwellers had just moved on.

"If there's people up there, then they got corn or squash growing around here someplace," Gardner said.

"I don't see no corn and squash," Lynch said.

"Don't mean it ain't there," Gardner retorted.

"Everybody wait down here by the bottom of the cliff while I figure out a way to get up there," Muriday commanded.

Ten minutes later, he had found a narrow trail along a ledge, which was virtually invisible from below, and was making his way up to the ancient adobe structures.

There were about a half dozen separate buildings neatly tucked into the crevice, each with one or more windows, carefully constructed with hewn cottonwood lintels. As he got closer, he could see pottery scattered around in the shadows. If a cliff dwelling was abandoned, the pottery was mere piles of shards. These pots, the color of the sandstone and marked with designs painted in black, were intact. He could also now smell the smoke of a recent fire.

There were people here.

He was being watched.

Down below, the others saw Muriday pull his revolver as he neared the first building.

Unlike the Apache, the pueblo people had the reputation of being peaceful. Some of those living in the large clusters of pueblo cities between Bernalillo and Santa Fe traded actively with the Anglos, and had traded with the Spaniards before them, but the pueblo people were mainly farmers who sought only to go about their own business and be left alone. They did not raid Anglo ranches to steal horses or cause mischief as the Apache did, but they were known to fight back if pressed hard enough.

Ben Muriday was here today to press as hard as it took to get what he wanted.

Swallowing with difficulty, he stepped through the door.

An old woman seated on the floor near a fireplace on the opposite wall made no indication of a move toward or away from him. She merely turned her head slightly to stare into his eyes.

His first impression was that she was the oldest person he have ever seen in his life, and she may well have been.

Her expression was one of defiance. She obviously could not stop the intruder, but likewise she just sat there, wrapped in a threadbare blanket and an old shawl, wordlessly telling him that she was not going to run away. Pitiful as it was, this tiny room was her house, and she was staying to stare down the trespasser.

Muriday looked around quickly and saw no weapon, or anything of the provisions that he sought.

Without saying a word, Muriday stepped out and carefully approached the second building, which appeared to be connected to the next one. A ladder led to its roof, so not wanting to risk an ambush, Muriday stepped on its second rung and peered onto the roof, his Colt tightly gripped in his hand.

A flurry of movement almost made him squeeze the trigger.

It was likely that his regret for having needlessly shot Stanton saved the lives of two children of about three years of age.

They were huddled on the roof, clinging to each other and trembling mightily, with their dark eyes the size of the opening in the top of a nearby pottery jar. It gave him a weird sense of exhilaration to have such power that he could instill such terror in these children — especially after facing the intractable insolence of the old woman.

The first room that he entered in the larger building was empty, but the door led to another room.

This one had the cluttered look of a place where people lived. Indeed, pressed against the far wall were a half dozen people. There were two children, a bit older than the ones on the roof, and two women. They were both younger than the first woman, and one was much younger. She had long, dark hair, a finely featured face, and an ample bosom which was barely covered.

Had no one else been present, Muriday

imagined the pleasure he would have taken at her expense.

In the front of the group were two men. One was clearly the elder of the group, though he was much younger than the old woman, and the other man was young and small, but with the hardened muscles of a man in his prime.

His eyes told Muriday without ambiguity that if no one else had been present, he would have wished to kill the white man with his bare hands.

"Look here," Muriday said, lowering his gun slightly. "We don't mean to hurt nobody. We just fell on some hard luck losing our pack horse and our provisions. We just need us some vittles for a three-day ride up yonder."

The little group merely stood and stared.

"Don't tell me *nobody* of your lot speaks English!"

Muriday repeated his request, this time accompanying it with gestures of pointing to his mouth, his stomach, and the distant horizon.

The people spoke among themselves, and soon there was a consensus that if they gave the white man the provisions he sought, the white man would go away and the nightmare would end.

The women went to work, gathering up some dried beans, some small bags of cornmeal, and even a fistful of dried chilies. This they packed into an old flour sack, which the younger woman handed to Muriday.

Having her body so close, and smelling her musky, sweet fragrance, was too much of a temptation. He reached out and touched her barely covered breast. Her garment fell away slightly, revealing her left breast in all its enchanting fullness.

As his hand closed to relish the touch of what his eyes beheld, he felt the sting of a hard and furious slap across the face.

Muriday turned to look in shock at the angry expression of the other woman, the woman who had hit him. She was probably the younger woman's mother.

He did the only thing he could think to do.

He raised his Colt and placed the muzzle directly on the center of her forehead.

CHAPTER 18

Bladen Cole had heard the single gunshot at a half mile distance from the pueblo, and had watched with his spyglass as a lone man emerged from one of the adobe buildings carrying a light-colored bag. He could tell by the red and white striped shirt that it was Muriday, and he wished that his optics gave him adequate resolution to see the expression on the man's face.

He wondered who got shot.

Cole knew, from having discovered the pack horse grazing on a hillside, that the foursome had lost their food supplies. This explained their having paused to rob the people at the pueblo. It seemed an almost whimsical irony that men who possessed $9,000 in gold were compelled by dread of hunger to steal from some of the poorest people on the continent.

The theft also confirmed what Cole had supposed, that they were provisioning to bypass the Anglo settlements in the Rio Grande valley. He was pleased. It would be a lot simpler to follow them in open country than through towns and villages.

They left the pueblo quickly, practically at a gallop, as though intending to make up for lost time.

With the halter rope of the pack horse secured to his saddle horn, Cole mounted up and followed. He passed some distance from the pueblo, but he saw the people standing up there watching, and he knew they saw him. He waved as he passed to the point where it was clear that he had no intention of stopping.

Nobody waved back.

"Gonna say who you shot up there?" Lynch asked Muriday as they plodded north.

The first time he had asked, the bloodshot anger in his partner's eyes told him to back off — but that was an hour ago.

It looked as though Muriday would avoid answering again, turning away from Lynch to spit a wad of tobacco which he was chewing.

At last, he turned back and said simply, "Nobody."

Lynch just nodded, as though to say that he would ask no more on the subject.

"Almost plugged an old lady up there," Muriday said at last, as though unburdening himself of an embarrassment.

"Why'd you almost do that?"

"Because I decided not to after my finger was already pullin' on the trigger. Put the slug in a wall."

"I mean why was you gonna pop the old lady?"

"Got slapped hard across the face."

"How'd that happen?"

"I was havin' a little fun with a young one up there. She didn't like me doin' that."

"Sure wouldn't mind having a woman myself about now," Lynch admitted.

"This was a fine one, all right," Muriday explained. "Fine and smooth and just right in all the right places. Don't feel right about killin' a woman, but you gotta use 'em for what they're made for. Had half a notion to take her along."

"That would have made things real complicated," Lynch said with a nod. "Last thing we need is having all these Indians out here mad at us . . . *and* chasin' after us."

"Plenty of time for women after we get us up to Santa Fe," Muriday said, spitting a cheekful of tobacco on the ground.

■ ■ ■ ■

Bladen Cole opened the pack saddle by the light of a growing moon and ate well, knowing that the foursome camped in the broad valley below were rationing their victuals. They had provisioned for two weeks in the wilderness, so there was plenty from which to choose. He even found a jar of dates. He enjoyed a few, then a few more, and packed the jar up for later.

It was about four o'clock, reckoned by the position of the moon, when he was awakened by a ruckus down below. He trained his spyglass on the fire circle and saw two men, Muriday and Lynch judging by the fact they were untied, running almost comically, in concentric circles. He saw another man, bound hands and feet, wriggle from a bedroll, but he saw no evidence of a fourth.

Someone had escaped.

Cole looked around cautiously, although it was unlikely that the escapee would have climbed to his elevation to get away. In such a situation it is a natural inclination to move as quickly as possible, and going uphill slows a man's pace.

One of the two untied at the campsite — Cole couldn't tell whether it was Lynch or

Muriday — fired two shots from a rifle into the air. Apparently the intention was intimidation, or he would have aimed at something.

Damned fool way to try to intimidate, Cole thought, shaking his head. The shots only served to alert the escapee to the fact that his absence had been discovered and to give him a precise idea of how long of a lead he had. If he was far enough away not to make detectable noise while running, he would continue to run until first light, because a search could not be mounted until then.

The circles in which Lynch and Muriday were wandering served to indicate that their biggest problem at first light was in which direction, in the 360-degree arc of possibilities, they should begin their search.

Cole pondered the same question. Returning back toward the south was out. How could this man go back, unarmed, toward the pueblo which his companion had just robbed? To the west lay virtually nothing but mountains and desert, where a man would probably not survive on foot. As Cole surmised, the best option for a man on foot would be to make for civilization, and the closet settlements were due east, less than a half day's ride away or longer on foot, on the banks of the Rio Grande.

For two nights, Jasper Gardner had lain in his bedroll, studying the ropes with his fingers, planning how he might untie the knot that secured his feet. His fingers could not reach the knots that bound his wrists, but he *could* get his fingers into those at his ankles. At last, as his captors both dozed, he seized the opportunity, and ran with it. More correctly, he tiptoed with it, straight toward the picket line, with his boots under his arm, and wishing that he could have untied his hands so that he could also have grabbed a gun.

As he reached the horses, he watched Lynch wake up, stand, look around, and stretch. He could have gone ahead with his plan to mount up and ride away bareback, but without a gun, there was no way that he could do this at night without being caught — and *shot*.

Faced with a choice of waiting patiently to be sure that Lynch fell asleep again, or getting away on foot sooner rather than later, Gardner anxiously chose the latter, and regretted it within a matter of minutes as he slowly crossed the moonlit desert in his stocking feet. There was, by then, no going back.

He stumbled onward, as quietly as possible, until he was far enough away to finally sit down, find a stick, and use it to pry open the knots on the ropes that secured his hands.

This done, he pulled on his boots and made for the Rio Grande, not yet sure what he would do when he got there but try to get someone to take pity on a poor man who wandered out of the wilderness with rope burns on his wrists. He would try somehow to get a horse and, hopefully, a gun. Then he could intercept the others and retrieve the gold — *his* gold.

Gardner thought of the injured Stanton, whom he had abandoned, but not for long and not hard. As they had since the day he sold his mother's home to the carpetbagger, Jasper Gardner's thoughts centered mainly on the welfare and aspirations of Jasper Gardner.

Muriday, Lynch, and Stanton mounted up under the loosest definition of "first light" that could be imagined. Indeed, the western sky was still as black as charcoal.

"Still say it ain't no time o' day to be tracking somebody," Lynch complained.

"Gotta find that sneaky devil," Muriday insisted.

"Why?" Lynch asked. "We still got his

partner, and we still got the loot."

"Because," Muriday explained angrily, "we can't go bringing back only half of the robbers and leave one at large. We might get only half the reward."

"Let's just tell 'em he was killed by Indians."

"Can't do that," Stanton interjected. "I'll squeal on you."

"Shut up or I'll blow off your head and we'll take you back dead instead of alive," Muriday shouted.

"Then there ain't no way to prove that *you* didn't take this dough in the first place."

Muriday had guessed correctly that Gardner was headed toward the Rio Grande, though he realized in the cold, dim light of the promised dawn that he faced a serious challenge. Finding a man in this vast patch of desert, studded by thousands of cactus and scrubby little bushes, all of which looked like a man standing when glimpsed at great distance, was like finding the proverbial needle in a sea of needles.

It drove him mad — in both definitions of that temperament — that he could at this moment be looking directly at Gardner and not see him. This was an observation which he chose not to share with Lynch, although it would have been hard for Lynch not to come to the same conclusion by his own observations.

CHAPTER 19

"Good evening, mademoiselle, and *merci beaucoup,*" Amos Richardson said as Therese de la Gravière poured him a glass of the blood red wine, all the way from France, which he had been favoring of late.

"*Pas de quoi,* you are most welcome, *Monsieur Doctor,*" she said, returning his smile.

"I don't see Nicolette here this evening," Richardson observed.

"We all need a night off once in a while," she replied. "She's at the Governor's Palace tonight."

"Well now, what takes her to the Governor's Palace?"

"There is a soiree, a reception for a government official who is visiting Santa Fe . . . a Mr. Schurz, I believe."

"Oh yes, Mr. Hayes's secretary of the interior, we knew him as *General* Schurz during the war," Richardson said with a nod of recognition. "He was on the *other* side, but that is no longer here nor there. I had read in the newspaper that he is in the city. He arrived yesterday on the Atchison, Topeka & Santa Fe. What, pray tell, is Nicolette's interest in visiting dignitaries?"

"She is on the arm of Mr. Waldron," Therese said, smiling. "She mentioned that she too had read about Mr. Schurz in the paper, and he invited her to the soiree."

"Does she seem to be finding his company pleasant?"

"*Comme ci, comme ça.* More than she will admit . . . at least to me . . . perhaps to herself. We'll have to wait and see. They have been to the theater as well. She was more pleased with the play, I think, than with the company, but I believe that she did find him agreeable."

"And you? Do you find Mr. Waldron to be agreeable?"

"Nicolette is of that age . . . I have told her as much . . . when she should be entertaining suitors. Mr. Waldron *is* a gentleman; a high-placed gentleman taking an interest in one's daughter is almost never a *bad* thing, although I *do* fear his taking her away to the East."

"You could perhaps join them back East?"

"My life is here," Therese said with a smile, looking at the doctor in a certain way.

"When we first came to Mexico, I pined for France. When we first came to Santa Fe, I yearned for France. Now Santa Fe is my home."

"May I present Miss de la Gravière, Secretary," Ezra Waldron said, introducing her to the guest of honor.

"Ah, de la Gravière." Schurz smiled, taking Nicolette's hand. *"Enchanté. Bonsoir, Mademoiselle de la Gravière."*

"Guten Abend," Nicolette said, returning the German-born cabinet officer's French with a greeting in his native tongue.

"Sprechen sie Deutsche?" Schurz replied, his eyebrows arched in surprise.

"No, sir," Nicolette replied with a smile. "But Mama has always told me that it is polite to greet people in the language of their birth . . . as you did with me."

"I see," Schurz said. "I daresay your English is superior to mine, even after twenty-eight years in this country."

"I am afraid that I have come more recently than you, sir, though I have spent most of my years in New Mexico."

"Which we are pleased to have more closely bound to the nation by means of the railroad, thanks to our mutual friend, Mr. Waldron."

"It will do great things for commerce, which pleases me personally," Nicolette told him.

"How is that, *mademoiselle?*"

"My mother and I . . . we own the restaurant Refugio del Viajero, which is nearby, and we anticipate an increasing number of customers from across the land. We would be pleased to welcome *you,* as well, sir, if your schedule permits while you are in Santa Fe."

"I would be honored, *mademoiselle,* though my visit to your wonderful city is regrettably short."

With one more handshake, they parted company and the secretary was introduced to another guest of the governor.

"I forgot to curtsy," Nicolette said.

"I don't think he cared," Waldron assured her. "Thank you once again for joining me at a moment's notice like this."

"Thank you for inviting me to join you. I enjoyed meeting Mr. Schurz. I do hope that he might have occasion to visit the Refugio."

"The schedules of politicians are, as I am sure you understand, not theirs to do with as they please."

"Of course," Nicolette said.

"Do you know Tobias Gough?" Waldron

asked her.

"I read his column in the *Santa Fe New Mexican,*" Nicolette said.

"Let me introduce you . . . Tobias . . . may I introduce you to Nicolette de la Gravière."

"Miss de la Gravière," the newspaperman said, turning to the young woman in the long crimson dress with lips the color of chilies. "It is a pleasure to meet you . . . although I believe I recognize . . . It's hard to forget a lovely face."

"Thank you, Mr. Gough, it is a pleasure to meet you," Nicolette said with a smile as she took his extended hand. "I *have* seen you a time or two at Refugio del Viajero."

"The restaurant," Gough said, trying to place her.

"Miss de la Gravière and her mother are the proprietors," Waldron explained.

"Of course," Gough said, making the connection. "That's where I've seen you."

"I enjoy your column," Nicolette said. "You have an uncanny gift for getting to the bottom of things."

"Thank you." Gough beamed, pleased to be noticed by such an attractive lady. "I try my best."

"Will you be accompanying the secretary as he tours the territory?"

"Well he *has* made news," Gough said.

"That's what one might expect from transferring the Indian Bureau from the War Department to his Interior Department. Quite controversial, I've read . . . but a wise decision in my opinion."

"You have an ear for current affairs, Miss de la Gravière," Gough observed.

"I read the paper, Mr. Gough," she said with a smile.

"Good evening, Ezra," a voice from behind Nicolette boomed. She turned to see the ample form of Joseph Ames, the noticeably overweight colleague of her escort.

"Hello, Joseph," Waldron said, shaking his hand. "You know Tobias Gough . . . May I present Miss de la Gravière."

"How do you, Miss Gravière," he said, nodding to Gough and gripping Nicolette's hand with his fleshy paw. "I'm Joseph Ames . . . of the railroad. You must be the lovely French girl from the cantina whom Ezra has mentioned."

"I must be indeed," Nicolette said with a smile.

"It's not a cantina," Waldron corrected him. "It's a restaurant, and a fine restaurant at that."

"Sorry, ma'am," Ames said. "I stand corrected. I'm new to the territory, and new to the . . . um, the native cuisine."

"You should visit the Refugio del Viajero sometime so that we may introduce you to the *native* cuisine," Nicolette said with a broad smile.

"I shall," Ames promised noncommittally. "Now, if you don't mind, young lady, I'd like to steal Ezra for a minute or two for some *man* talk?"

"Of course," Nicolette said, bowing her head slightly in mock deference, which Ames did not perceive.

"Has there been any news?" Ames asked. "Will these people be caught? Where is that bounty hunter that you hired?"

"There has been nothing," Waldron admitted. "I don't know that we *will* hear . . ."

"We *must* get that money by the end of the month," Ames said, visibly worried. "This thing is getting out of control. We should have hired more than one man . . . This is obviously beyond his ability."

"It is out of our control, Joseph," Waldron said firmly.

"I don't like seeing things *this* out of control," Ames retorted. "I believe that we must consider reporting this affair to the proper authorities and getting a sheriff's posse on the trail of these men."

"A trail gone cold and stale after a week's

time?" Waldron said sarcastically.

"A trail which must be followed, and the sheriff is the professional authority who *should have* been involved *before* this trail went stale," Ames asserted.

"We've made our bed, Joseph. We cannot afford to second-guess our own decisions."

Nicolette wandered the room, taking a flute of champagne, which she sipped. She thought of the difficulties in obtaining such goods in Santa Fe, and imagined how this would change with the coming of the railroad.

"Mademoiselle."

Again, a voice from behind her, and Nicolette twirled to a greeting from the guest of honor. Schurz introduced her to an elderly couple as his "fellow European émigré," to which she responded by commenting on the idea of a nation of immigrants.

"I believe the country is made stronger by its being a nation of immigrants, you from France, myself from Germany," the former senator explained, slipping momentarily into his politician vest. "I believe that we immigrants can accomplish tremendous things for the development of this great composite nation of the new world, if in our works and deeds we combine and weld the best that is in the character of our original homelands with the best that is in the American character."

"I agree, sir, though I remember little of the land across the sea," Nicolette said. "I would have to say, sir, that here in New Mexico, we view things a little differently than you do in the East."

"How is that?"

"The East, and by that I mean *both* North and South as they identified themselves in the late war, shares a common heritage in the same colonial power, and a common heritage in their fight for independence one hundred years ago. Here, we were part of a different empire, from which this territory was more recently removed, and many people still alive have memories of a culture quite different from the common civilization which is shared by all of those in the East. We all *still* feel like immigrants."

"I had not thought of it from this perspective," Schurz said thoughtfully.

"May I cut in," Ezra Waldron said, entering the conversation.

"Of course," the interior secretary said. "Sir, you are accompanied by a very bright young lady, here. *Mademoiselle,* I enjoyed our thoughtful chat. *Bonsoir.*"

"*Bonsoir,* sir, *Guten Abend,*" Nicolette

replied, remembering to curtsy.

"You seemed to have impressed Mr. Schurz with your conversation," Waldron said.

"We were speaking about this being a nation of immigrants, and how those of us in the territories all have the feeling of still being foreigners in America," Nicolette explained. "I suppose that this will change as the railroad arrives."

"Would you like to *see* it?"

"Pardon?"

"I would be honored to invite you to come down to see the railroad construction headquarters at Lamy," Waldron offered. "It is but an hour or so by carriage, and I think that you might enjoy seeing our activities before the spur is actually completed into Santa Fe."

"That would be most interesting, Mr. Waldron," Nicolette said. "I would very much like to see the Atchison, Topeka & Santa Fe as a work in progress."

CHAPTER 20

As Nicolette de la Gravière had gone to sleep on down pillows thinking about immigrants and railroads, five men had awakened in the dark desert with dust in their nostrils, and the anxiety of plans gone awry.

Bladen Cole had lost his fugitives to a rival even before they had become his captives. Ben Muriday and Simon Lynch faced the dilemma of a captive having become a fugitive, while that man faced the desert alone, with no gun, no horse, and the prospect of men possessing *both* in pursuit and hot on his heels.

Redressing the shortcoming of his lacking these most useful — indeed essential — of possessions was the highest objective for him as the new day began. Jasper Gardner could at least be thankful for his boots.

The sun, white hot and promising another scorching desert day, now burst over the Sierra Manzano, which lay on the eastern side of the Rio Grande. Somewhere ahead, and perhaps reachable before the sun passed through its noontime zenith, lay the river and its populated valley.

Somewhere behind, however, rode those who did not want Gardner to reach that river valley. He moved quickly, alternately running and walking, but his lungs burned from the exertion. He looked back often, knowing that if he was seen by those men on horseback, it would be the end of his escape. He could run, but he could not hide. They would be upon him within minutes — assuming, of course, that they did not simply put a .45-caliber Winchester round through his back.

Suddenly, at what seemed like an hour past sunup, he reached the edge of the plateau on which he had been hiking. From this crest, the terrain sloped gently down-ward toward the Rio Grande, which lay in the distance like a fiery snake, reflecting the fire of the morning sun. He paused to congratulate himself on not having been caught — yet.

The river was still very far away for a man on foot, but Gardner knew he need not reach its banks. All he needed was to reach some outpost of the scattering of settle-ments that filled its valley. There were many horses and many guns in the Rio Grande valley. He just needed one of each.

As he paused momentarily to take in the view, he leaned forward, his hands on his knees, and gasped to catch his breath. He coughed a dry cough that stung his windpipe like hot coffee. Jasper Gardner thought that hot coffee would taste good right now, but he desperately craved *water*. More even than a horse and a gun, he needed water.

As he stepped forward to descend the broad, shallow slope, he glanced back one more time. More even than water, he needed to know that his pursuers were not in sight.

They weren't — yet.

Bladen Cole studied the three men though his brass spyglass. He had looked in vain for the escapee, and he watched as the mounted men did the same. When the sun was on the cusp of breaking into the day, they did a broad search of the surrounding area before deciding on an eastward direction.

They searched for some time before heading toward the Rio Grande. He could not tell whether they had found the man's trail or had just decided to head out in his probable direction.

Cole tied the lead rope of the pack horse

to his saddle horn and followed, allowing them a generous head start.

Jasper Gardner found that his descent into the valley, however gradual, aided his pace, and it was not long before he saw a cluster of houses, and he made for them. They proved to have been abandoned, likely a failed attempt at a homestead, but from the vantage point of the collapsing front wall, he could see another group of houses. From these, there rose a promising column of smoke.

The distance deceived him, but at last he was near enough to see a man in a corral, shoeing a horse.

"Hello, friend," he called out, waving to the man.

The man looked up and waved, but did not return the greeting. He went back to work until Gardner was about thirty yards from the corral. He dropped the horse's foot and walked toward the fence.

"Good morning, sir," Gardner said in as friendly a tone as possible. "My name's Jasper Gar— Garrity."

"Name's Vargas," the man said, his English lightly accented with Spanish. "What brings you out this way?"

"Headed up toward Bernalillo."

"Don't see too many fellows walking out of the desert," Vargas said warily.

"I'm embarrassed to say I got robbed yesterday," Gardner said, repeating a story that he had concocted and rehearsed as he made his way across the desert. "They got everything . . . my horse . . . my gun . . . my dough."

"Looks like they let you live."

"Guess I'm lucky."

"Guess so."

"I'd be much obliged for a drink of water," Gardner said hoarsely.

Vargas pointed to a pump that was situated before his small clapboard house.

Gardner pumped, cupped his hand, and took a drink.

Even uncut whiskey never tasted so good.

He repeated this several times until the slosh of water in his empty, dehydrated stomach made him feel a bit sick.

Next, he rinsed his hands and cleaned the sores on his wrists.

"Looks like they had you tied up," Vargas observed, still standing inside the corral.

"They did."

"Lucky you got away."

"I sure am. Do you know where a fella might get hisself a horse?"

"Down that way about a mile and a half,

you'll see a house with one wall painted
kind of a light blue."

"You reckon he might have a horse to
spare?"

"Can't know without asking."

"Much obliged for the water."

"You bet."

Jasper Gardner staggered onward, down
the hill in the vague direction that had been
indicated as that of the house with one blue
wall.

The first time that he glanced back, Vargas was still looking at him. The next time,
he had disappeared.

It had been Gardner's intention to steal
the first horse that he saw, but Vargas had
not averted his eyes for even a moment and
had kept close to a Winchester that he had
laid across a wooden box near where he had
been working.

Maybe, Gardner decided, he would steal
the *second* horse that he saw. Maybe, if he
was lucky, that horse would be grazing
unattended.

"What the hell do you suppose that was?"
Simon Lynch wondered aloud, after he and
his companions suddenly heard a series of
three shots fired in rapid succession.

"Not sure," Ben Muriday replied, pulling

his rifle out of its scabbard. "Seems they came from down that way."

A few minutes later, they could see a shack about a quarter mile distant, with a corral nearby.

Three more shots rang out from that general direction.

As they neared the house, they could see a man with a rifle who seemed to be in the midst of target practice. Muriday replaced his rifle — no need in there being an unnecessary provocation — but kept his hand near the pistol in his holster.

"Mornin' " Muriday said in greeting as they came near to the man, who was watching them as he slotted more rounds into his Winchester.

The man merely nodded.

"I was wonderin' if you might've seen a stranger pass this way this morning."

"You boys the law?"

"No, but we're bringin' in a couple of robbers that would be wanted up north. One of 'em got away and we're trailing him . . . Right, Stanton?"

"I ain't got nothing to say," Stanton replied.

Vargas looked at Stanton, and at the ropes that bound his wrists. Then he looked at Muriday.

"Where you headed from?" Vargas asked.

"Yonder over by Luera," Muriday said, pointing to the southwest.

"Wish I could help you," Vargas said, returning to slotting rounds into his Winchester.

"Much obliged," Muriday said.

"You bet."

CHAPTER 21

Jasper Gardner was practically on top of the house with one blue wall before he saw it. At first, he couldn't understand why Vargas had sent him here, until he had walked around to the eastern side and seen a series of fields on the sloping hillside below. A man was working down there with two large horses hitched to a harrow. He was probably planning to harvest a second crop of squash before fall.

As Gardner surveyed the scene, he saw a small barn and corral about halfway down the hill from the house with one blue wall. There was a lone, unattended horse in the corral. This was exactly what he was looking for.

He made his way toward the lone horse, exercising caution lest the farmer should see him. As he approached close to the corral, Gardner looked around for a saddle. A grin creased his lips as he saw it, neatly

206

perched on a rack near the barn door. He chuckled to himself that the next thing he needed was an unattended gun.

"Where you headed?"

Gardner turned and saw the gun, though neither it nor — as it now turned out — the horse were unattended.

A short woman in a gray-green gingham dress was aiming a twelve-gauge shotgun at him. She appeared by her stance and her voice to be in her thirties, but the leathery texture of her face told of hard winters and hot summers that would make a person old beyond the years marked by a calendar.

"Just passing by," Gardner said, raising his hands shoulder height to that she could see he was unarmed. "Stopped to admire your horse . . . mighty fine horse it is too."

"You weren't thinkin' of admiring her out the gate were ya?"

"No ma'am . . . not at all. My intentions are honorable and I don't mean nobody no harm. 'Specially not a lady. No ma'am."

"What you doin' up this way?"

"Just passing though. Do you know a fella name of Vargas?"

"Lives up yonder. Why?"

"Well, here's the thing," Gardner began. "Me and him was talking . . . just this morning in fact. I said I was looking for a horse and he said you go on down to the house with one blue wall. When you get down by there . . . he told me this . . . when you get there you might find that they can help you get a horse."

"He said *that*?"

"Yes, ma'am. He done said that. He said this would be the place to come if I was lookin' for a horse."

"T'ain't."

"You wouldn't be able to help out a fellow down on his luck?"

"Not with no horse."

"If I could just explain . . ."

"You walkin' up like that with your wrists lookin' like you been hog-tied begs all sorta questions that no explainin' can answer."

"I was robbed," Gardner asserted. "Like I told Mr. Vargas, I was robbed and they stole everything and left me for dead."

"So you done come here hopin' to do a bit of horse thievery?"

"Not at all. I'd be happy to pay you for it."

"How much you offerin'?"

"How much you askin'?"

"Don't see that you got no way to pay for nothing."

"I'm rich," Gardner said in an exasperated tone. "Just as soon as I catch up to them robbers, I can pay you whatever you want. I promise."

"Don't believe none of that. Now, you better jus' git before this trigger finger gets itchy."

"Have it your way," Gardner said, turning to walk away.

He glanced back and saw that she had lowered the muzzle of the 12-gauge and was cradling it on one arm.

Now or never, he thought.

In one swift move, he leaned down, grabbed a two-foot piece of scrap lumber, hurled it at her as hard as he could, and rushed her.

She had already dropped the shotgun when he collided with her.

Both of them sprawled on the ground, then rolled and lunged toward the weapon.

She got her hands on the barrel and he grabbed the stock.

The woman winced in pain as he kneed her in the kidneys, but she would not let go.

He got a better grip on the stock as she twisted the barrel to pry the shotgun from his grip.

His fingers reached the trigger.

He was about to discharge a hellstorm of buckshot into her leathery little face when she pushed the barrel away.

The blast pulverized a nearby wooden barrel, but both combatants went unscathed.

Gardner pulled the gun free from her grip and had started to aim it when a shot rang out. The bullet narrowly missed his head.

"Drop it or the next one won't miss," Ben Muriday said. He and the others had ridden up as Gardner was brawling with the woman.

Gardner let the muzzle fall and felt the shotgun being taken from his hand.

He turned to see the face of the angry farmer a split second before a huge fist impacted his face. The pain was excruciating and accompanied by the sound of cracking bone.

Through the haze of blood and tears, he felt himself being helped to his feet.

Then the fist came again, and he felt himself falling again.

Gardner felt his body move at least a foot each time the farmer's boot hit his kidneys.

"Stop," demanded Muriday. "Stop. Don't kill him. I need the sonuvabitch alive."

"Are you the law?" the farmer asked angrily.

"No, but we're taking him in to a noose."

"Let him get finished off *here and now.*"

"Lookit, mister," Muriday pleaded.

"Lemme buy him off ya for one of these."

The farmer looked up to see that Muriday was holding a twenty-dollar gold eagle. He paused, sighed, and looked at his wife. There was venom in her eyes.

The farmer wiped his sweaty brow on his shirt and began to cock his leg to strike again.

"Eagle's got a friend," Muriday said.

The farmer looked up to see a second gold coin.

He looked at his wife. She looked at him, at Gardner, and up at the two coins that Muriday held. At last she spat on Gardner, nodded, and turned to walk away.

Muriday handed the coins to the man as Lynch climbed down from his horse to scrape Jasper Gardner off the ground.

CHAPTER 22

"I thought we were keepin' far enough away from the Rio Grande that we wouldn't run across nobody," Simon Lynch said in disgust as they looked down at the trading post. "Thought you said we was comin' up through the middle of nowhere by stayin' this far west of the river."

By the early afternoon of the day following the pummeling of Jasper Gardner at the house with one blue wall, the tattered group had reached a small outpost that lay near a ford across one of the eastward flowing tributaries of the Rio Grande.

"It figures they'd have a place like that at a ford," Ben Muriday observed, thoughtfully chewing a wad of tobacco. "Besides, I ain't never been this far north in the territory any more than you ever been this far north. How am I supposed to know everything?"

"Don't need no ford in late summer,"

Lynch pointed out, conceding that neither of them knew much about the lay of the land in northern New Mexico. "We can cross anywheres."

"You need provisioning, 'less you gonna be starving us to death," Gabe Stanton complained.

"Shut up, you," Muriday demanded. "Shut your damn mouth. I have half a mind to let you starve . . . but you ain't gonna starve to death just on account of you came up short of breakfast. Besides, we're gonna be in Santa Fe by suppertime tomorrow. Then you can eat your hearts out courtesy of somebody else than us."

"Bastard didn't steal enough from those damned Indians," Jasper Gardner interjected, his voice still nasal from his damaged nose. "What we gonna eat for supper *tonight* if we don't go down there and buy us some grub?"

"Shut your damned mouth," a frustrated Muriday demanded.

"I says one of us goes down yonder, and the rest goes and fords upstream somewhere," Lynch suggested.

"All right," Muriday said after taking a minute or two to think over his options. "I'll go down and get us enough salt pork to get us through till tomorrow when we're rid of these two. You go on upstream and get 'em across. I'll meet up with you a mile due north by that chalk-colored cliff up yonder."

Lashing his horse to the hitchrail, Ben Muriday stepped past, or over, several children, who were playing or doing odd jobs around the front of the main building, and made for the door.

In the coolness of the interior, he could see a long counter and, beyond it, ranks of well-stocked shelves. As he glanced around in the interest of being aware of his surroundings, his eyes took stock of a pair of young half-breed men who looked like ranch hands. They were sitting at a table with a bottle of something brown.

A plump young woman with dark eyes and freckles across her nose greeted him from behind the counter. She was dressed modestly, in the style of the Latter-Day Saints, and had her dark hair tied in a knot atop her head.

"May I help you, sir?" she said with practiced efficiency.

"I'll be having me some salt pork and some beans, enough for four . . . days . . . on the trail," Muriday said, catching himself before revealing that *four* men needed provisioning for *one* day.

"Yes, sir, I'll get that together for you at once," the woman said with a smile.

"You wouldn't be needing some tack, would you, friend?" an older man, with a long, unkempt gray beard, said, getting out of a rocking chair in the corner of the room.

"Don't reckon," Ben Muriday told John Jacob Smith.

For near to forty years, John Jacob Smith had operated his strategically located trading post here at this ford, catering to the citizens of nearby pueblo cities, as well as the increasing numbers of Anglo travelers who passed this way. He had made a good livelihood for himself and for his large family by catering both to the needs and to the wants of his patrons, and by having a unique knack for closing sales of the latter.

"Got us a special going on bridles," Smith suggested, moving in to interest his customer in doing more shopping than that for which he had planned. Smith had not been successful out here by allowing customers to walk out with pockets full of cash. "I can set you up with a real fine hackamore with some real attractive braiding done by a feller up in Colorado."

"No, I don't think I'll be needing —"

"Sometimes, ain't so much what a man needs, but what he might *want* to have. I

215

can show you while Molly gets your purchases together."

"No, sir. As much as I appreciate you taking an interest, all I need's the grub."

"Shot of something to ease the cares of the day, then," Smith suggested.

"Well . . . I reckon."

As a member of the Latter-Day Saints, who were not, by nature, given to taste liquor, Smith did not imbibe himself. However, as a merchant whose reputation was that of full service to his customers, Smith was happy to provide what those customers sought, and even to suggest when it might be needed.

Grinning broadly, the bearded man poured two fingers from a bottle that he took from behind the bar. Muriday could also see a grin on the face of the round young woman, who he took to be the man's half-breed daughter.

"Ooo-ee," Muriday said with a wince as the whiskey touched his tongue. "Ain't often had whiskey that's cut so little as this."

"Pride ourselves on a happy customer," Smith said.

Preparing himself for his second sip, Muriday relished the flavor and fiery feel of the bourbon as it rolled down his throat.

"Pour you another?"

"Just one," Muriday replied, indicating that he *would* have another, but only one finger this time.

"Can I set you up with a fresh bottle for those lonesome nights out on the trail?" Smith offered.

"No, sir," Muriday said, reaching in his pocket for some cash. " 'Tis just enough to have that taste in my memory . . . Thanks a lot, though."

"Fresh eagles," the proprietor said, examining the newly minted coins that sparkled on the counter. "You musta had a payday recently."

"Got me a bigger one comin' up," Muriday replied, feeling a bit unsteady on his feet. For a man unused to full-strength bourbon, three fingers was enough to round off a lot of the hard edges on his daily concerns.

It was also enough to make him unaware of the attention directed toward him by the two men at the nearby table. The mention of the freshness of his twenty-dollar eagles *caught* their attention, and the reference to a bigger payday coming *kept* it.

They waited until Muriday had collected a ten-dollar gold piece as change from his purchases and ridden off before they corked their bottle and made for their own horses.

■ ■ ■ ■

The sun had been down for an hour before Muriday and Lynch dragged their captives off their horses to make their camp and eat the Saints' salt pork.

"Suppose you can keep yourself awake long enough to take first watch?" Lynch asked crossly as Muriday stretched out with bourbon on his mind, his head on his saddle, and his belly full of salt pork. "Didn't think so. This'll be the last time I let you go for provisions and come back half-drunk. Least you could have brung the rest of the bottle back to share."

"Shut yourself up," Muriday shot back. "Tomorrow we's gonna be living high in Santa Fe and you can drink yourself silly if you wanna."

At that, Lynch shook his head in disgust and walked away as Muriday began to snore.

"We gotta get out of here tonight," Gardner whispered to Stanton when Lynch was out of earshot.

"You gonna wake me up and give me a chance like you *didn't* the other night?" Stanton responded in an angry hiss. "I don't trust you no little bit since you done run off without me."

Though Stanton's arm was still a bit stiff, and Gardner's nasal passages were still painful, the two men were gradually recovering from the pain of the injuries they had suffered over the preceding few days. They were certainly sufficiently mended to be anxious to make a success of their last nighttime escape opportunity before they were delivered to an uncertain future in Santa Fe.

"Like I told you yesterday," Gardner explained, "I *woulda* come back for you soon as I got a gun."

"That's crap."

"You can think that if you want . . ."

"You know damned well if there was two of us, you wouldn't have got yourself knocked on the ground by that *woman.*"

"She had a damned bird gun," Muriday explained. "You can't just walk up to nobody that's got a bird gun. You gotta outsmart 'em."

"You consider *yourself* a smart one?"

"Shut up and let's figure this thing. Gonna be in Santa Fe tomorrow. We gotta get out of here tonight. We got one of 'em out cold. If we take the other one, we can make for the horses."

"How we gonna do that with our feet all

tied up?" Lynch asked.

"Same as I did the other night. Pull your feet up and get to workin' on the knot tyin' your ankles together. You can't get to your wrists, but you sure as hell *can* get your ankles undid."

"How we gonna clobber him with our hands tied?"

"If we both get on him, one of us can choke him with tied hands."

"What do we do if Muriday wakes up?"

"Quit askin' questions. You got a better idea?"

CHAPTER 23

"Who's there?"

"Damn it . . . who the hell?"

K'pow. K'pow.

"Don't hit the ones who's tied up."

K'pow.

"Damn you, Muriday, shoot him!"

K'pow.

Bladen Cole awoke suddenly to the sound of gunfire and an angry crowd of shouting men in the arroyo beneath his campsite.

He had drifted to sleep with the quiet of a starry desert night, with the twinkling lights of Santa Fe in the far, far distance, and with the anxiety of knowing that no more sleeps intervened between this night and the day of finality and reckoning.

K'pow. K'pow.

Below him now the camp of the four men was a swirling nest of activity. At its center, half-standing and half-crouched, was Simon Lynch with his Winchester in his hands. The gray smoke from the smoldering campfire mixed with the bluish smoke of burnt gunpowder.

K'pow. K'pow. K'pow.

The two captives, one of them with his feet unbound, lay nearby, wriggling like awkward serpents as they tried to hug the ground to stay out of what were apparently several lines of fire.

Cole could see two other men, the same two Indians who he had seen ride out from the trading post the previous afternoon. They were on an gravel slope opposite Cole's position and attempting to crawl upward toward the campsite.

From what he could see in the moonlight, and by what was left of the campfire, Cole surmised that the two men had intended an ambush, but Lynch had heard them as they tried unsuccessfully to get across the gravel without making any noise.

K'pow.

One of them had risen to a crouch and fired at Lynch with his pistol.

He missed.

K'pow. K'pow. K'pow.

Lynch replied with three shots in rapid succession, also without hitting anyone.

"Damn you, Muriday . . . where the hell you at?" Lynch called, as he slotted more cartridges into his rifle.

At first, Cole did not see him, but at last he spotted the red and white striped shirt. Muriday was standing, naked from his waist to his ankles, beneath a scrub cottonwood near the picket line where the horses were tied. When the attack had started, he was caught, literally with his pants down, answering the call of nature. In so doing, he had also left himself naked of his firearms, and impotent in his being able to shoot back to aid Lynch.

After four days of riding and pondering how it would finally happen, Cole knew that it was time for him to make his presence known.

He did not relish the prospect of killing the two young fellows who were attempting to ambush the foursome. If they kept up the practices which had led them to this juncture, they were doomed not to be long for this earth, but he did not welcome for himself the role of being the agent of this inevitability.

K'pow. K'pow.

In the case of one of the young men, this fate was nearer than Cole could have imagined.

K'pow.

The man had risen to fire his gun and

223

caught a .45 round to his forehead from Simon Lynch's Winchester.

K'pow.

Showered by the bloody mess that spurted from this lucky hit, the other man had stood, fired one last time, turned, and run, plunging down the talus slope and disappearing into the darkness.

Under cover of this unfolding commotion, Bladen Cole had, by now, approached to within thirty feet of Simon Lynch.

"Drop the rifle," Cole demanded.

Lynch turned, the muzzle of his gun at a downward angle. He stared straight at Cole, looking him directly in the eyes.

It was one of those moments that seems to go on and on, but which actually goes by in the twinkling of an eye, as the two men stared at each other.

Lynch had no idea that he was staring at a man who had been looking at him from afar for more than a week. Cole, for the first time in all those days, could see the face of the man whom he had come to know only as a distant stick figure.

At last, Lynch opened his mouth as though to say something, but he did not. He coughed slightly as blood belched up from his innards and dribbled from his lips.

Lynch too, had been hit, suffering a painfully mortal wound that left him in the cold cocoon of shock.

As he fell forward, Cole turned his eyes into the darkness, looking for Muriday.

Lynch's partner had by now approached almost to the campfire, his pants pulled up, hoping to grab a gun and aid in the common cause, but he now realized that this cause was hopeless. Without a gun, he was virtually out of options.

As had been the case with Lynch a moment earlier, Cole was now face-to-face with Ben Muriday, a man whom he had seen previously only from a distance.

Yes, Cole was now seeing Muriday for the first time face-to-face.

A face.

The face.

That face!

A cold chill came over Bladen Cole as he stared with disbelief.

It was a chinless face with close-spaced eyes, a long nose, and a sparse, unkempt mustache. It was the ugly, haunting visage that had tormented his dreams and seasoned his nightmares since that terrible night in Silver City.

Ben Muriday was the rat-faced man who had killed his brother.

For a decade of his life, he had thought

about this moment and how he would finally *kill* the man who had shot Will down that night.

Now that moment was suddenly upon him, arriving with no warning.

The two men stared at each other in one of those moments that seem to go on and on, but which actually go by in the twinkling of an eye.

Cole was paralyzed — not from fear, or indecision, but from shock.

Ben Muriday had no memory of Bladen Cole. He saw only a man who held a gun when he had none.

He turned and ran.

Cole did not realize until he raised the rifle to his shoulder and gazed through the sights that his hands were trembling. He could not remember the last time that his hands had trembled. He found himself awash in a downpour of emotion and adrenaline not unlike the explosive thunderstorms of the past days.

Muriday was halfway to the picket line when Cole squeezed off a shot.

K'pow!

He missed.

K'pow!

He had run after the man, pausing to aim and fire a second time just as Muriday leapt on a horse and took off riding bareback.

Cole fired a third time, taking a shot that would have been nearly impossible under the best of circumstances.

K'pow!

Suddenly, a shot rang out from behind him.

He turned to see one of the prisoners trying to aim Lynch's Winchester with his hands still bound together.

K'pow!

Cole put a round into the dirt about eighteen inches from the man's head, and he dropped the gun.

CHAPTER 24

"Let's just split it *two* ways," Jasper Gardner promised, offering the same arrangement he had unsuccessfully proposed to Ben Muriday and the late Simon Lynch. "Don't even have to be *three* ways. You can have *half.*"

As with the previous negotiation, this idea fell on deaf ears. After a night of wrathful bickering between the two, mainly concerning Gardner's failure to include Gabe Stanton in his escape attempt, Bladen Cole had just turned to ignoring them.

After a week and a half on the trail, Cole finally had his prisoners in tow, with less than a day's ride ahead of him. As he neared the conclusion of this affair, however, the only thought that seemed to have staying power in his mind was the nightmare image of the face of the rat-faced man who had shot his brother.

Even as the sun rose into the day, and the

heat of the New Mexico summer made its presence felt, the cold chill of the night before remained. Seeing that face, that unmistakable face, in the mixture of firelight and moonlight made it seem in his mind's memory like a ghostly apparition, like that of the inhuman ghoul, which he had always imagined the rat-faced man to be.

Bladen Cole had seen his worst recurring nightmare — and it was real.

In the distance, Cole could see a group of men and horses. They had a wagon and were removing a number of medium-sized crates. Strange, it seemed, that they should be unloading a wagon way out here.

As he and his caravan of fugitives approached, he watched the men start to set up a tripod. By the time that he approached close enough to read the words ATCHISON, TOPEKA & SANTA FE RAILROAD written across side of the wagon, they were installing a surveyor's transit on the tripod.

"Morning, gentlemen," Cole said as he approached them.

"Good morning to you, sir," one of the men replied.

"I can tell by your cargo that there's a railroad coming," Cole commented, making conversation. His tone carried a tinge of dry irony, given that nearly everyone in the territory was aware of the arrival of the rails.

"That would be an accurate assessment, sir," the man said with a sense of pride of accomplishment in the tone of his voice. "We'll have the route into Bernalillo surveyed by month's end. After that, it's up to the work gangs."

"That'll be a big change to this country," Cole said, thinking back to the vast open spaces through which he had ridden over the past week.

"Folks'll be able to ride as far in an hour as a man on horseback can ride in a day," the man said proudly.

"I guess that'll make gettin' around a lot faster," Cole said. "Hope folks can figure out what to do with all that extra time."

"Looks like you got yourself some cargo of your own," the man said.

"These fellows have a rendezvous with the law, and I'm helping them in that direction."

"They look a little worse for wear," the man said, looking at the purplish-pink hue of Gardner's face and the bandage on Stanton's sleeveless arm.

"They lived a hard life over the past few days before they came into my care this morning," Cole said and smiled.

"You wouldn't have got your pretty face all busted up if you ain't got yourself on the

losing end of a fight with that *woman*,"
Stanton interjected, unable to ignore a
chance to get in a verbal jab against his
estranged partner.

"Shut your damned mouth," Gardner
shouted, indignant at being constantly
reminded that he had come to a draw in a
fight with a member of the female species.
"If I weren't all tied up, I'd kill you with my
bare hands."

"Like to see you try!"

"They're a lively pair," the surveyor said
with a smile.

"That's why I'm real anxious to be done
with 'em," Cole replied.

"Mr. Waldron," the man said, coming into
the railroad offices in Santa Fe. "I've got
some news you're gonna want to hear."

"What's that?" Waldron said, looking up
at Nathaniel Siward, who functioned as his
courier, aide, and all-around right-hand
man.

"We just got word from out where the
survey crew is working," Siward explained.
"There's a stranger riding this way with a
couple of pack mules that have packs
marked ATCHISON, TOPEKA & SANTA FE.
He's also got a couple of men all tied up
and he says he's taking them to the law in

Santa Fe."

Waldron knew immediately that his bounty hunter was finally returning. He wondered how three or four fugitives had become two, but he imagined there had been some gunplay involved.

"Thanks for letting me know," Waldron said, standing up and reaching for his jacket. "Now hightail it back down yonder and find this man. Tell him that Ezra Waldron wants to meet him and his cargo at my office down by Lamy. Use my name. I know this man. His name is Bladen Cole."

Waldron was amazed that the bounty hunter had prevailed. With the passage of a week and then some, the railroad man had assumed that he would never see Cole again. If it had been him, Waldron mused, he would have been strongly tempted to take the cash and keep going, rather than to return it for a lesser amount. As Waldron had once observed, honorable men were a rarity in the West. Of course, they were rarer still in the financial circles in the East.

With a quick glance at the wall clock, he made a beeline for the offices of the *Santa Fe New Mexican.*

"Is Tobias in today?" Waldron asked.

"You're in luck, he just came in," reported

the man at the front desk. "I'll go fetch him."

Waldron found himself pacing and listening to the clip-clop of the wall clock pendulum as he waited for the columnist. Three minutes passed, and then five.

"Mr. Waldron," Gough said in a jovial tone as he emerged from an inner office. "Pleasure to see you. To what do I owe the pleasure? It's still a trifle early for you to take me to lunch."

"I have something that you'll find to satisfy your appetite more happily than a steak at Delmonico's," Waldron said. "I have a news item for you, a 'scoop' as they say nowadays."

"My ears are all yours," Gough said, stifling an overt display of eagerness.

"I'd like you to join me in taking a little ride down to Lamy," Waldron insisted.

"When?"

"Now."

"Now? I have a —"

"You'll *want* this story."

"What is it?"

"I'll fill you in on the details," Waldron promised. "But we must go at once."

The farther Cole rode with his disheveled caravan of outlaws and gold, the more he

233

saw of the work crews of the Atchison, Topeka & Santa Fe. There were men with teams of horses grading the roadbed, and wagons loaded with rock and gravel to level the ground ahead of those who were grading. At one place, they were constructing a wooden bridge across a small arroyo.

There were so many men and horses coming and going that he almost did not notice a rider coming in his direction at a gallop. Nor did he notice, until the man was but a short distance away, that he was coming to meet him.

"Mr. Cole? Bladen Cole?" asked the stranger.

"Who's asking?"

"My name is Nathaniel Siward," he replied. "Mr. Waldron . . . Ezra Waldron . . . sent me to meet you."

"That was nice of him," Cole said.

"Mr. Waldron asked me to come out here to take you to meet him at the construction headquarters over by Lamy. He has an office there."

"How far is that?"

"Less than an hour. It's closer than Santa Fe."

Cole nodded that he would follow Siward. His suspicions had initially been aroused, but the man looked like someone who carried messages for a man like Waldron — *and* he was not carrying a gun.

"How'd he know I was out this way?" Cole asked as they rode.

"One of the crews reported that they had seen you," Siward said. "With two men tied to their saddle horns and pack saddles carrying railroad markings, you gotta admit that you stand out."

"Reckon we do," Cole said with a smile and a glance back at his tattered prisoners. "He say anything else?"

"Just that he seemed pretty sure that you were Bladen Cole and that he wanted to meet you at Lamy. He did seem surprised . . . *and* pleased to hear about you coming."

CHAPTER 25

"Mr. Cole, I presume," Ezra Waldron happily said as Bladen Cole rode up to the large canvas-topped structure that served as his office.

Tobias Gough scribbled earnestly. Waldron had just paraphrased a celebrated quote from the pages of the *New York Herald* just six years earlier when their correspondent, Henry Stanley, had located the long-missing Dr. David Livingstone in the heart of darkest Africa.

Waldron had just handed Gough a wonderfully usable line.

"Didn't expect such a welcoming committee," Cole said skeptically as about a dozen Atchison, Topeka & Santa Fe employees gathered around to gawk at his ragtag crew.

"This is Mr. Gough of the *Santa Fe New Mexican*," Waldron said, introducing the journalist. "He's here to chronicle your success . . . and to write that the forces of law and order are taming the uncivilized West."

Cole could tell by Gough's expression that this line, fraught with hyperbole, would probably get a rewrite. He was surprised, and more than a small bit mystified, to find Waldron greeting him in the company of a newspaperman — after he had explicitly told Cole that he wanted no one to know about the robbery. Apparently a lot had changed in the ten days that Cole had been on the trail.

"Two mules packed with bags carrying railroad markings," Siward said, pointing out the animals carrying the bags of gold.

"Bring those packs into my office," Waldron ordered the gawkers standing nearby. "Siward, see to it that those two characters are locked up."

As Cole looked at Stanton and Gardner for what he hoped would be the last time, he noticed a peculiar expression on Gardner's face. He was staring directly at Waldron with a sort of directed rage that suggested strongly that they were acquainted.

"Come into my office, Mr. Cole," Waldron suggested congenially, turning his back to Gardner. "Let us get you a cold cup of water . . . and perhaps something a bit stronger?"

"Much obliged," Cole said as one of Waldron's minions immediately handed him a tin cup of water. He savored it and handed it back for a refill as he removed his hat and wiped his brow with his bandanna. It was only slightly cooler to be out of the direct sun and under the canvas.

"Please have a seat," Waldron invited, as he and Gough sat down.

"Thanks, but I think I'd rather stand," Cole said. "Been doin' a lot of sittin' last few days."

The pack saddles were brought in and dumped with a series of clanks on the wooden floor.

"Should be close to all of it still there," Cole said. "They were dipping into it to buy whiskey and provisions before I caught up to 'em, but there won't be *much* missing."

"How much did the thieves take?" Gough asked, taking notes.

"Round nine grand," Waldron said.

"Do you have an exact number?"

Waldron looked at a man with a string tie, who pulled his spectacles down from his forehead, consulted some papers. and said, "The total that we have is $9,094.80."

Siward knelt and untied one of the bags.

A river of uncirculated gold eagles flowed out onto Waldron's floor. Siward opened another, found bundles of currency, and nodded when he examined the bank markings on the wrappers.

"Looks good," Waldron said and smiled. "While Siward here counts out your reward money, could I offer you a shot of Kentucky's finest?"

"I'd be obliged," Cole said with a nod.

"Tell me of your manhunt, Mr. Cole," the journalist asked. "Do you have names for these two?"

"The skinny one goes by Stanton, Gabe Stanton. The big one with the plum-colored nose is called Jasper Gardner."

"Where and when did you catch them?" Gough asked

"Followed 'em as far as the Mogollons before I caught up to 'em. They were movin' pretty fast. Reckon they planned to hide out down there."

Cole deliberately held back the interlude in the narrative that was inhabited by Muriday and Lynch, considering this information superfluous to the circumstances of the manhunt's conclusion.

He also withheld mention of the Dutchman's gold. If he had survived this quest, Otto Geier should be left in peace.

"Mr. Waldron said that there were three men involved in the robbery . . . and possibly four," Gough continued. "You rode in with two. Where . . . ?"

"You'll find them, or more rightly, you'll find their bones, about a day's ride south," Cole explained. "The buzzards had already been workin 'em, and I figure the coyotes have gotten under the rocks I piled on 'em by now."

"What happened? Did you . . . ?"

"Greed's a funny thing," Cole began. "It's a peculiar thing. It'll drive a man to most anything. On the other hand, maybe it's a simple, straightforward thing that'll drive a man to do arithmetic. The two that you're locking up over yonder decided on the *first day out* that half of nine grand was worth more than nine grand split four ways."

"What about Indians?" Gough asked. "The Mogollons are Apache country. Readers are interested in Indian stories."

Cole shook his head and finally acquiesced to take the chair that Waldron had offered earlier.

"Well, there *were* a couple of scalps lifted," the bounty hunter said as Waldron refilled his shot glass. All eyes were on Cole in anticipation of the continuation of the story as he took a sip of the bourbon whiskey.

"Who was scalped?" Gough asked with a

quizzical expression. "These men you brought in were in pretty rough shape, but as I saw, they both have their hair."

" 'Twas Jasper who done the scalping."

"Who?" Gough asked. Out of the corner of his eye, Cole saw Waldron tense, and a concerned, almost fearful, expression came over his face.

"Two Mescalero boys who ambushed 'em. Trying to steal horses, I suspect."

This revelation produced a pause in the conversation, which Nathaniel Siward used to step across the room and hand Cole a bag of gold eagles.

"Much obliged," Cole said with a smile.

"You're welcome to count it," Siward offered.

"Not necessary," Cole replied. "It feels right . . . and besides, I was watching you over there . . . and I saw you count out nine piles of ten."

"Good man," Waldron laughed.

"Well, I reckon I've imposed on your hospitality long enough," Cole said, standing again. "It's time for me to head on up to Santa Fe and spend some of this gold on a store-bought bath. Thank you much for the whiskey."

Had Nicolette de la Gravière taken a different route as she drove the buckboard south from Santa Fe that day, she would have crossed paths with Bladen Cole as he was coming north, but she did not.

As previously arranged, she had accepted Ezra Waldron's invitation to visit the Atchison, Topeka & Santa Fe construction headquarters at Lamy, and she arrived less than hour after the bounty hunter had departed. Nicolette parked her vehicle near some other buckboards that were tethered by a centrally located canvas-roofed structure that appeared to be more important than the others.

"I'm here to see Mr. Waldron," she said with a smile as she stepped inside. "He is expecting me."

"He's not here right now," a man with a string tie said as his expression said that he was startled to see a woman at the construction camp. "He's down at the cages. I expect him back shortly, if you'd care to wait?"

"Thank you, sir," she replied, glancing at a large clock and noting that she was exactly on time. "I don't mind going to where he is . . . if you might direct me."

"This camp's not really . . . I mean . . . for a lady . . ."

"I'm sure that I'll be fine," she said, continuing to smile.

Armed with directions, she made her way through the bustling camp, ignoring the occasional whistle and one catcall that was more absurd than obscene. She passed piles of rails and heavy, rough-hewn wooden ties. Men were loading these, as well as weighty barrels of railroad spikes and other commodities, onto small work trains which departed from sidings and chugged off into the distance where the actual laying of tracks was taking place.

Finally, she reached the place at which she had been told that "if you look left, you can't miss it."

Indeed, she looked left and saw what looked like a series of cages set onto a flatcar. The railroad maintained its own jail, organized along the lines of a military brig, which was used mainly to lock up and cool off men involved in brawls. Today, it hosted the former captives of Ben Muriday and Bladen Cole.

Nicolette could see Ezra Waldron, standing on a platform, speaking to the men who were in two of these cages.

"Damn it, I don't want to argue about that!" Waldron shouted.

One of the other men shouted back, his words unclear, sounding to Nicolette as though something was wrong with his nasal passages.

"Mr. Waldron," she said as she approached.

He turned, a look of surprise on his face.

Waldron seemed now to suddenly remembered that today was the day of her visit.

"Miss de la Gravière," he said, the look of surprise melting into a red-faced embarrassment which he tried in vain to conceal. "I'm so glad that you could come."

"I'm *so* glad that you could come," mimicked one of the men in a cage, taunting Waldron.

"What's a lady doin' out here?" Gabe Stanton said teasingly. "Hey, sweetheart . . . did you come over here to see *me*? Come a little closer . . . let me touch that sweet satin . . ."

"Shut up!" Waldron demanded, leaping off the platform and rushing toward Nicolette.

"I apologize for this," he said as he reached her. "You should *not* have to listen to this."

"Think nothing of it," she said without blushing. "Men with the loudest bark usually have a feeble bite."

"You shouldn't be out here in this part of the camp without an escort," he said, blushing. "This is no place for a lady."

"So I've been told," she laughed.

"Please let me show you around," he said,

regaining his composure.

"Thank you," she said, smiling. "It is all very grand, and on such an enormous scale. I have never seen anything quite like it."

CHAPTER 26

In a perfect world, a chapter in the life of Bladen Cole should have closed then, and a fresh one begun with the newly risen sun now streaming through his hotel room window. A soak in a bathtub and a night on a mattress, between real sheets, should have been the relaxing turn that set his mind at ease, and his body free to get on the trail north to Durango, Colorado.

In a perfect world, there would not have been the nightmares, refreshed by the image of the rat-faced man, seen so abruptly, and so grotesquely, in the moonlight.

A cup of coffee — hot coffee made in a proper pot and not boiled over a campfire or drunk cold to avoid the smoke of a fire — should have set the tone for a fine day the promise of which would have been serenaded by the call of meadowlarks. But for Cole, the nightmares did not end when his eyes were opened and a razor was drawn across a cheek.

He grabbed a newspaper, abandoned by its owner as he departed from an adjacent table in the hotel dining room. The headline on the front page of the *Santa Fe New Mexican* read ROBBERY ON THE AT & SF R'ROAD: THIEVES CAUGHT. The byline was that of Tobias Gough. Bladen Cole was quoted. So too was Ezra Waldron.

Mr. Bladen Cole, who ran the perpetrators to ground and returned them to face justice, had pursued them to the Mogollons, where he surmises they had intended to hide themselves. Most of the loot, originally totaling $9,094.80, according to railroad sources, was returned. Mr. Cole explained that the bandits had spent part of their ill-gotten booty on drink and supplies.

Mr. Ezra Waldron, an executive of the road, told this reporter that this theft illustrates the difficulty of doing business in what he calls the lawless West.

Cole put the paper down and stared thoughtfully, recalling the words that Waldron and his colleague, Joseph Ames, had used when they made the decision to utilize the services of a bounty hunter rather than a sheriff's posse to hunt the bandits. One of the words that still resonated was "discretion."

Waldron had gone to great lengths to explain that if the capital markets were to get wind of a robbery of this size occurring within twenty miles of Lamy, potential investors would close their wallets to providing the cash that was the "lifeblood" of the railroading business.

If that was true, and it seemed reasonable to Cole that it *was,* then why did Waldron *invite* a newspaperman to publicize the robbery? This anomaly made no sense, but he shrugged it off as being Waldron's business and none of his own. Cole had other things on his mind that were of much greater importance.

He had to *find* the rat-faced man.

Were it not for the renewed and persistent nightmares of the man, Cole would have been checking his roan out of the livery stable and riding out of town, but the nature of that nightmare had changed the course of his life, just as the original glimpse of the rat-faced man a decade back had changed its course. As much as he had been haunted all those years by the image of that ugly face, the thing that haunted him even more was that he had never been able to *find* the man. Now he was able to imagine himself on a trail not cold by years, but as fresh as a day and a half.

Relishing the feel of the new shirt purchased the day before at the dry goods store, Cole entertained the thought of abandoning the two dusty, sweat-stained ones that he had dropped at the Chinese laundry, but his thrifty streak intervened.

"One dollar," the man said. "Very dirty shirts."

"One dollar." Cole smiled, placing a coin on the counter and taking the paper-wrapped parcel.

"Found this in pocket," the laundryman said, handing Cole a small folded piece of paper.

"What?"

Inside the folded the paper, he saw the two Denver & Rio Grande passes that he had found on the two dead men on the first day of his pursuit.

"Oh yeah," he said. "I forgot about these. Thanks much."

Cole had already opened the door when he had a thought. He turned back and asked the man whether he had seen a chinless man with close-spaced eyes and a long nose.

"No," the man said thoughtfully. "Would recognize a man like that. So ugly."

"Thanks," Cole said, placing two more coins on the counter. "I'd be much obliged if you kept an ear and an eye out for him. I'll check back with you in a day or two."

The man smiled for the first time, nodded once, and scooped up the coins.

Making his way up the street, Cole glimpsed the Refugio del Viajero, where he had somewhat enjoyed his supper the night before. The *carne asada* treated his taste buds with perfection, but he would have enjoyed his dining experience much more had he chanced to lay his eyes on a certain young woman with lips the deep crimson of the chilies. The other girl waiting tables had said that it was Nicolette de la Gravière's day off.

Cole thought of the man who had recommended the restaurant to him in the first place, and decided to pay a call on his fellow Virginian, Dr. Amos Richardson.

"Señor Doctor," Domingo announced as Cole stepped through the door. "Señor Cole is here."

In the other room, he could see that the coroner was with a "patient," but one who would not object if the doctor interrupted his exam.

"Good to see you, Mr. Cole," Richardson

said, extending his freshly washed hand. "I was reading of your adventures in the paper this morning."

"Yeah, it's a little awkward for me talkin' to those fellows. Never know what they're gonna write. I just kept it short and to the point. Bringin' back the money and the robbers sort of speaks for itself."

"That it does, sir." Richardson smiled. "Care for a cup of coffee?"

"Thank you," Cole said and nodded.

"It seemed that Mr. Waldron was happy to have his money back," the doctor observed as he poured his own cup.

"That he was, and for good reason, I'll grant you that, but there's something that confuses me."

"What's that?"

"You were there when the railroad men said they wanted this robbery kept quiet. They were sacred that news of it would spook the money men . . . remember?"

"Yes, I *do* remember that. As I recall, they were quite adamant about keeping it quiet."

"What do you suppose changed?"

"I reckon the fact that you brought back the cash and the perpetrators trumped their fears of people knowing about the thievery," Richardson said with a grin.

"Reckon so," Cole said as Richardson

topped off his coffee cup. "None of my concern on any account."

"Mine neither," the coroner said. "What are your plans now?"

"Well, I had been looking forward to a plate of *carne asada* over at the Refugio . . . and I made good on that plan last night."

"Was Nicolette de la Gravière there?" Richardson asked.

"No," Cole said with a tinge of wistfulness. " 'Twas her night off."

"Probably just as well," Richardson said, picking up on Cole's pensiveness. "She's been seen around town with Mr. Waldron of all people. Not sure if it's serious."

"Wouldn't have minded laying eyes on her again before I left town," the bounty hunter admitted.

"I had figured that you would be on your way north to Durango already," the coroner said.

"Looks like that'll have to be postponed," Cole said. "I've got another man that I need to find down here in New Mexico."

"What's *he* wanted for?"

"Killin' a man."

"Who?"

"Ummm," Cole answered hesitantly before deciding to share the facts with the doctor. "He killed my brother."

"Your *brother*?" Richardson asked, his brow furrowing with concern. "Where? When?"

"It was a few years back . . . down in Silver City. I had pretty well given up on ever finding him again. Then I saw him the night before last."

"Where? What was he doing?"

"The long story, which I figured was more than the newspaperman needed to know, is that the two I brought in, Gardner and Stanton, fell in with two others down toward the Mogollons. They rode together for a while until there was an Indian ambush. One of the second two got killed, and the other one was the one who killed my brother."

"Are you sure . . . I mean after a number of years?"

"No mistaking that face," Cole said, shaking his head. "He's got a face like a rat . . . pointy nose, beady little eyes too close together . . . no chin. Even his whiskers look like whiskers on a rat."

"What happened to him after you saw him?"

"He got away," Cole said dejectedly. "I fired and missed. Reckon my hand was shaking, which I'd rather not admit, but I have to admit it to myself. I couldn't chase him at the time on account of the two train robbers."

"Let's take this to the sheriff," Richardson said. "He can get a wanted poster out. With a face like that, this fellow won't be hard to find."

"Don't reckon we can do that," Cole said. "It was ten years back, and there's nobody to say he done it except me. If the law took it up, it would be my word against him. Will is long dead and long buried."

"I understand," Richardson said.

He did.

This was not Virginia. Sometimes in the West, scores needed to be settled between just the two men involved.

CHAPTER 27

Having rented a deposit box at bank for the safekeeping of his reward money, Bladen Cole departed Santa Fe, riding not north toward Colorado and tomorrow, but west, toward yesterday.

He rode not in search of the dreams embodied in a new chapter of his life, but in search of the worst nightmare from his past.

To succeed, he needed to descend into the depths of the nightmare. He needed to get inside the mind of the man who haunted his dreams.

A decade back, the last time that Cole had gone in search of the rat-faced man, he had done so with no idea from where he had come, and less of an idea of where he was headed. Back then, nobody with whom Cole spoke as he searched had seen a rat-faced man. There was no trail on which to chase him, and even the absence of a trail went impossibly cold.

He had failed then.

He was determined not to fail his second chance.

This time, he returned to the place where he knew the trail began. Riding alone, unencumbered by pack mules laden with gold and a pair of fugitives, Cole was able to get back to the campsite in a couple of hours. It was easy to find. He just looked for the buzzards.

There was virtually no chance of an ambush here now, but he nevertheless studied the area with his spyglass for a long time before approaching the place from which he had watched the opening exchanges of the gun battle on that fateful night.

The body of the young man from the trading post whom Simon Lynch had killed was gone. It had probably been retrieved by his friend who had gotten away.

Lynch's remains, which Cole had ordered Stanton and Gardner to cover with rocks, had been uncovered and dragged a short distance away, probably by the second ambusher when he came back for his late friend. Lynch's body had been mutilated, perhaps originally by this man and certainly, for the past day and a half, by the buzzards.

About this, Cole cared little. His only concern was to pick up Muriday's trail. As he walked through the camp to the place where the tracks showed the man galloping away from the picket line, he noticed that Muriday's saddle was missing. Cole had abandoned it where it lay as too cumbersome to carry.

The bounty hunter had taken Muriday's abandoned boots for spite, and all the guns for practicality, but the saddle was just too bulky. Examining the area where it had been, Cole discovered that Muriday had doubled back and retrieved it. He had then ridden north, away from the direction that Cole had taken with Stanton and Gardner. With no boots and no gun, he had prudently decided that ambushing Cole was out of the question.

Cole imagined that Muriday was wishing now that he had taken the opportunity to simply abscond into oblivion with the money. However, as with a man who has tasted success at the tables, the lust for still more success clouds rational judgment.

Greed is the fuel that feeds the fire of greed.

Nearly two hours later, as he trailed the northward march of the rat-faced man, Cole came to the outbuildings of a small ranch, where two men were shoeing a horse.

"Afternoon," Cole said in greeting.

"Afternoon," one of the men said as they both stood to watch him approach.

"I was wonderin' if you might have seen a man ride through here yesterday," Cole asked, as a way of opening the conversation, rather than as a question, because Muriday's tracks led straight to this spot.

"Said he got caught in an Indian ambush," one of the men confirmed. "He a friend of yours?"

"Yeah," Cole lied. "I was supposed to catch up to him up north around Tesuque. Passed the place where the shooting took place this morning."

"Well, he was sure in a big hurry," the other man said.

"Youda been too," the other man said. "If the Indians had got your damned boots . . . and killed your partner."

"Buzzards are pretty much done with *him*," Cole said with a nod. "Terrible sight . . . something you never get used to seeing. Glad my friend got away."

"Least he's got boots," the first man said.

"Damned *expensive* boots," the second man laughed. "He done paid me a ten-dollar gold piece for an old pair I had layin' up in the barn and had been figurin' on get-

258

tin' rid of."

Cole laughed along with the two men who thought the idea of a man paying that much for old boots was hilarious.

"He wanted to buy hisself a gun too," the first man said. "Couldn't help him out there, though. Don't have no old ones of those layin' around."

"Glad you could help him out with boots, though," Cole said and nodded.

"Hope you catch up to him pretty soon," the man said.

"Me too," Cole said and he rode away.

Cole continued north, as the day waned and the light began to fade.

It is always easier to trail somebody in the late afternoon, because the low angle of the sun casts long shadows that make the tracks easier to see, but when the sun sets, the tracks virtually disappear.

When this happened, and the night quickly darkened, Cole could see lights in the direction that the tracks had been leading, so he rode toward them.

The source of the lights turned out to be a tiny hamlet dominated by a low-roofed general store. This being cattle country, Cole imagined that this place was probably a boom town during roundup and branding time, but it was little more than a backwater to the economic life of the area during the remainder of the year.

As he rode up, he could see two men drinking at the bar inside the store, and took a long look at their boots. Their posture told him that they were regulars.

"Do you for?" a man asked as Cole dismounted.

His demeanor, as he pitched methodically in a rocking chair outside near the doorway, explained that he was the proprietor.

"Wondering if you might've seen a friend of mine yesterday?"

"Might have."

"Ugly little character?" Cole said, describing Muriday. "Long pointy nose?"

"No chin?"

"That's him," Cole confirmed.

"Real jumpy little feller," the proprietor offered as though adding to the description.

"Well, he *did* get jumped by Indians."

"Thing that really got him hoppin' was reading the newspaper," the man explained.

"What newspaper?" Cole asked.

The man nodded toward a paper that was lying on a table just inside the door.

"Big news down in Santa Fe," the man continued. "Everybody's been talking about it."

"What's that?"

"Somebody robbed the railroad for some number of thousands . . . forget how much."

"That so?" Cole asked, as if making conversation.

"They got the bandits . . . Some bounty hunter brought 'em back. Everybody's been talking about it."

"You say my friend was all excited about this?" Cole asked.

"Yeah, he said it was somebody he knew . . . the bounty hunter that he had met. Probably somebody you know too."

"Don't recognize the name," Cole lied as he picked up the paper and read his own name.

"Can I do somethin' 'bout your thirst?" the man asked, lifting his rheumatism-tormented frame out of the chair.

Lumbering inside, he called to the bartender.

"Delgado . . . a whiskey for my friend."

"Lemme buy *you* one too," Cole offered.

"Mighty kind of you. Delgado, make it *dos.*"

As he drank with the man, Cole's new friend rambled on, drifting with a train of thought that meandered from past to present and back again. At last, the conversation came back to the railroad, the robbery, and Cole's jumpy acquaintance.

"He got real excited," the man explained. "He started out talkin' to me like he was in a real quandary about gettin' attacked by Indians and losin' everything. Then he read that article and decided that nothing was gonna make him happier than settin' things right with this bounty hunter down in Santa Fe. He acted like this bounty hunter owed him some money, but he was more interested in setting things right."

"Those were his words?"

"Those were his words. He wanted to set something right."

"Did he say what?"

"Something he needed a gun for."

"A gun?"

"Yeah, I sold him a .45 and four dozen rounds," the man said. "He said the Indians got the one he had. Guess they didn't get his dough. He paid me a gold eagle for that piece."

Bladen Cole camped about a mile from the general store where he had shared a couple of shots with the proprietor. That night, he fell asleep in the bosom of his nightmare, but with the exhilaration of knowing that the trail was not cold.

A decade back, Cole had gone in search

of a rat-faced man with no idea from where he had come, and less of an idea of where he was headed. This time, he knew where the rat-faced Ben Muriday was headed.

This time, the rat-faced man would be hunting Bladen Cole. He was coming after the man who had cheated him out of reward money and legitimacy.

The hunted just had to get to the hunter *first.*

CHAPTER 28

Making her rounds of daily errands, Nicolette de la Gravière left the general merchandise emporium with a new skillet for the Refugio del Viajero under her arm. After spending yesterday afternoon touring the Atchison, Topeka & Santa Fe construction headquarters, and the evening dining with Ezra Waldron and his colleagues under the stars, she was back to her routine, her apron, and her duties at the restaurant.

She wondered whether her evenings spent with this railroad man yet constituted her entertaining him as a "suitor," as her mother was eager for her to do. She did admit that he *was* a gentleman, with all the qualities of politeness and cordiality that accompanied the term. He was not condescending, as men so often were, when she spoke of her own affairs, and she greatly appreciated that.

As much as she was growing fond of Mr. Waldron, however, nothing about him had yet manifested itself as that intangible something that would make her feel an exhilaration in his presence. The sight of him did not bring a flush to her cheeks or, in Shakespeare's words, "bewitch her bosom."

It was the unnamed cowboy who had "stolen the impression of her fantasy."

Of course, as her mother pointed out, in the *long term,* it was a gentleman who was a provider who would furnish a lady with a future of security and contentment. A drifting cowboy might inflame her passions and cause her heart to soar, but in the *long term,* a drifting cowboy provided only disappointment, loneliness, and heartache.

The sad thing was that Nicolette knew her mother was probably right.

As it happened, the route of her return from errands took her past the offices of the Atchison, Topeka & Santa Fe. Was this, she might have wondered, by chance or by subconscious design? Perhaps there *was* a bewitching in her bosom, consciously repressed, at the thought of Ezra Waldron.

In any event, the route that took her past the offices of the railroad naturally led to a glance inside, and when he happened to be there, and their eyes met, she *did* feel a flush come to her cheeks.

In an instant, she was faced with the quandary — should she stop in for a quick hello?

Would that be too forward — or would the impoliteness of *not* stopping in for a quick hello be a greater *faux pas.*

Not being a shy girl, for no one who waits tables in a popular restaurant can long be timid in personal interactions, she opened the door and entered.

Almost immediately, Nicolette wished she had decided otherwise.

It quickly became evident that Waldron and his colleague, Joseph Ames, were in the midst of an argument.

"I'm sorry for intruding, gentlemen," she said, making the most of the choice she had made. "I don't mean to interrupt, I was just passing, and did not want to be so rude as to not convey a greeting . . . so having said hello, I shall continue . . ."

"It's fine," Waldron said. "We were just discussing railroad business . . ."

"Which as you might imagine, Miss de la Gravière, is none of your concern," Ames said.

"Of course," she said, opening the door. "Good day, gentlemen."

"You needn't be curt with the lady," Waldron interjected.

"I was not being curt, I was stating the obvious."

"Your choice of words represents poor judgment."

"When it comes to poor judgment, I believe that *yours* in the affairs of this road is an extreme example of this," Ames said as Nicolette closed the door behind her.

"You missed that *vaquero* last night," Dolores Herrera mentioned casually as she and Nicolette set the tables for the evening meal at the Refugio del Viajero.

"What *vaquero*?"

"That one who so enchanted you when he dined here a week or so before."

What *vaquero*? Nicolette wondered. Suddenly she felt her face go red. *That vaquero. That* cowboy.

"He was *here*?"

"Last night," Dolores said with a nod. "I waited on his table. He tipped very good."

Nicolette swallowed hard.

She would say no more, at least until she had a chance to speak to her mother alone.

"You didn't tell me he was here," Nicolette said pointedly.

"Who was here?"

"The cowboy, Mama . . . *the* cowboy . . . last night."

"Oh that's right," Therese recalled. "He was."

"Why didn't you tell me?"

"Slipped my mind . . . You're not truly interested, are you?"

"You said he would never come back, Mama," Nicolette replied. "You were *so* sure that he would drift away and never be seen again."

"It's just by chance . . . a coincidence."

"Did he ask after me?"

"Nicolette," Therese exclaimed sarcastically. "Certainly you don't think that every man who catches your eye is going to take a fancy to *you*?"

"He *might.*"

"What about Monsieur Waldron? I thought that *he* was courting you."

"We just went to the theater . . . *one time,*" Nicolette replied. "Is *that* courting?"

"And to the Governor's Palace for a reception for . . . what was his name?"

"Mr. Schurz . . . Mr. Carl Schurz."

"Mais qui," Therese said, wrinkling her brow. *"L'homme Allemand."*

"He's not German anymore," Nicolette corrected her mother, who disliked *all* Germans, even though the Franco-Prussian War had been over for more than ten years. "He's American . . . he's in Mr. Hayes's cabinet. He lived here during the war . . . so did *you.*"

"So I did," Therese said and nodded, unconvinced of her daughter's logic. "But you changed the subject. I was speaking of Monsieur Waldron and his intentions. What would Mr. Waldron think if he knew that you were longing for a cowboy while you were keeping company with him?"

"It would be none of his business," Nicolette said defiantly. "I *do* like Mr. Waldron, but I am not *married* to him. I may think about who I please."

"It displeases your mother to see you pining after a broken heart."

"Mama."

"I'm sure that Monsieur Cole has more important things to concern himself with than a *jeune fille* who once served him *carne asada.*"

"And I'm sure that I am not a *young girl,*" Nicolette insisted. "And how do you know his name?"

"I did not mean to mention it . . ." Therese said, sorry indeed that she had mentioned Cole's name.

"Why?" Nicolette demanded.

"Because he's a *bounty hunter,* my girl," Therese admitted. "Because he is *the* bounty hunter who was written about in the newspaper."

"You mean the railroad robbery?" Nicolette asked, flabbergasted. "*He* is the man who brought the railroad bandits to justice?"

"I mean that this man, Bladen Cole, is not merely a drifting cowboy," Therese said sternly. "He is a man of exceptional violence, and *not* a man I wish to have associated with *my* daughter."

CHAPTER 29

Ben Muriday rode into Santa Fe armed with a slightly used .45-caliber Colt and a determined aspiration to exact vengeance on the man who had cheated him of the glory for which he longed. He imagined that the bounty hunter Bladen Cole was drinking and womanizing and enjoying himself in the territorial capital. He imagined this poser basking in glory, and enjoying the touch of tender female flesh, which *rightfully* belonged to Ben Muriday.

He checked into a fleabag hotel, knowing that lodgings more commensurate with this image of himself awaited him when he had found the bounty hunter and taken the reward money he rightly deserved.

There were still gold eagles in his pocket, but having paid too much, in his desperation, for shoes and a weapon, he was conserving his resources. This was only temporary, of course; he intended to be flush as soon as he caught and killed this damnable bounty hunter.

Muriday blamed the man for cheating him of a reward that was rightfully his, and he blamed the bounty hunter for attacking the camp and killing Simon Lynch. He assumed that Cole's arrival and the ambush at the campsite by the two Indians from the trading post had been somehow coordinated, when these events were merely coincidental.

Muriday had ridden with Lynch for the past two years. They had engaged in mischief, had made some modest scores, and having learned of the Dutchman's gold, they had planned to become fabulously wealthy — that is, until Muriday came up with the plan that they should rehabilitate their reputations and become heroes by turning in a pair of robbers.

Now Lynch had paid with his life for Muriday's crazy notion. It wasn't the first time that Muriday had lost a partner in a gunfight. There was that time down in Silver City about ten years back. They were drinking in a bar and got into an argument with a couple of hotheaded cowboys. Muriday had shot one and had gotten away, but his partner left the bar feet first.

Since then, he looked at partnering up with somebody as a business arrangement.

Getting friendly was always secondary to getting the job done. He was sorry to see Lynch get himself killed, but Muriday kept his eye on the plan. He considered the avenging of Lynch's demise to be a mere by-product of finding and killing the bounty hunter to get the reward money.

However, getting the cash wasn't the only thing on his mind. Muriday's plan was also frustrated by the riddle of how he might redress that other wrong he had suffered and secure for himself the notoriety the bounty hunter had stolen from him, the notoriety accorded to this Bladen Cole in the pages of the *Santa Fe New Mexican.*

After many days of camping in the mountains and deserts, a new shirt and a bath in a real bathtub can do wonders for a man's disposition, and they did wonders for the temperament of Ben Muriday.

He was in so good a mood, in fact, that he hardly noticed when the man at the Chinese laundry gave him a strange double take. It was as though the man *knew* him, but so what? This man was merely a Chinaman.

With these chores behind him, Muriday set out upon his quest. Where better to learn the affairs of the day, Muriday thought, than that nexus of all rumor, gossip, and talk of the town, the nearest saloon?

"Sure could use a whiskey," he said, placing a coin on the bar.

As the bartender fussed at his back bar, getting down a bottle for his first sale of the morning, Muriday eyed the decorations above the mirror that rose behind the bar. There was a line of figurines, each about a foot tall, made out of cottonwood sticks, pieces of cloth, and animal fur. Some of them had feathers and animal teeth attached. They all had dreadful faces painted on them, each one competing for ferocity and eeriness with the one beside it.

"What's all them about?" he asked.

"Kachinas," the man said. "The Indians out at the pueblos make them."

"What the hell for?" Muriday asked with disgust. "They're ugly as sin . . . look like devils."

"They're for some kind of magic . . . according to the man that sold 'em to me."

"Where'd he get 'em?"

"Out at the pueblos, I reckon."

"They supposed to be for good luck?"

"Reckon not."

"Why?"

"Feller who sold 'em to me got hisself shot just after he sold 'em to me."

"Damn," Muriday said. "Ain't you scared

of havin' 'em?"

"Don't much believe in magic," the man said as he returned to the bar with an open bottle.

"Much obliged," Muriday said as two welcome fingers of amber magic flowed into a glass set on the bar before him.

"Sure been readin' a lot about those train robbers lately," he said as the bartender placed his change on the bar.

"Folks been talkin' about little else," the bartender said. It being early in the day, there were few customers in the place, and he was in the mood for discourse. "Been articles in the paper for the last couple days."

"When they gonna put 'em on trial?" Muriday asked, making conversation. He really did not care when the trial happened, or what happened to Gabe Stanton and Jasper Gardner.

"Don't reckon I know," the bartender said thoughtfully. "I figure that as soon as they bring 'em to Santa Fe, they'll get 'em before a judge to be arraigned."

"Bring 'em to Santa Fe?" Muriday asked. "Thought they was *already* in jail."

"They got 'em down by Lamy at the Atchison, Topeka & Santa Fe camp," the bartender said. "The railroad's got theirselves a brig down there."

"Why are they there and not in jail?"

"That's where the bounty hunter brought 'em. It was the railroad and not the law that offered the reward. They're gonna be there until the sheriff can go down and get 'em on up here."

"What's keepin' him?"

"With all that publicity, there'd be a lot of gawkers gettin' in the way. He needs to put together a posse to ride herd on 'em coming up here. It's the better part of a day's ride."

"I see," Muriday said thoughtfully. "Speaking of that bounty hunter," he added after a thoughtful pause. "I s'pose he's been livin' it up in town lately."

"Never saw him in *here,*" the bartender said. "Guess he was drinkin' somewhere else. Folks did see him around, though. He was eatin' over at the Refugio del Viajero the other night. Last I heard, he's gone. He rode out yesterday . . . according to what I heard."

"Where you reckon he's off to?"

"Reckon he's off to spend his money somewhere besides around here."

"Where's he from?"

"I've heard Colorado . . . but somebody said something about him coming from down Silver City way."

"What can I help you with?"

"Come to see the sheriff," Muriday told the deputy.

In Muriday's mind, the idea of recapturing the elusive esteem associated with bringing the thieves to justice had moved to the forefront of his list of objectives.

There was no better way to achieve this, he decided, than to include himself as a member of the posse that brought Stanton and Gardner to Santa Fe. It was not that this, in itself, would provide the desired renown, but his being part of the posse would provide him with the *opportunity* to distinguish himself for all to notice.

"What business do you have with the sheriff?" the deputy asked.

"Wanna be on that posse what's gonna bring in the train robbers," Muriday said proudly.

"I see," the man said with a tone that explained that Muriday was far from being the first man to volunteer for this duty.

The man finished what he was doing, then stood and walked toward a door that led to an inner office.

"Wait here," he said.

Muriday waited, listening to the monotonous *click-clunk* of the wall clock and watching several other people transacting other business.

Finally, the deputy returned with a tall man wearing a five-pointed silver star.

"Sheriff Reuben Sandoval," the man said extending his hand.

"Muriday . . . Ben Muriday. I wanna be on that posse they say you're raising to fetch them fellas up from down at Lamy."

"You from around here?" Sandoval asked.

"Nope. Just passin' through."

"Where you from?"

"All around."

"Where mostly?"

"Been down in Lincoln County for the past year," Muriday said. "Before that in Grant County for a while and over around Parker County, Texas."

"You get around some, then," the sheriff observed.

"That I do."

"What sort of work do you do?"

"Cowboying mainly," Muriday said. "Whatever needs doin.' "

"What interests you in being on this posse?" Sandoval asked.

"Reckon I wanna be a part of being on the side of bringing these bad men to justice."

"That's very commendable, Mr. Muriday," the sheriff said. "But I already got as many men as I am going to need for the posse. If you could leave your name and how to get hold of you with the deputy here, I'll get in touch with you if there's anyone who can't make it. Thanks a lot for takin' the interest though."

"Thank you for takin' the time, sir," Muriday said, disappointment in his voice as he took the sheriff's extended hand.

"Mr. Muriday," came a voice behind him as he crossed the street from the sheriff's office. He turned to see one of the men he had seen inside.

"Mr. Muriday, my name is Nathaniel Siward," he said, extending his hand. "Couldn't help overhearing you generously volunteering to join the posse."

"Was you aiming to get on the posse yourself?"

"No. I just happened to hear you."

"Good thing you ain't lookin' to get on the posse," Muriday said. "Seems like he's got all the men he needs for the job. Ain't hirin' nobody else."

"How'd you like to be on the posse?"

"Like to be, but if he ain't hirin', he ain't hirin'."

"He's not the *only* one getting up a posse," Siward said.

"How's that?"

"I work for the Atchison, Topeka & Santa Fe, and as you can imagine, we've *also* got us an interest in seeing these men brought to justice."

"So?"

"We need a man of our own to ride along to support the sheriff's posse and make sure that nothing happens," Siward explained. "I'd like to hire you to ride as part of the railroad posse."

"That's an idea, all right," Muriday said.

"Pay you in gold," Siward said with a smile. "The sheriff's volunteers are just getting expense money. We're paying a gold eagle for a day's work."

"Well, I reckon that suits me fine," Muriday said. "I'm your man."

"Welcome to the Atchison, Topeka & Santa Fe," Siward said, shaking Muriday's hand again. "You just get yourself down to Lamy by dawn the day after tomorrow, and you're riding with us. If you wanna get down tomorrow night, look for me and we'll feed you supper and breakfast and give you a place to bunk, so you're fresh-faced when we ride out."

Ben Muriday could not believe his good

fortune. Luck was obviously riding with him to put him in the sheriff's office at the right time to be overhead by Nathaniel Siward. Being hired on by the railroad was better that riding with the sheriff. There was the gold, certainly, but it was with the railroad, not the law, where the bounty hunter had gotten his reward *and* his recognition.

If he was lucky, Muriday thought, he might even get some information from the railroad men as to where he could go to find that damned Bladen Cole.

CHAPTER 30

"Oh no," Nicolette de la Gravière said as she read the *Santa Fe New Mexican.* "This is terrible."

She was supposed to be helping to sort the fresh produce, but the headline caught her eye.

"What's terrible?" Dolores Herrera asked.

"It's the Atchison, Topeka & Santa Fe. Their shares on the stock market back in New York have fallen."

"Don't those things go up and down all the time?"

"But they fell a lot. According to the paper, they have lost a third of their value."

"Why is that?"

"It's the robbery," Nicolette said, reading intently. "It says here that 'investor confidence collapsed,' when the news of the robbery reached New York."

"What does that mean?"

"It means that the financial people are

pulling their money out of the Atchison, Topeka & Santa Fe and putting it somewhere else."

"How do *you* know all this?" Dolores asked quizzically.

"Because Ezra . . . Mr. Waldron . . . explained it to me."

"He is now '*Ezra*'?" Dolores laughed. "I didn't think you were courting yet."

"We're not," Nicolette said, blushing. "He's just . . ."

"I thought your *corazón* was throbbing for the handsome *vaquero*?" Dolores said teasingly. "And now Señor Waldron is 'Ezra'?"

"I like Mr. Waldron," Nicolette admitted. "He is a gentleman . . . Mother likes him. She approves because he is a gentleman."

Dolores smiled knowingly, reading between the lines as she carefully arranged a group of tomatoes which the cooks would use later to prepare the fresh salsa that afternoon.

"I feel so bad for Mr. Waldron," Nicolette said as she organized the pots and pans on the grill. "His job is in the financing of the railroad. This will reflect badly on *him*."

"I'm sure that he knows what he's doing," Dolores said sympathetically, putting her hand on Nicolette's shoulder. "He is a smart man. He knows more about these things than we do."

Nicolette nodded.

As soon as the morning prep work was done and the boys had come to fill the fireboxes with mesquite, Nicolette pulled off her apron and made her way down the street to the Atchison, Topeka & Santa Fe offices.

Ezra Waldron was at his desk, as were several of the clerks. Joseph Ames, with his overbearing nature and his soft, fleshy hands, was not there.

"Mr. Waldron," she began, unsure of how one expressed commiseration in circumstances such as this. She noticed a copy of the *Santa Fe New Mexican* on his desk and nodded to it. "I see you've read the news today . . . I was so sad to see this. You must be absolutely devastated."

"Miss de la Gravière," he said, looking up, surprised to see her. "What are you doing here . . . I mean that I am very glad to see you . . . but I *am* surprised."

"When I read this . . . I just had to come to see you and offer a word of . . . empathy."

"You are so kind, Miss de la Gravière," Waldron said softly, taking her hand in his. "I certainly appreciate your kindness."

Nicolette was both startled and soothed

to feel her hand in his, and him continuing to hold it, both gently and firmly. It was as though, for a moment, he was consoling *her,* and she felt comforted by his warmth.

"Mr. Waldron," Nathaniel Siward said, bursting through the door.

"Oh . . . I'm sorry if I'm interrupting . . ." he said when he saw his boss with Nicolette de la Gravière.

Seeing Siward, Nicolette quickly pulled her hand from Waldron's tender grasp.

"No, it's . . . no interruption," Waldron said, grasping for words as her hand slipped from his. "Miss de la Gravière was just expressing her sympathy for us in the current financial downturn. I was about to explain that these things happen . . . that we hope for a timely reversal of bad fortune."

"I see . . ." Siward said nervously.

"What were you about to tell me?"

"The prisoners, sir," he said. "The sheriff is going to Lamy to get them on the day after tomorrow."

"That's good," Waldron said, speaking as much to Nicolette as to his employee. "We won't be sorry to see them leave our custody . . . will we?"

"No, sir."

"Will we have our men involved as we

planned?" Waldron asked.

"Yes sir, I'll be riding along myself . . . and I've just hired another man."

"Who is he?"

"His name is Muriday, sir," Siward explained. "He seems to be just the sort of man we're looking for."

"That's good to know," Waldron said, his voice relaxing somewhat.

"If you gentlemen will excuse me," Nicolette said, stepping back. "It sounds as though you have much to discuss, and I must get back to prepare the Refugio del Viajero for opening."

She had seen Joseph Ames coming up the street, and he made her nervous.

He reached the door before she did, and his immense bulk seemed to explode through it.

"Ezra, I assume you have read the news?"

"That I have, Joseph."

"Our worst fears have been realized," Ames insisted emphatically. "Your foolish decision, a decision which you will recall that I called foolish when I learned that you had made it, has destroyed us."

"I would not characterize this as having *destroyed* us," Waldron replied.

"Ezra, you did a *damned* fool thing by trumpeting to the press that we'd had so serious a theft . . . especially after we had *agreed* that it should be kept quiet," Ames said. "Once again, as I have before, I see the young lady on the premises, and I do apologize to the young lady for the strong language . . . but, ma'am, if you insist on frequenting these offices where men speak freely . . ."

"I was just leaving," she said, ducking through the door.

"I'll be going as well," Siward said, following her out the door. "I need to get back to Lamy by nightfall."

"That was rude, sir," Waldron told Ames when the others had left.

"If you are going to be keeping company with her, you should not be doing so under the pretext that you are not a fool, sir," Ames retorted.

"Stock prices go down, and stock prices go up," Waldron said.

"Correction," Ames shouted, thrusting the yellow paper of a telegram across Waldron's desk. "Stock prices go down, and stock prices *plummet*. This just arrived from New York. This will not appear in the *Santa Fe New Mexican* until tomorrow, so the young lady will be spared the embarrassment of

287

being associated with you for that length of time."

Waldron studied the telegram. The Atchison, Topeka & Santa Fe share price had continued to fall, and the Denver & Rio Grande Western moneymen were reaping the fruits of a tide of shifting capital.

"It is not enough that we are falling like a stone," Ames said in disgust, "but at the same time, our worst rival is *surging.* What, pray tell, were you saying about your damned fool decision having *not* destroyed us?"

Nicolette de la Gravière glanced at the clock. There was less than a half hour until closing time, but it had already been a very long and exhausting day.

In the beginning of their acquaintance, Ezra Waldron had carried himself with an air of superiority about his being in the lofty heights of high finance, while her own Refugio del Viajero was minuscule by comparison. Now, having watched the fortunes of his mighty railroad tumble, she was thankful for the proceeds that she saw in the cashbox tonight.

Noticing someone enter the front door, she put on her hostess's smile and glanced in that direction.

"Mr. Waldron," she said, startled to see him. "Please come in. Please, let me get you a table. Right this way. I hope you are feeling better . . ."

"I've not come to dine, Miss de la Gravière," he said, returning her smile with one of his own. "I have come to offer you this rose, and to ask that you join me once again at the theater two nights from now . . . they're presenting *Macbeth.*"

"I would be most pleased to accompany you to the theater, Mr. Waldron," Nicolette told him, although in light of the tumult of the day, which was likely to continue, she questioned whether so gloomy a play as *Macbeth* would do much for their respective moods.

However, she remembered his gentle touch, and the empathy which she felt toward him.

She bade him good night, and as he departed, she paused for a moment to admire and to contemplate the single, long-stemmed rose which he had presented to her.

As she turned, Nicolette noticed her mother across the room, watching her with a smile. Therese was pleased with what she was seeing.

As Nicolette put the rose aside and returned to her work, and to a table that was wishing to settle up its tab, she wondered whether she and Ezra Waldron might actually be meant for each other after all.

CHAPTER 31

Bladen Cole had come full circle. He had ridden out of Santa Fe into the mountains and deserts in his search for the trail of the rat-faced man.

Now he was riding back *into* Santa Fe on a fresh trail of a man with a .45 and four dozen rounds who was hell-bent on "setting things right" with a bounty hunter he expected to be lingering in Santa Fe, spending reward money and living it up.

Cole chuckled when he pictured Muriday imagining himself as the hunter, gunning for Cole, not knowing that Cole had been hunting *him* for years. Cole *knew* that *he* was the hunter. He knew that at last, he was closing in on the final resolution of his most persistent nightmare. The rat-faced man was within his grasp, and this time he would *not* get away — because this time, *he* was looking for Bladen Cole.

As he had ridden that full circle that now

brought him back to Santa Fe, Cole had tried to picture where Muriday would look for the man who'd cheated him out of the reward money he felt was his due.

Reaching Santa Fe as the sun stood high in the sky, Cole's first stop was the Chinese laundry. The proprietor nodded his recognition as Cole entered. The man remembered him.

"Saw your man," he said. "Ugly with no chin."

"That's good news," Cole said, reaching into his pocket. "When was he here?"

"This morning," the man said as he heard coins clinking in Cole's pocket.

"How long ago?" Cole asked, placing two gold eagles on the well-worn counter.

"Three hour," the man said, looking at his clock. "He left here and went to saloon . . . there."

"Thank you much," Cole said, gently and almost formally placing another coin on the table.

Back outside, he cast his gaze down the street, where he could see the Refugio del Viajero. The sign on the front door read CERRADO. They would not be open for several hours. He wondered where he would be then, and how long it would be before he glimpsed those dark eyes and those lips the color of chilies.

As he stepped across the street, Cole instinctively fingered his holster. Muriday might still be at the bar. If so, the showdown he had imagined in his mind for a decade could come within a matter of moments.

After seeing that his quarry was not inside, the second thing that captured Cole's gaze upon entering the saloon was the eerie line of kachina dolls presiding over the room from above the mirror behind the bar.

"How can I brighten your day, sir?" the man behind the bar called out in an usually cheerful tone.

"You're in a good mood," Cole observed, returning the man's grin.

"No reason not to be. 'Tis a sunny day and I'm going to spend it under a cool adobe roof."

"Well, in that case, I'll stay for a while and let you brighten my day with a cold beer."

"Good choice," the man said, maneuvering a glass mug beneath a spigot.

"Good beer," Cole said and nodded after he'd taken a long, satisfying drink.

"Brewed right over yonder by Probst and Kirchner's," the man said. "Reckon they make the best beer in town."

"You got quite a collection there," Cole

said, pointing at the figurines.

"Yep. They serve as a wonderful conversation piece . . . or pieces . . . I reckon that not one person in five who comes in here fails to make mention."

"Never seen so many in one place before," Cole said as he savored the frothy refreshment.

"Feller got 'em out at one of them pueblos . . . or maybe at a couple of pueblos. They say they got magic in 'em."

"Do they?"

"I never seen no magic out of 'em 'cept they get folks a-talkin' . . . and stayin' to buy another drink."

"Speaking of fellers," Cole said, putting his half-full glass back on the bar as a signal that he would not be having a refill. "I'm tryin' to catch up with a friend o' mine. I think he might have come in here this morning."

"Been several fellers . . ."

"This one would've been . . . well . . . kinda ugly."

"Beady eyes?"

"Yep."

"No chin?"

"That'd be old Ben Muriday," Cole said with a smile.

"It seemed kinda funny him callin' my

kachinas ugly," the bartender recalled. "With him being . . . like he is and all . . . not that I reckon he can help it."

"How long ago did that old rascal head on out of here?" Cole asked.

"Couple hours, I reckon. He only stayed for one drink when I told him about the posse."

"What posse?"

"You've heard about them two train robbers that everybody's been talking about?"

"Hard not to," Cole said, pointing to a couple of copies of the *Santa Fe New Mexican* that were laying at the other end of the bar.

"Well, the railroad's got 'em caged down at Lamy, and the sheriff is gettin' together a posse to go down there tomorrow to bring 'em on back up here to Santa Fe to stand trial."

"So Muriday's gonna try and get himself into that posse?" Cole asked.

"Soon as I told him about the sheriff lookin' for folks, he got all excited and said he was gonna do that. You know, you might want to get your own self over there and try an' get hired on. Least you'll catch up with your friend that way."

"Much obliged," Cole said, draining the half-filled glass and heading for the door.

"What can I help you with?" asked the deputy as Cole stepped into the sheriff's office.

"I'm asking about the posse that's being put together . . ."

"Being put together to escort those two train robbers up from Lamy, right?"

"Yup," Cole confirmed.

"There was just a fella in here an hour or so ago askin' about that," the deputy explained. "Sheriff told him he's got everybody he needs. Sorry . . . you're outta luck."

"Thanks anyhow."

"One thing I can tell you though," the deputy added. "That being that I seen that fella talkin' to Nathaniel Siward of the railroad. I've heard that the railroad might be gonna have their own posse ridin' along too. You might try gettin' on with them. Between you and me, the railroad is gonna be payin' more than the sheriff would."

"Much obliged," Cole said.

Ben Muriday arrived at the big Atchison, Topeka & Santa Fe construction headquarters at Lamy, finding it a chaotic hive of commotion the likes of which he had never seen. For a man used to riding in country lightly populated, if populated at all, to suddenly be surrounded by hundreds of scurrying workmen and massive thundering machinery was both fascinating and unnerving.

He asked around for Nathaniel Siward and was directed to a large tent about a quarter mile away along a section of track.

"Reportin' for duty," he said when he finally made eye contact with Siward.

"Good," Siward said. "You're just in time for supper."

"That's what I was hopin'," Muriday replied.

"Listen, I gotta go take care of something. Lennox here will take you down to the chow line and tell 'em that you work for the road, and you're not just another . . . er . . . fellow walking in out of the desert."

Siward had considered using the phrase "not just another strange face" to describe Muriday, but looking at the man's unsightly, rodentine appearance, he decided that politeness demanded that he phrase it differently.

"When did you hire on?" Lennox asked.

"Just yesterday," Muriday replied. "Done got myself on the posse that's gonna be taking them two bandits up to Santa Fe."

"Ain't that the talk of the camp," Lennox said. "Nobody never knew there had been a robbery, and here comes this bounty hunter with the banditos . . . and bags of gold too."

"Sure woulda figured that folks would have knowed about a robbery of that size."

"Guess the bosses kept it quiet," Lennox said with a shrug. "Reckon they was wishin' they could *still* keep it quiet."

"What do you mean?"

"There's talk all over that there's a big ruckus back East about the road gettin' hit with a big old robbery."

"What kind of ruckus?"

"Don't rightly know," Lennox admitted. "All I care is that I keeps a-mannin' a boiler wrench, and they keeps a-payin' me."

"Speakin' of them robbers," Muriday asked. "Where they keepin' them at?"

"Down at the cages."

"What's the cages?"

"That's where you get sent to cool your heels if you get caught fightin' or raisin' hell."

"Can you show me?"

"Sure," Lennox said. "We can wander on down there after chow."

Mounted on a flat car, the cages had been shunted to a siding far from the main camp, where they were under guard by a man with a rifle.

"What you doin' down here, Lennox?"

The man queried as the two men came close and their faces became visible in the light of the lantern. "Ain't nobody supposed to be comin' round the prisoners."

"The more the merrier," came a shout from within one of the cages. "This sonuvabitch ain't keeping us company."

Muriday recognized the nasal voice of Jasper Gardner.

"Shut up," demanded the man with the rifle.

"Whatcha gonna do? You gonna shoot me?"

"Awful arrogant for a condemned man," Lennox said.

"Ain't condemned yet," Gardner asserted. "Ain't never gonna be once I get time alone with that boss of yours up in Santa Fe."

"What's he mean by that?" Lennox asked the man with the Winchester.

"Hell if I know. He just keeps on a-sayin' that he plans to talk to the bosses. Maybe he figures on killin' a boss or two. Maybe he figures on bein' pardoned . . . fat chance of any of that happening."

Muriday tried to keep his face in the shadows so that he could size up Gardner and Stanton without being recognized. The contraptions in which the two men were being held were literally cages, like those in which an animal would be kept in a zoo.

"Hey, Muriday? Is that you?"

Damn it. He realized that he had been made. Perhaps it was just as well. He would have had to cross this bridge tomorrow with Siward watching.

"Looks like you've got yourself caught, Stanton."

"You *know* these men?" Lennox asked.

"Reckon I do."

"They friends of yours?"

"Sure would not use *that* word," Muriday said.

"We're *great* friends," Gardner said teasingly. "Know him all his life . . . since this ugly toad of a sonuvabitch was a tadpole."

"Looks like you ain't gonna be knowin' much of anybody from now on 'cept a judge and hangman," Muriday shot back.

"How is it that you know these two?" Lennox asked.

" 'Twas back . . ."

"This sonuvabitch was tryin' to take us in before that other bounty hunter ambushed him and chased him off," Gardner explained.

"That true?" Lennox asked.

"You think anything this weasel says is *true*?" Muriday laughed.

■ ■ ■ ■

Ben Muriday was relishing the rarity of a hot breakfast when the sun first peeked over the horizon.

"Hey, Muriday," Nathaniel Siward called from across the area where about two dozen men were putting away their first meal of the day. "Time to saddle up."

"Already saddled," Muriday replied, turning to Siward, proud to be ahead of the game. "Are the sheriff's men down from Santa Fe already?"

"We're gonna meet 'em on the trail," Siward said. "Say, Lennox tells me that you *know* these two prisoners."

"Me and my partner ran across 'em a while back," Muriday confirmed. "New Mexico's a small place. When you got as few people as we got here, it makes sense that you're gonna cross paths with somebody more than once in your life."

"I reckon," Siward said, nodding at what seemed to be a reasonable explanation.

As they mounted up and headed in the direction of the cages, Siward resumed the conversation.

"You sure they ain't *friends* of yours?"

"I can guaran-damn-*tee* you that they

ain't friends of mine."

"Reason I ask is this," Siward said in a serious, confiding tone. "I ask because I want to be sure that if need be, you wouldn't mind shooting these men?"

"You mean if they try to escape?" Muriday asked.

"Yeah, *anything* like that. Sometimes a man hesitates to shoot to kill somebody he knows."

"You reckon on having to *kill* these two?"

"When Mr. Waldron hired Mr. Cole to bring them in, he said he wouldn't mind one bit if they came back dead, but he brought 'em back alive."

"Your boss *hired* that bounty hunter?" Muriday asked.

"Yeah, did you think he just *found them* out in the desert somewhere?"

"Reckon I did," Muriday said with a nod, not letting on that he had *seen* Cole "just find them."

"You got no hesitation about killing them, then?" Siward repeated.

"If they try to escape . . . wouldn't we wanna try and catch 'em first?"

"If that didn't work . . ."

"Got no problem killin' 'em if that's what it takes," Muriday confirmed.

"Good."

Siward looked at Muriday, trying to read his expression, but it was hard to figure out anything from his caricature of a face, with its narrow-spaced eyes and strangely shaped mouth.

Gardner and Stanton had already been mounted on horses by the time that Siward and Muriday reached the siding where the cages had been parked.

"Look familiar?" Jasper Gardner shouted to Muriday as they approached, holding up his hands, which were tethered to the saddle horn.

"You talkin' to me?" Muriday asked.

"Was *you* who was doin' just this same thing to us a few days back."

"You got me mixed up with that bounty hunter who done brought you in," Muriday laughed.

"No, I ain't," Gardner retorted. "I never forget a face . . . especially one as ugly as *yours.*"

"I may be ugly, but at least I ain't wearin' hemp bracelets and headed to judgment day."

"What's he talkin' about?" Siward asked Muriday.

"Last time I seen him 'twas in a cantina down in Santa Rita," Muriday lied. "The only thing touching his wrists down there was the top of the bar."

CHAPTER 32

"Miss de la Gravière," Ezra Waldron said, rising to greet Nicolette. "Such a pleasure to see you."

"Mr. Waldron," she said with a smile, entering the Atchison, Topeka & Santa Fe offices with a large tray. "I hope you don't mind. I brought you a bit of lunch."

"I don't mind in the least. This is so delightful. It smells *wonderful.*"

He watched eagerly as she folded back a cloth napkin to reveal a plate of tortillas, accompanied by sliced meats and tomatoes. *What a delightful girl,* he thought to himself.

"I waited until Mr. Ames departed," she said. "I fear he does not like me."

"It's not that he dislikes you. It is that he's consumed with the ongoing financial difficulties and deeply angered by this turn of events."

"And yourself?"

"I'm troubled as well, of course," Waldron

said. "But I hope that my worries are unaccompanied by unwarranted discourtesy toward you."

"No, sir . . . but Mr. Ames . . . It certainly displeases *him* that I call on you at your place of business."

"I call on *you,* Miss de la Gravière, at your place of business."

"Thank you . . . Thank you *so* much for the rose," she said with a smile. "And the opportunity to accompany you to the theater tomorrow."

"As far as my colleague is concerned, you may certainly consider his bark worse than his bite."

"It still makes me nervous to come when he is here."

"You are welcome here at any time, Miss de la Gravière."

"Thank you . . . and if I may be so bold, sir, you may call me Nicolette."

"Thank you, I shall call you Nicolette, and you may certainly feel free to call me Ezra."

"Thank you, Ezra," she said, feeling the way the word flowed from her lips in conversation.

He stood to get a cup of coffee and offered her one.

"Thank you, Ezra," she said, giggling slightly at the repetition.

"I hope that you do not find the difficulties of the railroad unduly troubling, Nicolette," he said, savoring the feel of her name as its three syllables rolled across his tongue.

"Except as it affects you," she said. "It is always troubling to see someone whom you . . . whom you know, facing difficulties."

"Nothing to worry about," he said in a reassuring tone.

"Mr. Ames does not share your confidence," she noted. "He feels rather strongly about your decision to publicize the robbery."

"He is entitled to his opinion."

"What made you change your mind?"

"Well, um," he said, almost as though he had not considered what it was that had caused him to do so. "I suppose it is not good to conceal facts . . . facts that might cause greater embarrassment if revealed at a moment not of one's choosing . . ."

"I have heard that the perpetrators will be brought here to Santa Fe later in the day," she observed, changing the direction of the conversation, if not its subject. "I saw the sheriff and several of his men depart earlier as I was on my way to the post office."

"They'll be in jail here tonight," Waldron said in a tone that suggested concern.

"When do you imagine the trial will start?" she asked.

"I don't know," Waldron said, seeming distracted, as his eyes drifted to the window and gazed down the street toward the courthouse. "It would have saved the people of New Mexico a goodly sum had Mr. Cole decided to bring them back dead, rather than alive."

"Ezra . . ."

"I'm sorry," he said, startled to have caught himself in a perceived indiscretion. "I'm *so* sorry, I did not mean to discuss such subjects as killing in the presence of a lady."

"Ezra," she said again. "The 'lady' does not take offense at discussion of dead bandits, who for all we know, deserve a hangman's noose, only at the thought that you would advocate a bounty hunter serving arbitrarily as an executioner."

"That's not what I meant, of course. It was merely an observation that a trial of obviously guilty men is expensive."

"I'm not quibbling about their guilt," she clarified. "But are not trials as much a means of ascertaining the *truth* of the circumstances as they are about determining *guilt*?"

"Absolutely," Waldron said, nervously.

"The truth is paramount, of course."

"I know little of the matter aside from what I read in the newspaper," she said. "And *you* were there when the bounty hunter delivered his prisoners and his report."

"As you read, the bounty hunter *did* report evidence of these two men having murdered a pair of their confederates."

"Did his evidence seem credible as offered?" Nicolette asked.

"It seemed as much," Waldron replied with a nod. "And on top of that, they had been killed in cold blood . . . shot in the *back.*"

"That's disgusting," she said, an exaggerated grimace creasing her lips the crimson of chilies.

"Indeed," Waldron agreed.

"I suppose the bounty hunter will be called to testify in the trial," she said, realizing as she articulated this thought that it flowed from that place deep inside her where her bosom was still bewitch'd by the thought of Bladen Cole. If he was in town for the trial, would he return to the Refugio del Viajero?

"Probably . . . it is probable that he would be called."

Nicolette turned abruptly at the sound of

the door opening, fearing that it was Ames, for whose return she had stopped watching.

She breathed a sigh of relief. It was Tobias Gough of the *Santa Fe New Mexican.*

"Is this a bad time?" the newspaperman asked of Ezra Waldron. "If it is, I can come back."

Waldron glanced at Nicolette, who shook her head slightly. Her curiosity about what Gough had on his mind outweighed any concern she might have had over an interruption of a light lunch with the man with whom she was *almost* courting.

"What can I do for you, Tobias?"

"The sheriff will be back by the end of the day, and the perpetrators in the crime will await justice," Gough said, setting up the premise for his question. "This closes the circle on this affair. What are your thoughts?"

"We were just discussing this," Waldron said. "I would have to say that we at the railroad are pleased that these men will be tried in a court of law, and that justice will be done. The fact that these men were apprehended demonstrates that New Mexico Territory is not the uncivilized and lawless place that is portrayed in the Eastern press."

"Very good," Gough said as he scratched feverishly in his notebook.

"And now, Miss de la Gravière," Gough continued after he had scribbled Waldron's entire quote. "As a member of the public, how do you view the apprehending of these men and their being brought to justice?"

"I view it as Mr. Waldron does," she said. "I believe that the 'public' sees it as excellent news indeed that the robbers were caught, and that a significant robbery has not gone unresolved."

"And thieves have been brought to justice," Gough interjected, leading her.

"Of course," she continued. "The public will await the trial with considerable eagerness."

"The public will be delighted to see justice prevail," Gough added in a way that invited further comment.

"Justice and *truth,*" she said with a smile.

"I imagine that you'll be following the trial intently," she said after giving him a pause to scribble down her last comment.

"I plan to be in the courtroom each and every day," he said. "Our readers will have a keen interest in the proceedings."

"I've enjoyed your articles, Mr. Gough," she said.

"Thank you," he replied to the unanticipated compliment.

"I recall one in particular that you wrote

two months ago . . . about Delmonico's," she said with a broad smile.

"Yes . . ."

"I was wondering if I might invite you to consider writing one about Refugio del Viajero?"

"Yes . . . of course . . . That would be . . . That's a very good idea," he said. "I believe that would be a wonderful idea."

With this, Gough folded up his notebook, mentioned his deadline, thanked both of them for their time, and scuttled out the door.

"I believe that I too must be moving on," Nicolette said. "I have tables to set and chores to do before this evening."

"Thank you once again for coming," Waldron said. "Thank you also for bringing the lunch. It was so kind of you."

"Think nothing of it. I thought you deserved some cheer in light of everything which has transpired."

"Once again, it was so kind of you. I hope you drop in often . . . with or without lunch."

"I will be delighted."

"As I have said, you are welcome here at any time, Nicolette. If I am not here, you are welcome to await my return."

"Thank you . . . Ezra."

CHAPTER 33

"When you reckon we'll meet up with the sheriff?" Ben Muriday asked Nathaniel Siward.

The monotonous ride through the rolling hills north of Lamy invited the making of conversation.

"Reckon we'll see him in an hour or less," Siward replied, appearing a bit anxious.

"What's troubling you?" Muriday asked. "You're seeming a bit nervous. Like you never been this close to criminals before."

"As a matter of fact, I have *not,*" Siward admitted.

"Well . . . they's both tied up and they ain't goin' nowhere. If they do, we's the ones with guns."

"Yes, I know." Siward nodded.

The ride continued uneventfully. They passed a couple of freighters in wagons loaded with supplies bound from Santa Fe, but other than greetings shouted to these men, Siward and Muriday now rode mainly in silence.

They crested a low ridge and saw an open trail ahead for at least a mile. Muriday yawned.

Suddenly, Gabe Stanton and Jasper Gardner, riding ahead of their captors, reined their horses to opposite sides of the trail and turned.

"What the hell?" Muriday shouted, grabbing for his gun.

Hours of boredom suddenly exploded into fast, confusing action. Lulled practically to the verge of napping, Muriday's reflexes had been dulled.

Before he could react, Stanton had ridden up to him and was grabbing for the pistol that he was drawing from his holster.

How did he get untied?

Muriday's horse reared, and he tried to break his fall. As he leaned sideways to get away from Stanton's grab, he was tipped off balance and could not help but slide from the saddle as the horse bucked. As he fell, he felt his Colt tumbling from his grasp.

K'pow! K'pow!

When he heard the shots, simultaneous with his hitting the ground, Muriday's first thought was that his own gun had gone off when it struck the ground.

However, when he stared up through the dusty haze, he saw Jasper Gardner holding Siward's rifle.

How did *he* get untied?

He raised it, aiming it straight at Muriday.

K'pow!

Muriday felt the pain in his cheek, and the pain in his throat as he gasped and inhaled a swirling cloud of dust.

"Ride! Ride!" Gardner shouted.

There was the chaotic pounding sound of sixteen prancing hooves all around him, then the rhythmic thundering as half that number were spurred into a gallop.

Muriday sat up, feeling his cheek, which was soaked with dust-caked blood. It felt as though half his face had been shot away, but he quickly determined that he had been hit not directly, but by gravel kicked up by a ricochet.

He stood up, looking at the scene.

Siward was on the ground, and their horses were a short distance away.

"Ooooh," Siward moaned, writhing it pain.

"Where you hit?"

"I ain't . . . He missed . . . hurt my back fallin'."

Muriday stepped to his aid.

"Never mind me," he shouted through his anguish. "Go . . . Go after 'em. You gotta stop 'em. *Stop 'em with a bullet.*"

Muriday retrieved his Colt from where it had fallen and ran toward his horse.

The two fugitives had left the main thoroughfare, but he could see their dust in the distance. He kicked his horse into a gallop, bent on revenging his honor from the ignoble tumble that he had experienced when Stanton rushed him.

Also on his mind as he raced in pursuit was his *plan.* As much as he cursed that which had just happened, he realized that it potentially turned the tide of events in *his* favor. Ten minutes ago, he had expected to have been *part* of a posse that delivered Gardner and Stanton into the cold embrace of the law. Now he had been handed the splendid opportunity to be *the* man, and the *only* man, to bring them into Santa Fe.

Muriday licked his dusty lips at the thought.

Their lead was measured in minutes, so he had every reason to believe that he would catch up to them sooner rather than later.

As he watched them in their distant dust cloud, his right hand moved to his holster, but he decided against it. Taking a pistol shot at this distance would serve only to waste ammunition.

He had them outgunned, a rifle and a

pistol to their one long gun, but he had no way of knowing how many rounds they had left. He wished that he had asked Siward how many rounds he generally kept in his Winchester.

Muriday also wished he knew how both Stanton and Gardner had gotten their hands untied. He had ridden with these two men for four days, and only once had Gardner gotten free — and when he did, he had not managed to free his hands until after his escape.

Damned fool railroad people! Can't even tie knots right.

Horses cannot gallop forever, and within a half hour, the pursuer and the pursued were riding at a walk.

They remained close enough to see each other, less than a mile apart, but too far to shoot — or so Muriday thought.

Pop . . . tzing!

The sound of a distant shot was followed by that of a bullet coming near.

Damned fool is a pretty good shot — or a lucky shot, Muriday thought to himself.

Muriday considered retaliation, but thought again about the futility of returning fire at this range. Good shot or lucky shot, whichever phrase described Gardner, Muriday knew that he was *neither*.

As the fairly open country gradually became more rugged, Muriday periodically lost sight of his quarry, who now moved in and out behind boulders and clusters of short pine.

He kept his eyes glued to the distance.

There they are.

There they aren't.

There they are again.

There they aren't again.

They still aren't.

Where are they?

He breathed a sigh of relief as they re-emerged.

This went on, and on, for what seemed like an hour, but which was probably much less.

Then came the inevitable moment when he realized that he had not seen them for much too long.

Had they gotten clean away?

Knowing the hotheaded Jasper Gardner as he did, he knew that he was not a man to go away quietly when he had a gun.

An ambush was the only answer.

Muriday studied the distant terrain nervously.

Somewhere out there, Gardner was drawing a bead on him.

Where?

How long had it been since Gardner and Stanton had stopped?

It couldn't have been more than a minute or two.

Muriday tried to calculate the place where he had last seen the two. Having done this, he tried to figure out where near this place he would set up for an ambush if it was him doing the setting.

There were a couple of places, rocky areas of high ground near to one another, that offered both good cover and good visibility, so he rode forward, screening himself, as much as possible, from this area.

It was one of those cat-and-mouse moments when the passage of time literally stopped in its tracks.

Had it not been for the impulsiveness of Jasper Gardner, Muriday would have been practically on top of them before the first shot was fired, but restraint was not in Gardner's nature.

K'pow!

Punctuating the stillness of the windless midday desert, the shot startled Muriday, even though he'd known that it would be coming.

He turned to see a whiff of powder on a small cliff less than fifty yards away.

As he slid off his saddle, he expected a

second shot.

K'pow . . . tzing!

Muriday had covered most of the fifty yards before his nemesis fired again.

K'pow!

It was Muriday's turn to squeeze off a round.

"Betcha runnin' low on ammo," Muriday shouted.

K'pow . . . tzing! came the reply.

For a moment, the only sound that Muriday heard was his own measured breathing.

Then there was the noise of gravel falling on a slope.

Gardner had gotten tired of waiting for his target to appear in his sights.

Muriday moved toward the sound.

K'pow . . . chunk!

The bullet hit a pine limb an inch from his head.

Muriday looked into the wild eyes of Jasper Gardner, just twenty feet away. The Winchester was on his shoulder, and his hand was on the lever.

It would be less than a second before he fired again.

Muriday aimed and squeezed.

K'pow!

He saw Gardner fall backward and the rifle fall from his grasp. A growing, dark red stain had appeared on his shoulder.

"Damn you, Muriday," he said angrily through the pain. "What the hell are you doing?"

"What I shoulda done a long time ago," Muriday said, walking closer and pointing his gun at Gardner's head.

"You're outta your *mind,* damn you," Gardner said, realizing that Muriday was aiming to deliver a *coup de grâce* to a defenseless man. "What the hell . . . ?"

K'pow!

Muriday's shot, aimed by a man who was, by his own admission, a poor marksman, was intended for Gardner's forehead, but it struck his neck instead.

Jasper Gardner's last moments of life were extraordinarily painful.

Muriday quickly grabbed the rifle and scrambled up the hill looking for Stanton.

The second fugitive had not waited to see what happened next. He was already running, but he had not gotten far.

K'pow! K'pow!

Muriday's rifle shots did not hit Stanton, but they unnerved him.

Beginning to run erratically, he tripped and fell.

K'pow!

Again, the shot missed, but again it frightened the intended target.

"I give up," Stanton shouted, raising his hands from a seated position. "You got me. Don't shoot."

Muriday did not, but he kept the rifle ready as he walked slowly forward.

Through his mind ran the words that Siward had used.

"I want to be sure that if need be, you wouldn't mind shooting these men . . . Stop 'em . . . *Stop 'em with a bullet.*"

"You got me," Stanton repeated. "I said you got me . . . Put down the damned gun you crazy sonuvabitch."

K'pow!

The bullet struck Stanton's gut.

He looked up at Muriday with pain and anger in his eyes.

As Muriday came closer, Stanton coughed, and blood spilled out onto his chin.

K'pow!

Fired from point-blank range, the bullet struck Stanton's forehead, and he toppled backward into the dirt.

CHAPTER 34

"You're late," Nicolette de la Gravière said crossly as the produce man braked his wagon at the rear entrance to the Refugio del Viajero.

"But *señorita,*" he insisted, as he began to unload the morning's consignment. "I cannot be late by more than a few minutes."

"Late is late," she grumbled. "And what of these tomatoes? They are quite small today . . . are they not?"

"Regrettably," he said in agreement, although he could see no difference between these and yesterday's tomatoes, which the young woman had accepted with a smile on those lips the color of chilies.

"What has gotten into you this morning?" Therese de la Gravière asked her daughter when the produce man had finished unloading and driven off. "You nearly tore off the poor man's head."

"The produce was late, and the tomatoes

are small," Nicolette replied.

"What's *really* gotten into you?" Therese asked, inspecting the tomatoes, which *did* appear to be the same size as yesterday's tomatoes.

"The produce was late, and the tomatoes are small," Nicolette repeated.

"Nicolette."

"I'm just thinking about the bandits," she admitted.

"What is it about bandits that has my daughter so out of sorts that she feels she has to bark at the produce man?"

"They were brought in *dead,*" Nicolette said.

"By all accounts, they were dangerous men who had disregarded human life and had even *taken* human life."

"Now," Nicolette lamented, "there will be no trial."

"Do you imagine that those men were *not* guilty?" Therese replied in an almost teasing tone.

"Did you read in the paper what I told Mr. Gough?" Nicolette asked.

"*Yes,* and I am so proud to see my daughter quoted in the newspaper," Therese said with a smile. "I am also pleased that you insisted that he write of Refugio del Viajero. I'm looking forward to his visit."

"We'll see *that* when we see it," Nicolette said. "But did you read what I *said*?"

"About justice . . . about seeing justice done?"

"I told him that there is *more* to a trial than justice," Nicolette said, stopping what she was doing and staring into her mother's eyes. "Am I just a naive girl?"

"Ce qui?"

"Mama, am I naive to think that a trial can be more than just a forum for determining *guilt*? Am I naive to think that a trial can also be about finding the *truth*?"

"Mr. Waldron, they're already gathering in the Plaza," Nathaniel Siward said, coming into the Atchison, Topeka & Santa Fe offices.

"Then I must go quickly," Waldron said, shoving some papers aside. "We must thank Mr., um . . ."

"Muriday. The man's name is Ben Muriday."

"We must thank Mr. Muriday on behalf of the Atchison, Topeka & Santa Fe Railroad for apprehending the bandits and removing them finally and *completely* from our lives."

"You got this one on the cheap," Siward reminded him. "You had to pay Cole two grand to bring those two in. You retained

Muriday for twenty dollars."

"What irony," Waldron said. "I think I'll find a way to pay him a bonus for relieving us of this curse once and for all."

Waldron grabbed his coat and hat, and the two men walked quickly down the street toward the Plaza, the central square of Santa Fe.

"Is Tobias Gough . . . ?"

"He was already there when I stopped by fifteen minutes ago," Siward confirmed. "He was asking people what they thought. He'll probably want to interview Mr. Muriday."

"I want you to handle *that*, Nathaniel. Muriday does not sound like an especially articulate man . . . I don't think he should be left alone with Gough. Stay with him. Help him. Suggest phrasing."

"On the subject of articulate phrasing, I read the interview with Miss de la Gravière in the paper this morning," Siward said. "It would seem that you have a well-spoken young woman on your arm."

"She is smart as a tack for sure," Waldron said with a nod. "And she is very well read."

"Seems a shame," Siward said, shaking his head.

"What's a shame?"

"Seems a shame that those kinds of brains are wasted on a woman."

■ ■ ■ ■

As Waldron and Siward reached the Plaza, there were already about a hundred people on hand, and more trickling in.

In the hours since Ben Muriday had ridden into Santa Fe late yesterday, leading two horses with bodies strapped across the saddles, he had been the talk of the town.

For a number of hours last night, the *talk* of the town had been the *toast* of the town. Muriday had stopped into a saloon for a drink, and had found himself prevented from paying. This being the type of saloon where men celebrate such things, he had been greeted by an offer to buy him a drink. Before that drink had even reached his dust-encrusted lips, there had been a second offer, and then a third.

When Muriday entered the Plaza this morning, he was showing the effects of having not stopped accepting the largesse of the saloon crowd with that third drink — or even with the sixth.

Seeing Muriday, Siward escorted him to where Waldron was. In turn, Waldron swept him up onto the bandstand.

"The grateful Atchison, Topeka & Santa Fe Railroad wishes hereby to express its deep indebtedness to Mr. Ben Muriday for recapturing those two bandits who had twice escaped, and who have finally been dealt their irrevocable punishment," Waldron said, holding Muriday's right hand high.

There were a few polite claps, but most people were present out of curiosity, rather than celebration. Only from among a gaggle of Muriday's drinking companions of the night before was there any real applause.

"Much obliged," Muriday mumbled, staring sheepishly at the deck of the bandstand. As much as he had long yearned for this very moment of glory and adulation, he was paralyzed with stage fright.

"To thank you for the service you have rendered to the Atchison, Topeka & Santa Fe . . . and to the *people* of the Territory of New Mexico, I am pleased to present you with this pass, which provides unlimited free passage on the Atchison, Topeka & Santa Fe . . . in *perpetuity,*" Waldron shouted, giving emphasis to words he felt were deserving of emphasis.

Muriday stared blankly at the pass. He didn't know what to think. He had never been on a train in his life, and had never had any desire to be.

"And now I'd like to get on to that part of

our business which I am sure Mr. Muriday is *most* anxious to transact," Waldron announced to the assembly. "Two days ago, this road hired Mr. Muriday to be part of its contingent in the posse bringing these two heinous thieves and killers to justice. At that time, I offered to pay Mr. Muriday a gold eagle for a day's work. I now formally hand him that sum for a job well done. *Because* of his heroism and his going above and beyond the call of duty, I herewith *double* that sum in the form of a bonus . . . Having done that, I am going to double it *again*!"

"Much obliged," Muriday mumbled, staring sheepishly at the four glittering coins in his hand, and remembering the canvas bag holding hundreds of these which he had once had in his possession. As he listened to the smattering of applause, he pondered the fact that his plan had finally come to its moment of completeness.

This was *it*.

As Waldron was shaking Muriday's hand a final time, Tobias Gough swept in.

"Wonderful remarks," he said, patting Waldron on the shoulder.

Next, he introduced himself to Muriday.

"Mr. Muriday, I'm Tobias Gough of the *Santa Fe New Mexican.* Could you tell me what it was like to hunt those dangerous criminals yesterday?"

"I dunno . . ."

"Just tell me in your own words," Gough said encouragingly. "Our readers will want to know exactly how it happened from the man who was *there*."

" 'Twas just ridin' along with Siward, when they got theirselves loosed somehow. We got blindsided. Siward done got knocked down and his rifle took. I went a chasin' 'em, caught up to 'em. They fought back hard. *I feared for my life.* Got nicked on the face from a ricochet . . . see here."

"Tell me of the climactic moment," Gough asked, glancing at the scar on Muriday's face, over which some gauze had been taped.

"Well, 'twas them or me," Muriday said soberly. "Nearly got myself shot more than once. They was well hid . . . and a far piece away . . . but bein' a good shot, I was able to hit 'em. That sonuvabitch Stanton, he kept a-comin'. I hit him. He flinched a bit, but that didn't stop him. He just raised his damned gun and pointed it straight at me."

"That sounds frightening."

"You're damn right," Muriday said, getting into his role as storyteller. " 'Twas him or me. I just fired once more just as he shot at me. That's when I nailed the sonuv-abitch."

"That's an amazing story of survival, Mr. Muriday," Gough said. Waldron could not tell by his tone whether or not he was taking the yarn with a pinch of salt. Nevertheless, in the final analysis, all that mattered was the results.

Bladen Cole stood unnoticed at the fringes of the crowd in the Plaza as Ezra Waldron acclaimed Ben Muriday and applauded the deaths of Stanton and Gardner. As Muriday was presented with the railroad pass, Cole was reminded of those two Denver & Rio Grande passes that he had found on the bodies of the two dead men, and which he still had in his pocket.

He was also reminded of Waldron's words the first time that they had met. The railroad man had said that he would not be disappointed if the robbers came in feet first. Now, thanks to Ben Muriday, Waldron had gotten his wish.

CHAPTER 35

"May I help you?" asked the clerk in the Atchison, Topeka & Santa Fe office.

"I'm here to see Mr. Waldron . . ." Nicolette de la Gravière said hesitantly.

"He's not here. He just left with Mr. Siward. Expect him back soon.

"May I wait?" Nicolette asked. "He said that I am welcome to do so."

"You bet. Go ahead and make yourself at home."

Nicolette had missed Waldron by less than a minute as he and Siward hastened to the Plaza to reward Ben Muriday.

She took a seat in the chair next to his desk where she usually sat when she came calling, and prepared to wait. Her eyes wandered idly from the large clock on the wall to the equally oversized calendar posted near it, then to Waldron's desk, piled high with papers and ledger books.

The minute hand on the clock moved slowly.

Nicolette daydreamed. She crossed her legs one way, then rearranged her skirts and recrossed them the other way.

She yawned.

The clerk smiled as he came to Waldron's desk to look for something, and nodded slightly as he took the ledger book that was on top of the pile in the center of the desk.

As the book was removed, a delicate rustling of air slightly rearranged the papers beneath it.

Nicolette's eyes wandered idly to the large clock, to the oversized calendar, and then back to the papers on Waldron's desk.

Out of the corner of her eye, she saw a piece of correspondence on the letterhead of the Denver & Rio Grande Western Railroad. It struck her as odd and out of place to see the letterhead of the rival road here in the offices of the Atchison, Topeka & Santa Fe, but assumed there was a good reason.

Nicolette glanced back at the clock, with its slowly moving minute hand, and decided to wait three more minutes — no, four. She was nervous that Mr. Ames might burst in at any moment. She was also nervous about appearing to be too eager for Ezra Waldron's company.

Meanwhile, though, she was growing more curious about the Denver & Rio Grande letterhead.

What hurt could it do to just take a quick peek?

She reached across the desk and tugged it out from beneath several other sheets.

Not wanting to be seen picking it up to read it, she left it on the desk, turning her head at an angle to make out the words:

Dear Mr. Waldron:

Thank you very much for your excellent work yesterday, and throughout this entire affair. New York is already reacting favorably, and our cause is greatly improved. Your own shares should also be performing well. As promised, we have quietly deposited your $5,000 in the account you specified. The next installment will be paid to you when the two loose ends are eliminated.

Sincerely yours,

J. Smith

Nicolette could not at first grasp the meaning of the letter. What sort of "work" could Ezra Waldron be doing for the Denver & Rio Grande? What could he have done for which he would be compensated so generously by a railroad that was such a bitter rival of his own?

What were the "loose ends"?

What was this about "New York reacting favorably"?

When was "yesterday"?

She looked at the date.

The letter was dated one day after Ezra Waldron had made the decision to publicize the robbery.

A cold chill came over Nicolette de la Gravière as the pieces came together.

Could it be?

No, it couldn't, she insisted, kidding herself.

She reread the letter, beginning with the date.

Unimaginably, it now appeared without a doubt that Ezra Waldron had been *paid* by the Denver & Rio Grande to publicize the robbery in order to cause the Atchison, Topeka & Santa Fe stock to crash.

She remembered now his words that the *next* war between the Denver & Rio Grande and the Atchison, Topeka & Santa Fe would be won or lost not in New *Mexico,* but in New *York.* This is exactly what he had meant.

How could this be?

No wonder Ames was so angry, and Waldron had been so sheepish in justifying his actions.

Then she realized that she had been so absorbed in the letter that she had not noticed that another sheet of paper was attached to the letter with a banker's pin.

Glancing furtively toward the clerk, she turned over the letter, and looked at the second sheet.

This page turned out to be a monthly statement from a stock brokerage firm called Ripley, Storey & Bledsoe. Nicolette was not well versed in business, but she *did* know how to read a balance sheet.

The statement showed that Ezra Waldron had purchased five hundred shares of Denver & Rio Grande stock at the beginning of the month, and an additional two hundred shares around the time of the holdup. The share price fluctuated slightly over the earlier days but spiked abruptly on the date of the announcement and went up even further on the day after, which was the closing date of the statement.

Ezra Waldron had bet on the rival road and had *more than doubled* his investment.

With a trembling hand, she turned back to the letter to read it yet again.

Could this be?

Her eyes fell on the phrase in the last sentence about the "two loose ends." She now realized that these were the two robbers, shot and killed before the sheriff took custody of them yesterday.

The man with whom she had gone to the theater, the man whom she had found to be such a gentleman that she had succumbed to his charms, had been paid to have these two men *killed*.

Beads of cold sweat stood on her forehead, and she felt herself shaking as though it was below zero in the hot, stuffy room.

She had to get out of this place.

Nicolette did not know what to do. She did not know where to go.

She dabbed the tears on her cheeks with her handkerchief and tried to compose herself.

Out of force of habit, she was walking in the direction of the Refugio del Viajero.

What would she tell her mother?

What could her mother do?

Should she tell the sheriff?

Would he believe such an implausible tale?

It would be her word against Waldron's, and whom would the sheriff believe? Would he take the improbable word of a girl barely out of her teens over that of a prominent businessman?

She could tell her mother, but what could Therese de la Gravière say to the sheriff? Would he take the word of a widow woman — or *any* woman for that matter — over that of a prominent businessman?

Tears of despair rolled down Nicolette's cheeks.

After all of Waldron's lofty words about bringing criminals to justice, and all her own self-righteous words about *truth,* it came down to this.

She had been keeping company with the worst criminal of all, and there was nothing to be done.

Suddenly, Nicolette had a brainstorm. If there was any *man* of prominence in Santa Fe who would believe her, it was Dr. Amos Richardson.

"Let me get this straight," Richardson said after Nicolette had tearfully told him of her inconceivable discovery. "The Denver & Rio Grande specifically *thanked* Mr. Waldron for a service rendered to them on the date that he disclosed a huge theft?"

"And the letter said that five thousand dollars would be deposited, *and* deposited *quietly,* in his account," Nicolette said eagerly, wiping away her tears.

"The letter also said that 'New York' was responding beneficially, and mention was made of shares?"

"Yes," Nicolette nodded. "And the second page showed that he was buying shares of the Denver & Rio Grande, and they were going up."

"You need look no farther than the newspaper to see that Denver & Rio Grande shares have more than doubled in the past days," Richardson said, pointing to a copy of the *Santa Fe New Mexican* on his desk. "At the same time, Atchison, Topeka & Santa Fe share prices have fallen."

"Then there is the matter of the two loose ends," Nicolette reminded him. "That would certainly be the two men."

"Assuming for a moment that everything else you've surmised is true, why then would killing the two thieves be so important?" Richardson asked.

"Maybe they were *all* involved somehow?" Nicolette suggested. "When I was out at Lamy, I heard them arguing as though they knew one another from before, and he seemed especially nervous that I had overheard them arguing. The other day, when we were talking about the robbers being brought to Santa Fe to stand trial, he was especially outspoken in saying that they should have been delivered dead rather than alive . . . *and* he did hire the man who later killed them."

"As much as I am willing to grant the superiority of a 'woman's intuition,' none of this constitutes what one might call evidence," Richardson said.

"You don't believe me!" Nicolette exclaimed.

"I didn't say that," Richardson asserted crossly. "I didn't say that I did not believe you. As you yourself pointed out as you were describing the letter, this is a matter of your word against his, and of the probability that his word would be considered more credible. In fact, I *am* inclined to believe you. I only lament the absence of anything sufficiently tangible to support the object of convincing anyone else."

"Thank you. You have no idea how good it makes be feel to have someone think my story to be other than crazy."

"Is there any chance of you getting your hands on that letter?"

"Surely he would find it missing."

"There must be another angle," the coroner said thoughtfully.

"Maybe . . . maybe you could ask Mr. Cole to help investigate . . . unless you believe *him* somehow involved?"

"No. I do not," Richardson replied. "I was there when Mr. Waldron hired Mr. Cole. I watched their interaction. There was no hint of . . . *In fact* . . . now that I remember, Mr. Waldron was quite adamant when he said that the robbers were 'wanted, dead or alive' that he preferred . . . he meant *'dead.'* Then, Mr. Cole delivered those two *alive.* So no, Mr. Cole is not a party to this cabal."

"Then we shall ask Mr. Cole . . . no, we shall *hire* Mr. Cole," Nicolette said excitedly. "I'll take my money, I'll convince Mama to let me take money out of the Refugio del Viajero to *hire* Mr. Cole to discover the *truth.*"

"He would probably do it gratis," Richardson said. "*If* he were around."

"What . . . where . . . ?"

"I doubt that we shall see Mr. Bladen Cole again," Richardson said, his tone a bit wistful. "He has departed Santa Fe for good. He is on another quest. He has gone in search of the man who murdered his brother."

Nicolette simply stared into space. She felt her shoulders slump. A moment ago, thoughts of the bounty hunter, long suppressed by her conscious mind, had come thundering back from her subconscious; like a knight in shining armor, he could be the

341

very emblem of her deliverance. But just as quickly, he was gone.

Gone where? What quest could be more noble than to avenge the death of one's brother? Nicolette could think of but *one*. The most towering of tasks undertaken by knights under the code of chivalry — of which she had read in the storybooks — involved the knight and his lady, but she was not, alas, this knight's lady.

"I almost forgot," Nicolette gasped in horror, as she thought of her bosom bewitch'd by a knight.

"What?"

"I'm supposed to be attending the theater with Mr. Waldron . . . *tonight.* How can I . . ."

"Just calm down," Richardson advised. "Take a breath. You are the most composed young woman I know. Perhaps, while the production is ongoing, you'll think of something."

"Perhaps I will. If I do have a brainstorm, I'll share it with you . . . as the Bard would say . . . anon."

"What production are you seeing?" Richardson asked.

"*Macbeth.*"

"I see," the coroner said with a droll expression.

"I know what you're thinking," Nicolette said, sizing him up.

"What's that?"

"Something about irony . . . and something about the treachery which permeates that play."

"A woman's intuition," Richardson said with a smile.

CHAPTER 36

"Mr. Waldron," Joseph Ames said sternly, rising to greet his colleague as Waldron returned to the Atchison, Topeka & Santa Fe office.

"I have just received this telegram from the home office."

Waldron took the yellow Western Union flimsy in his hand. The message was addressed to Ames and it read:

FOR YOUR PROMPT ATTENTION STOP E WALDRON TO BE RELIEVED OF DUTY AND ORDERED REPORT HOME OFFICE IMMEDIATELY STOP

"Good day, sir," Ames said, picking his hat up from his desk. "Good day . . . and good riddance. Let the home office sort out the bitter fruit of your incompetence."

With that, Ames stormed out of the office, slamming the door behind him. Ezra Waldron stared at the telegram, devastated but not defeated. He *would* leave Santa Fe. What Ames did not know was that he had already planned his exit. Tomorrow, he would ride to Lamy for the last time. Tomorrow, he would climb aboard the afternoon train for Kansas City for the last time.

There was much about New Mexico Territory that he would not miss, but there were still things that he *would* miss. Among them, the smell of sweet perfume and the sight of lips the color of chilies.

In the scenario proscribed by his employers in their telegram, Ezra Waldron was to travel to the home office like a whelp with his quivering tail tucked between his quivering legs. He would then ascend the steps of the home office to be called upon the carpet, violently berated, then fired and banished forever from a job that had been the reason for his existence for the eighteen years that seemed to have lasted a century. Losing his job was a terrible blow, but it was not the end of the world. Indeed, he would not be going back to that world — nor would he be going to Kansas City.

Waldron had already made plans that were *not* those proscribed and imagined by the home office. Waldron's plans included climbing no steps, nor standing nervously upon any home office carpet. In *his* scenario, he would detrain at La Junta, Colorado, and simply disappear. He'd try Denver for a while, because that was where his bank accounts were, but deep down inside his soul, he knew that he would eventually wind up in San Francisco. Still fueled by the glittering fortunes of the Gold Rush and Comstock years, it offered all the opportunities of a financial hub — *and* it was the city of fresh starts.

He hung up his coat and hat and sat down at his desk.

"Who's been disturbing things at my desk?" Waldron asked in a deafening roar.

"I just took the account ledger," the clerk replied meekly from across the room. "You told me to use it to do those sums from last month."

"So I did," Waldron said, glowering at the man.

"Has anyone *else* been at my desk?"

The clerk thought for a minute and replied, "Miss de la Gravière was here to see you. She said that you said that she could sit in the chair next to your desk."

"That I did," Waldron said, retreating into his spinning head.

As his head spun, his eyes stared straight down at the letter that lay on top of the pile of paperwork on his desk for all the world to see.

The letterhead was that of the Denver & Rio Grande Western, and the contents, when viewed privately, had been a promise of wealth that had been the pot of gold at the end of the rainbow, the pot at the end of eighteen long years.

The contents, when viewed through the eyes of anyone else, such as the dark eyes of Nicolette de la Gravière, were, alas, an indictment of one Ezra Waldron for stock manipulation, conspiracy, and being an accessory to murder.

When he had left his desk in a hurry to rush over to the Plaza, he had tossed the ledger and a random stack of papers on top of these critical documents, assuming that the ledger, stack of papers, and critical documents would remain in exactly that same unrifled order until he returned.

Now there was no doubt in his mind that the gorgeous young woman with the beautiful smile, with whom he was on the verge of falling in love, had seen the letter and the brokerage statement.

There was no doubt in his mind that the bright and intuitive young woman whose insights he found marvelous, had *read* the letter and had seen the brokerage statement and had understood how and why it constituted an indictment of one Ezra Waldron for stock manipulation, conspiracy, and being an accessory to murder.

He looked at the last sentence of the letter and reread the part about the elimination of the "two loose ends." He almost cried when he realized that now, there was a *third* loose end.

He looked up. While he had been absorbed in his predicament, Nathaniel Siward had returned to the office and gone to the desk that he used when he was not at Lamy.

"Don't take off your coat, Siward," Waldron said. "We have an errand to run."

"We've got a problem," Waldron said quietly as they walked down the street. "Or I should say I've got a problem, which means the same thing . . . that being that *we* have got a problem."

"What's that?"

"Another loose end."

"What? Who?"

"I think that this is the most difficult thing I have *ever* had to do," Waldron said, looking at Siward with genuine, gut-wrenching anguish in his eyes.

"What's that?"

"You need to go find your friend Ben Muriday. Get him before he takes another drink, or get him dried out. You need to tell him that we have five hundred dollars for him. Tell him that we need him tonight. We have another job for him and *his gun.*"

"You don't seem yourself, *ma chère fille,*" Therese de la Gravière said to her daughter. "It is your night off, and you're going to the theater with a gentleman . . . but you look like you've just lost your best friend."

"Oh, Mama," Nicolette sighed. "I don't know . . ."

"What don't you know?"

"*Macbeth* is such a gloomy production," Nicolette complained, having decided not to tell her mother about her discovery on Waldron's desk.

"You're not going to the theater to see a play," her mother corrected her. "You're going to the theater to *be with a gentleman . . .* a gentleman who is courting you."

"I have not yet decided that we are in a courtship."

"By the time that a gentleman takes a lady to the theater *twice,* it's courtship," Therese explained. "By the time that a young woman brings lunch to a man at his workplace, it's courtship."

"Oh, Mama," Nicolette said, rolling her eyes.

"I have to get ready to run a restaurant tonight, and my daughter, who is going to the theater tonight, complains that she isn't sure that she's being courted. I wish a man would ask *me* to the theater."

"*Mama,* what man?"

"Any man. It's a figure of speech. Or *no* man, because that's the way it is."

"Mama, I didn't realize that you wanted . . ."

"That's because you're a young woman . . . and I am an old woman who should have forgotten such things long ago."

"Mama, you're still beautiful."

"Not that anyone notices . . ."

"*Ha!* You've seen the way Dr. Richardson looks at you," Nicolette said. "Do you think he comes to Refugio del Viajero twice a week only for the *carne asada?*"

"Yes. He is a very loyal customer."

"Oh, Mama, you're impossible."

"It is *you* who is impossible. Now, quit moping and get ready for Mr. Waldron."

"Mama, can I ask you a question?"

"Of course," Therese said. "When do you have to ask to ask me questions?"

"Do you think it was a mistake for Mr.

Waldron to tell the world about the robbery? Mr. Ames has been saying that it was
a terrible mistake.

"I'm not in the railroad business," Therese
said. "I don't know. What do you think?"

"I'm not sure. As I have read in the newspaper, it has driven down the price of his
railroad's shares."

"Then it was a mistake," Therese said with
a shrug.

"Unless it was on purpose."

"Why would a man hurt his own company
on purpose?"

"To help a competitor?"

"That's ridiculous," Therese said dismissively. "It would be as though I poisoned
my own salsa to send my customers streaming over to Delmonico's."

"You're right, Mama," Nicolette said
agreeably. "There would be no reason for
you to do that."

It *did* seem improbable.

"Nicolette?"

"Yes, Mama."

"Why are you putting on a black dress?"
Therese asked. "You should be wearing
azure or lavender."

"Because *Macbeth* is *such* a gloomy play,
Mama."

CHAPTER 37

"Mr. Cole, what a pleasant surprise," the coroner shouted cordially from the adjacent room when Domingo had announced the visitor. "Pardon me for not extending a hand in greeting. I'm with a patient."

The bounty hunter had decided to pay a visit to his fellow Virginian, if for nothing else than for the sake of conversation.

"I'm attending to some friends of yours, Mr. Cole," Dr. Amos Richardson said in a quieter voice as Cole stepped to the doorway. "If you are not offended by the presence of death, as I presume you are not, I invite you to step in to observe."

Cole came into the room to see the lifeless bodies of Gabe Stanton and Jasper Gardner. The deep purple of the latter's injured nose stood out in stark contrast to the pasty paleness of the rest of his face. Cole had no emotion upon viewing these faces, now in quiet repose, after what he had seen of them in life. He had harbored no desire to see them dead without their days in court, nor was he sorry to see that their lives' journeys were at an end.

"I assume that you have seen that this man you have been seeking has become a minor celebrity here in town," the doctor said as he worked.

"That I have, though I 'spect his time in the limelight will be short."

"I reckon you to be correct on that point."

"And here are two other of my recent acquaintances in your care," Cole observed, looking down at the bodies.

"The stories of their demise, which *they* have told me since their arrival on my table, are considerably different than that which Mr. Muriday has been telling around town," Richardson said.

"That's interesting . . ." Cole said, his tone asking the doctor to please go on. "How so?"

"Mr. Muriday has been telling a story of a gun battle with two armed men."

"So I've heard," Cole replied.

"If it does not offend you, smell this," the coroner instructed, holding up the right hand of the late Jasper Gardner.

As Cole placed his nose near, his first thought was that this was the hand that had so recently lifted two Mescalero scalps. His second thought was of the aroma of sweat mixed with the pungent and unmistakable stench of burnt gunpowder. He had smelled it so many times on his own hands.

"You would have no doubt that this hand had fired a gun?"

"None," Cole agreed.

"Now," Richardson continued, holding up Stanton's right hand. "Smell this hand."

The stench was that of sweat alone.

"And now this," the doctor said, holding up Stanton's left.

Again, there was no hint of the acrid spice of gunpowder.

"So you think Stanton never shot a gun?" Cole asked.

"Certainly not in the recent exchange, and probably not for many days prior. Mr. Muriday was in a gunfight with one man, not two."

"Wouldn't put exaggeration past him," Cole said.

"Let me direct your attention to another feature," the coroner said, continuing with his demonstration. "Note the nature of the bullet wound in Mr. Stanton's forehead."

"Looks to be close-range," Cole observed.

"Near point-blank," Richardson confirmed.

"Muriday shot an unarmed man at point-blank range?"

"That's about the size of it."

"You gonna tell the sheriff?"

"It will be in my report," Richardson said with a shrug. "Not that he will do anything. A dead fugitive is a dead fugitive. It just confirms the character of the man who you saw shoot your brother."

"That it does," Cole agreed.

"What are those?" Cole asked, pointing to a side table.

"Personal effects. I took them from the pockets of these two."

What had caught Cole's eye were two passes issued by the Denver & Rio Grande.

"I took *these* off the dead bodies of two dead men who pulled a railroad job with Stanton and Gardner," Cole said, pulling out the two railroad passes that he carried and placing them on the table.

"Four passes from a rival road," Richardson observed. "Two from Stanton and Gardner . . . two more from the others. All four of the men who robbed the Atchison, Topeka & Santa Fe carried passes from the rival road . . . These are given only to employees."

"That's what I thought until this morning," Cole said. "That was until I saw Ezra

Waldron hand one to Muriday as a *reward* for services rendered."

Richardson stared silently for a minute before he spoke.

"I had a very interesting visit this morning from a friend of yours," he said.

"A friend of mine?"

"Well, she *did* speak your name."

"She?" Cole asked, trying to think of any female friend he might have in Santa Fe.

"Nicolette de la Gravière . . . from Refugio del Viajero."

"What . . . How is *she* my friend? I only saw her once and without a formal introduction," Cole asked. "This is not to say that I would object in any way to her friendship."

"She too recalls your visit to the Refugio, and she went on to mention you by reputation."

"How so?"

"It's a long story," Richardson cautioned.

"I've got time."

"She's been seeing Ezra Waldron of the Atchison, Topeka & Santa Fe," Richardson began, ignoring the slight twitch of Cole's eyelids. "This has naturally involved her calling on him at the railroad's offices. This morning, she was there when he was not, and in the course of her waiting she happened upon some documents which caused her alarm."

"What kind of documents?" Cole asked, intrigued.

"She said that she found a letter to Mr. Waldron from the Denver & Rio Grande, thanking him for his service and advising him of a 'quiet' five-thousand-dollar deposit in his account at an unspecified location."

"Payment for what?"

"As near as I can figure, based on the date of the letter, it was for publicizing your capture of these two gentlemen, and the detrimental effect that this had on the Atchison, Topeka & Santa Fe share prices."

"How exactly?"

"Investors were panicked by the fact of such a large robbery," Richardson explained. "Lack of confidence on the part of investors drove capital to the Denver & Rio Grande. According to the documents that Miss de la Gravière saw, Mr. Waldron was heavily invested personally in the rival road and he made a great deal of money."

"I understand," Cole said. "Investing in rival roads is pretty lousy, not to mention disloyal, but I don't figure that it's illegal . . . is it?"

"I'm a doctor, not a lawyer," Richardson replied. "But I don't reckon that it is. Another thing that Miss de la Gravière said she found was a part in the letter about Mr. Waldron getting more money deposited in his account when he took care of 'two loose ends.' "

"What two loose ends?"

"I believe it meant the two gentlemen who arrived in my care this morning shortly after Miss de la Gravière departed."

"You think Waldron was behind Muriday killing these two?"

"I don't know," Richardson replied. "I honestly don't know. I remember being in the room when Mr. Waldron told *you* to bring them back dead rather than alive."

"I have not forgotten that," Cole said with a nod.

"Muriday was on assignment with the railroad when he finished the job *before* either man could stand trial. One might assume that Mr. Waldron had been paid by the Denver & Rio Grande to stage the robbery in the first place, and that he wanted to make sure there were no 'loose ends' to tell the tale. As I told Miss de la Gravière, without that letter, there is no evidence to support such a theory."

"Until there were *four* Denver & Rio Grande passes laying on your table," Cole pointed out. "They could have been hired guns from anywhere, but the fact that *all four* were carrying Rio Grande passes tells me that they had all *probably* worked as hired guns for *that* road."

"Possibly," Richardson said thoughtfully, looking at the passes. "The evidence *does* point in that direction. It certainly *looks* like there's a connection. If only the dead could speak."

"You didn't tell me how *my* name came up in your talk with Miss de la Gravière," Cole said.

"Oh yes, I meant to tell you," Richardson began. "She said that she wanted to take money from the family business to *hire* you to find the evidence."

Bladen Cole sat on a bench beneath an overhanging arcade on the opposite side of the street from the saloon in which the back bar was presided over by a rookery of kachinas, the saloon where he could glimpse Ben Muriday being treated to drinks and being toasted for a dubious distortion of heroism.

He would wait for the rat-faced man, and for the opportunity to confront him. It might be tonight, and it might be tomorrow. Sooner or later, Muriday would be alone. Sooner or later, the time would be right, and Cole was determined to be there when it was.

As he waited, his eyes wandered up the street in the direction of the Refugio del Viajero, and his mind drifted to Nicolette de la Gravière, and how he wished to see her face once again. He would, he told himself, go back to the Refugio del Viajero when his business with the rat-faced man had been resolved, and he *would* see her smile, and he *would* smile back. Would merely seeing her be enough, or could more come of it?

During the long days on the trail, Cole had allowed his mind to fabricate images of a future in which he became part of her life. He closed his eyes, pictured the smile on those lips the color of chilies, and knew that he could never tire of a face like that. Naturally, such a scenario would require a reciprocal interest on her part, but when a man is imagining during long days on the trail, he's in a playground of the imagination, where everything is possible.

Cole had allowed himself to cavort in the playground of such imaginings many times over the years since Sally Lovelace passed from his reality. It had been Sally who had changed his life by turning a wandering man into a man who indulged the notion of being a settled-down man. Then too it had been Sally who turned him back.

Sally had not so much cursed his life, as she had painfully exposed the curse that had been there all along. Cole was not meant to be long in one place.

Then again, as Doc Richardson had mentioned, Nicolette *was* rendered unavailable by the fact of her "seeing" Ezra Waldron, who *was* by all appearances a settling-down sort of gentleman — or at least he had apparently seemed so until Nicolette saw the strange missive from the Denver & Rio Grande. Perhaps when he saw her again, Cole would mention to her what the coroner had said of her expressed interest in hiring him. Perhaps he would allow himself to be hired, though for her there would be no hiring, but merely his offer to assist her without cost.

That would be a situation that might make for some interesting moments — helping a woman, to whom he was attracted, in the investigation of her gentleman suitor.

Then too Cole's own curiosity had been aroused, both by Nicolette's urgency about the letter and the compounding mystery illustrated by the four Denver & Rio Grande passes.

How long his mind had been drifting and wandering these roads of imagining, Cole did not know, but he was abruptly jerked back to the reality of the moment, and the reality of his single-minded obsession with the rat-faced man.

Muriday was being pushed through the swinging doors of the saloon in the company of a fairly well-dressed fellow Cole recognized as one of the men he'd seen at the Lamy railroad camp when he delivered Stanton and Gardner to Ezra Waldron.

They left the saloon, not meandering as drinking buddies would, but moving with a sense of purpose — *or rather,* the railroad man moved with the momentum of purpose, while Muriday was brought along in tow.

Through the window of a cafe near the Plaza, Cole watched the railroad man buy Muriday a cup of coffee, and then another. It became clear that the purpose of the coffee was medicinal, not social. The rat-faced man, having had some number of drinks of another nature, was being sobered up.

Having hired Ben Muriday to deliver the prisoners dead or alive, the Atchison, Topeka & Santa Fe apparently still employed him as part of its posse, and his work was evidently not yet finished.

Assuming that the "loose ends" hypothesis proposed by Nicolette de la Gravière and restated by Richardson was correct, Cole wondered what *other* loose ends might still be left in this affair.

Fed and caffeinated, Muriday left the cafe with the railroad man after more than an hour. It seemed later than it was because the late afternoon cumulus clouds had gathered in the west.

The clouds were dark, a menacing gray that carried the suggestion of rain. At the same time, the air too carried the dusty, pungent fragrance that told of the imminence of showers.

As the sky grew darker, the reflected flash of lightning within the clouds seemed brighter, and the rumble-mumble of thunder came closer upon the luminous heels of the white-hot flash.

"It's getting close," commented a woman to her companion as they passed near to where Cole was sitting.

Indeed it was, Cole thought, instinctively touching his holster and sizing up the rat-faced man across the way.

CHAPTER 38

Wearing a vested suit and a warm smile, Ezra Waldron arrived at the bottom of the narrow staircase leading to the second-floor apartment above the Refugio del Viajero. Nicolette de la Gravière had seen him coming. She now descended the stairs to greet him and to accept the small bouquet that he had brought.

The slightest hue of indigo in the fabric of her dress, revealed in the fading light of the day, took the edge off its blackness.

Her smile betrayed nothing of the mood of darkness that had been her cloak since her discovery earlier in the day. With the encouragement of Dr. Richardson, who had called her "composed," she had decided on a course of action that had her behaving as though nothing had happened, as though she had not seen the damning letter.

Likewise, Waldron's smile betrayed nothing of his having discovered her discovery.

Nor would his words betray any indication of the fact that he had been summoned to the home office to be fired, and that, tomorrow, he would be leaving Santa Fe forever. Tonight, he decided, would be played as though nothing had changed, and as though this night were the harbinger of all succeeding nights, nights which would involve a courtship.

As they small-talked, calling each other by first name, it seemed as though all of the earlier events were merely part of an illusory dream, like a scene from a play.

As they walked, dark clouds gathered above as not-so-distant thunder rumbled. The air smelled thick with rain, but the ground remained as dusty dry as it had been in the cloudless middle of the day.

Inside the theater, as the curtain went up on Act I, the three witches came onstage to a theatrical approximation of the gathering thunderstorm outside. Tin pans clattered offstage to suggest thunder, just as the real thunderstorm erupted outside, shaking the theater. Several people clapped, and there was a small ripple of laughter. Nicolette could see that, through her thick makeup, one of the witches had a grin on her face.

"Fair is foul, and foul is fair," the trio said, setting up the theme of duplicity that would prevail throughout the evening. Nothing, they implied, was as it seemed.

Nicolette glanced left, and thought about the man seated next to her, who had seemed the fairest of men, only to now be seen as a man most foul. His calm, congenial manner contradicted everything she had read in that letter and caused her to doubt her own instincts.

On the stage, the bearded actor portraying Macbeth strutted and postured, so consumed with lust for power that he almost immediately turned on King Duncan, who had only just promoted him in rank. Beside her, Nicolette saw the bearded villain portraying the gentleman wishing to court her, a man so consumed with lust for wealth that he had turned on the employer who had promoted him to a position of great accountability.

In both instances, the promotions to posts of greater prominence had only increased an appetite for more. Greed is the fuel that feeds the fire of greed. For Macbeth, this culminated in Act I with his decision to murder Duncan.

The hotter the fire burns, the more likely it is to consume the finer qualities of rational thought, and to tip the greedy toward the witch's cauldron of madness. In a speech near the end of the third scene, came Macbeth's realization of this fact.

"Why do I yield to that suggestion whose horrid image doth unfix my hair and make my seated heart knock at my ribs, against the use of nature?" the actor asked. "Present fears are less than horrible imaginings: my thought, whose murder yet is but fantastical, shakes so my single state of man that function is smother'd in surmise, and nothing is but what is not."

As the words washed over him, Ezra Waldron swallowed hard. He felt his hands grow clammy. He wished that it was all a nightmare, and that, as in the theater, the curtain would go down and the lights would chase away the visions in his head.

At the act break, he wiped his hand on his vest and managed to cast a weak smile toward Nicolette.

"How are you enjoying the production?" he asked through parched lips.

"Very nice," she said, returning the smile.

Her lips formed a smile, but there was something in the depths of her dark eyes that he could not read.

For Ezra Waldron, the action unfolding upon the stage was only a perpetuation of a nightmare striking close to home. To cover Duncan's assassination, Macbeth was compelled to murder his two bodyguards — *his* two loose ends.

Waldron cast a forced smile at Nicolette as onstage, Macbeth lamented, "Away, and mock the time with fairest show: False face must hide what the false heart doth know."

The theater company, aspiring to the pretense of sophistication, while operating in the reality of being on the doorstep of the wilderness, did the best that it could with what it had. The actors were eager, but the staging verged on the farcical. The scene in which Macbeth beheld the apparition of a bloody dagger was more amusing than frightening, but one person *not* laughing was Ezra Waldron.

"Is this a dagger which I see before me, the handle toward my hand?" asked the man portraying Macbeth, as a ripple of giggling coursed through the audience at the sight of a man in black carrying a wooden knife across the stage. "Come, let me clutch thee. I have thee not, and yet I see thee still. Art thou not, fatal vision, sensible to feeling as to sight? Or art thou but a dagger of the mind, a false creation, proceeding from the heat-oppressed brain?"

Waldron's "dagger of the mind" was not a false creation, but the sharp edge of his own conscience.

As Act III focused on Macbeth's hiring assassins to do away with Banquo, who suspected him of Duncan's murder, Waldron's mind turned to the endless, haunting succession of loose ends.

While Ezra Waldron's mind had fixated on the blood of the serial homicides, Nicolette de la Gravière's mind settled on allegories of greed and duplicity.

Nicolette projected herself into Macbeth's speech about the nature of men.

When the assassins described themselves as men, Macbeth observed that "in the catalogue ye go for men; as hounds and greyhounds, mongrels, spaniels, curs, shoughs, water-rugs, and demi-wolves are clept all by the name of dogs."

Men, she thought, *what is it that motivates them?*

However, Nicolette was quickly reminded that it was Lady Macbeth who was the prime motivator of her husband's ambitions.

" 'Tis safer to be that which we destroy, than by destruction dwell in doubtful joy," the actress told herself.

Greed, Nicolette realized, was a *human* propensity, not an imperfection intrinsic to men alone, and in Shakespeare's telling, it was the gateway to madness. For Macbeth, this madness would be Banquo's ghost; for Lady Macbeth, the bloody spot, the "damned spot" that could not be washed away.

CHAPTER 39

Bladen Cole had followed the rat-faced man as he parted company with the railroad man and headed down a street leading away from the Plaza. Walking past a theater, Muriday paused. Through the window, a well-illuminated lobby could be seen, but the doors were closed. A check of his father's pocket watch compared to the time posted on the marquee, told Cole that the evening's performance of *The Tragedie of Macbeth* had begun nearly forty minutes before.

It seemed incongruous to see a man like Muriday studying the marquee of a theater, and stepping onto the boardwalk to scrutinize the posters. Cole had not taken the rat-faced man to be someone with an interest in Shakespeare.

Cole had never seen a Shakespeare play himself, although he recalled having been compelled to read one or two in school. Perhaps he would have been obliged to read more had the war not come around the time that he entered his teens. There was little room for much more than reading, writing, and 'rithmatic — if that — with a war raging within earshot of your classroom.

Cole watched Muriday linger for a long time then scurry away as a small number of people emerged for the intermission. The way that the rat-faced man eyed the crowd and the doorway told Cole that the remaining loose end was attending the theater tonight.

Some of the well-dressed men lit hand-rolled cigarettes, and everyone glanced at the sky, which was now pitch-black and still rumbling ominously. The first heavy splats of rain now began hitting the ground, and the people hastened back inside.

The doors were closed, and the rain began to pour.

Cole nestled himself into the shadow of a protected alcove and saw Muriday do the same across the street. As he watched the rat-faced man, the rat-faced man continued to watch the doors.

Who was the loose end?

Cole wondered if it might be Ezra Waldron himself. Had the railroad learned of his association with its rival and decided to dispose of the traitor?

Alternately, was the traitor aiming to remove yet *another* impediment to his scheme? Could it be Joseph Ames?

The rain came down with furious intensity for a long while but stopped as quickly as it had begun. The roar of the torrent impacting roofs and streets was replaced with the sounds of water dripping from eaves and rushing through downspouts.

The air was suddenly filled with that freshness that always follows a desert storm.

Cole chose this moment to leave his narrow sanctuary. His goal was to circle the block, to position himself on the same side of the street as Muriday, and there to confront him.

Circling the block took longer than he'd expected, but at last he entered the narrow alley that led directly to his quarry. He could see Muriday ahead, silhouetted against the glow of kerosene lights that lined the street.

As the lights came up at the end of the play and the audience moved into the reception hall for brandy and sweets, both Ezra Waldron and Nicolette de la Gravière were in somber moods. After all, as Nicolette had told her mother that afternoon, *Macbeth* is *such* a gloomy play.

"You don't look well, Ezra," she said, imagining her own expression was not one of buoyant cheerfulness.

"A little upset in my stomach," he admitted. "Nothing a glass of seltzer wouldn't remedy."

"How did you find the play?" she asked as he handed her a sparkling water. "You were looking very engrossed all evening."

"Was I?"

"You *were*," she said, catching herself smiling at his nervousness.

"I found it a reminder of the dangerous times in which we live," he said. "A reminder of how little society has changed since the Dark Ages."

Waldron looked into her eyes and wished for everything else to go away. It seemed so unreal that this beautiful young woman would not live to see another sunrise. Her relaxed demeanor suggested that perhaps she *might not* have perceived the letter and the brokerage statement as an indictment — but just random business correspondence. He wished that circumstances were different, but he was single-minded in his determination that his own self-preservation trumped any other emotion or distraction. He could take no chances.

"Shall we?" Waldron said at last, and they

stepped out into the New Mexico evening.

The rainstorm that had threatened earlier had come and gone, and with it went the unsettled rumbling in the clouds.

It was a clear, cool night, with that freshness that comes to the desert after a rain shower. Beyond the flickering kerosene lamps, a few stars twinkled. Beyond the area immediately surrounding the theater, few people were about on the streets.

"Lovely evening," Nicolette said, because it seemed to be the right thing to say.

"That it is," Waldron said nervously.

"You need to relax," she said. "You're so tense. The play was just a play, and the play is over."

"The play is over . . ." he repeated, letting his voice trail off.

They walked in silence for a few moments.

She *knew* the nature of his darkness, and she was growing more and more angry with herself for playing the role of a naive companion. It was, she decided, time to confirm her suspicions about the contents of the letter.

As he moved through the alley, carefully and quietly, Bladen Cole was startled to hear voices out on the street. The production had ended, and people were leaving the theater.

375

His eyes were fixed on the alcove where Muriday was. Cole had *hoped* to get to him before the crowd appeared, but he would now have to make the best of the circumstances.

Closer he came.

Thirty feet.

Fifteen feet.

Out on the street, Nicolette was ready to say something to Waldron, to probe the conundrum of the letter, when she heard a scraping sound to her left and sensed the presence of someone emerging from the darkness.

She turned to see the most frightening of apparitions, more real and more tangible than any evil that had been conjured up within the theater.

The man's face, with its closely spaced eyes and exaggerated nose, its dreadful appearance sharpened in contrast by the shadows cast from nearby gaslights, was like a hideous, ugly mask that disappeared into his collar without a chin.

Most terrifying of all was the gun which he held.

Its muzzle was pointed straight at her face.

Bladen Cole was one step away from calling

out to Muriday when he saw the man raise his gun and step forward.

In the lamplight beyond the silhouette of the gunman, he saw Nicolette de la Gravière on the arm of Ezra Waldron.

Cole's immediate thought was that he had been correct in his assumption that Waldron himself had become the loose end.

However, when Waldron pushed free of Nicolette's hand on his arm and scrambled away, Muriday's gun did not follow him.

Instead, it remained pointed at Nicolette's terrified face.

"Muriday!" Cole shouted so loud that a sharp pain stung his vocal cords.

The man turned quickly, the muzzle of his Colt now trained on Bladen Cole.

K'pow-tzing!

The sounds of the gunshot and of the bullet whisking past Cole's cheek came as one.

Cole looked into the hideous face of the rat-faced man, grotesquely distorted by the streetlights and made yet more monstrous in Cole's mind by ten years of accumulated emotions which now surged over the bounty hunter like a tidal wave.

K'pow!

The bullet caught the rat-faced man in the right shoulder, effectively rendering his gun arm useless. The orders issued by Muriday's conscious brain demanded that a finger squeeze a trigger, but the message could not get through.

The weight of 250 grains of lead knocked Muriday off balance, and he toppled to the ground.

"This," Cole told him, as he aimed his own Colt at the man, "is for William Cole, gunned down by *you* in Silver City ten years back."

Muriday looked up pitifully through the excruciating pain.

Cole hoped that Muriday remembered that night down in Silver City. He could not know that the memory of that gunfight was among Muriday's last thoughts, but he *could* read in the rat-faced man's narrow-spaced eyes, that he did realize *tonight's* gunfight had been his last.

Cole saw the rapidly growing pool of darkness beneath Muriday's shoulder and knew that an artery had been nicked and the man did not have long to live. Cole lowered his gun and was in the midst of holstering it when he felt himself slammed by a force that nearly knocked him off balance.

In an instant, Cole realized that he was enveloped in the embrace of Nicolette de la Gravière.

He looked down into the tears flowing

from those beautiful dark eyes, and heard the lips the color of chilies tell him:

"You saved my life!"

Her arms clung to him with an urgent, almost desperate, strength. He felt that he had no choice but to wrap his own arms around her.

She closed her eyes and placed a warm, moist kiss on his cheek.

Her eyes flickered open, then quickly closed.

The lips the color of chilies met his own, and time stopped.

CHAPTER 40

"Why?" Nicolette de la Gravière demanded furiously of the helpless man on the ground, tears streaming down her cheeks.

"The girl," he gasped. "Gotta kill the *girl.*"

"Why?" Nicolette repeated as she clung tightly to Bladen Cole.

"Gotta kill the girl . . ."

"Why?" Cole demanded. "Why kill the *girl?*"

"Kill the girl . . . three hundred bucks .. kill the *girl.*"

"Who?" Nicolette shrieked, the whites of her teary eyes now the color of chilies. "Who paid you to kill me?"

"Ssssuuuu . . ."

"What?" Cole demanded.

The narrow eyes of the rat-faced man looked up into the eyes of the younger brother of William Cole.

It was the last sight they would ever behold.

Nicolette pressed her face into Cole's shoulder and moaned with deep hiccupping sobs. He held her tight, running his hands over the satin fabric that cloaked her shoulder.

His eyes looked up for the first time since he had holstered his Colt. Several dozen people, most of them theatergoers, had gathered around to observe the spectacle.

When Cole's gaze met that of one of the women in the crowd, she spontaneously began to clap her hands. Another joined her, and then another, and soon Bladen Cole was receiving a standing ovation.

"What's going on here?"

Everyone looked around to see Sheriff Reuben Sandoval pushing his way through the throng.

"That man saved her life," one of the women shouted, pointing at Cole.

From outside the small crowd, there came a voice declaring, "An attempt was made on my life!"

Everyone turned to look at Ezra Waldron.

"That man tried to kill me," Waldron said, arriving breathlessly.

"No, he didn't," a man shouted angrily. "He was pointing his gun at the girl."

"That's right," another man told the sheriff.

"You ran away as soon as he came out with his gun," a woman scolded Waldron. "He was pointing his gun at *her.*"

"That's the way I saw it," said someone else from the opposite side of the crowd.

"He even *said* that he was gunning for the girl," another man said.

"I heard it too," a woman confirmed. "This man saved her life!"

"I reckon you're mistaken, sir," the sheriff told Waldron.

"But . . . but . . ." the railroad man sputtered.

"Is that the way you saw it?" Sandoval asked Cole.

"It's the way *I* saw it." Nicolette interrupted, still clinging to Cole with trembling arms. "*That man* was pointing a gun at my face."

"The dead man shot first," someone added.

"Okay," Sandoval said with finality. "I guess I got the picture. Would somebody mind going to get a tarp so we can get this out of here?"

Turning to Cole, he added: "I reckon this lady is lucky you were around tonight."

"*Cole* . . . Bladen Cole," Waldron said, recognizing him for the first time. "That's you. I want to thank you greatly for saving my life . . . *and* the life of Miss de la Gravière. You are a true hero, sir."

"What does that make *you,* Ezra?" Nicolette asked.

"What?" Waldron asked.

"Where were *you*? You ran away and *left* me. If Mr. Cole had not been there, it would be *me* lying in that dirt."

"I feared that his bullet was meant for *me,*" Waldron insisted. "Because of my position with the railroad, I have enemies, especially among the shareholders."

"Muriday doesn't look to be a typical shareholder," Cole observed as someone arrived with a scrap of canvas to wrap the body for removal.

"How do you know him?" Nicolette asked Cole.

"He killed my brother."

"*Oh no . . .* When?"

"A long time ago," Cole admitted. "More recently he's been an employee of Mr. Waldron here."

"He works for *you*?" Nicolette asked angrily.

"He's not actually an employee, he's a railroad *contractor . . .*" Waldron stammered.

"He's the man who brought back the dead train bandits," Cole explained.

"It was *him*?" Nicolette asked. "*He . . .*

killed the bandits?"

"He shot them in self-defense," Waldron explained.

Cole bit his tongue, deciding that now was not the time to reveal what he had learned from the coroner about Stanton having been unarmed when he was killed.

They all stood without speaking, having said everything that could be said.

The crowd had largely dissipated, and the sheriff was supervising the loading of the mortal remains of the rat-faced man onto a cart.

"I must once again thank you profusely for saving Miss de la Gravière and myself this evening," Waldron said to Cole. "But if you'll excuse me, I believe that it is time that I must escort her to her home."

"I'm sorry, Ezra," Nicolette said with regained composure. "I believe that I will ask Mr. Cole to escort me home, thank you."

"Um . . . er . . ." Waldron sputtered.

"Thank you for escorting me to the theater, Ezra," she added, smiling weakly with her lips, but not with her eyes.

When they had passed out of view of the theater, it was Cole's turn for a thank-you, delivered intimately and passionately, straight to his lips.

■ ■ ■ ■

"Mon chère fille!" Therese de la Gravière exclaimed as her daughter came though the front door of the Refugio del Viajero. "They wouldn't let me come!"

"When we learned that you were safe after the shooting, we insisted that Therese wait here and remain safe herself," Amos Richardson said, placing his hands on Therese's shoulders as she embraced her child.

"We have learned that I have *you* to thank for saving my daughter's life," Therese said to the man she once dismissed as a drifting cowboy.

"Yes, ma'am." Cole nodded, as Therese embraced him. She had tears in her eyes, and so too did Nicolette.

Several other people, most of them regular patrons, clustered around Therese, offering moral support by their presence. Nicolette noticed that her mother squeezed one of Richardson's hands and did not let go.

"You've got a new patient headed your way," Cole told Richardson.

"Domingo is there," the coroner replied. "He'll know what to do. I can linger here long enough to buy you a brandy."

"Much obliged," Cole said.

"Dolores!" Therese shouted across the room. "Bring this gentleman a plate of *carne asada.*"

"Mr. Cole, please join me at my table," Richardson said, following his invitation with a gesture inviting Nicolette and her mother to do so also. Dolores promptly dropped a bottle of brandy and four glasses on the table.

She winked at Nicolette, who had her arm entwined with Cole's. Nicolette blushed and smiled as she averted her eyes from Dolores's. The other patrons edged back to their tables, but one man patted Cole on the shoulder and insisted on shaking his hand.

Therese closed her eyes and sighed deeply as Richardson filled her glass first.

"To Mr. Cole," the doctor said, raising his glass.

"To Mr. Cole," Nicolette seconded quickly.

"Thank you for . . . for my daughter," Therese said, starting to cry again.

"I take it that you finally caught up to the man you were seeking," Richardson said as he and Cole passed the Plaza on their way to the coroner's office from the Refugio del Viajero.

"I did," Cole said, feeling strangely empty after having had the weight of ten years lifted from his shoulders.

"I also could not help but notice that Mademoiselle de la Gravière finally caught up to the man that *she* was seeking," Richardson said with a chuckle.

"We didn't have an opportunity to discuss the business arrangement that she mentioned to you."

"I *did* notice by the smeared lipstick that she was more preoccupied with other arrangements," Richardson said with a smile.

"Waldron said that he thought *he* was the intended victim," Cole said, changing the subject and self-consciously wiping his face on his sleeve.

"Can that be true?"

"He ran off like a scared rat," Cole said with a disgusted shake of his head. "If Muriday would have been gunning for *him*, though, he would have chased him, or at least shot after him, but he kept his .45 aimed straight at Miss de la Gravière's . . . Nicolette's . . . head. His dying words were that he was paid three hundred bucks to 'kill the girl.' It was her that he was there to kill."

"Who would have paid him to kill *her*?"

"I have an idea," Cole said. "At daybreak,

I aim to make it my purpose to find out for sure."

CHAPTER 41

The first rays of a new day's sun colored the adobe buildings of the territorial capital with the deep orange tint of fire as Joseph Ames lumbered from his home to the nearby offices of the railroad. It was the only exercise that he got, but even though it winded him, he decided that it was something he must do. He cursed his unmanageable bulk, and wished that he weighed less, and tired less, but this was a curse he had carried, with great difficulty, for most of his life.

As was the case with his erstwhile colleague, Ezra Waldron, Ames was an Easterner who had come west to guide the Atchison, Topeka & Santa Fe toward the goal of making it one of the greatest railroads in the West. Together, he and Waldron had weathered storms from the Panic of 1873 to the war with the Denver & Rio Grande Western in the canyons of Colorado.

Ames had come to admire Waldron's insight and his business acumen. Waldron was a man who had always seemed instinctively to know the right thing to do, and the best means of getting it done.

Then came that day when Ames picked up the *Santa Fe New Mexican* and discovered that Waldron had trumpeted to the world that the railroad — *their* railroad — had been laid as vulnerable as a newborn babe to a robbery of staggering scale.

What the hell were you thinking, Ezra? Ames had thought as he threw up his fleshy arms in exasperation.

This was no small misjudgment, it was a serious miscalculation which jeopardized the road in the near term, and might cost it its very existence in the long term.

Why had he done it?

Nothing he had said seemed to Ames to provide a valid answer.

Ames heaved a great sigh of relief as he reached the offices and fumbled in his pocket for his key. He had always taken pride in being the first one to work. He believed that it set an example.

"Good morning, Mr. Ames."

He looked up to see a man approaching him from across the street.

"Mr. Cole," Ames said as he turned the

lock. "You're up at the crack of dawn."

"I'm here to have a word with your friend, Ezra Waldron," Cole explained.

"You'll not find him here, I'm afraid," Ames said as he opened the door and nodded for the bounty hunter to come into the offices. He was exhausted and did not want to enter into a conversation about Waldron while still on his feet.

"He's not here," Ames repeated as he lowered himself into his substantial desk chair and began dabbing the sweat from his forehead with his handkerchief. "And he will *not* be coming back."

"What?" Cole asked incredulously. "I just saw him last night. Where did he go?"

"I received a telegram yesterday from the offices of Mr. Thomas Nickerson, president of the railway," Ames began, making sure that Cole understood that Ames was sufficiently important to be in direct communication with the president. "His instructions were that Mr. Waldron was to be relieved of his duties here in Santa Fe and that he was to report to the home office."

"Why?" Cole asked.

"For a thorough dressing down on account of his imprudent and reckless revelations to the press about the robbery. This cost the road significantly in the confidence of our investors . . . not to mention stock value. Mr. Waldron, *of all people,* should have known better."

"Makes sense that your bosses would want to call him in," Cole said. "Why do you reckon he did it?"

"Took leave of his senses?" Ames speculated.

"You reckon he might have been doing it to help the competition?"

"To help the Denver & Rio Grande?" Ames said with surprise. "I cannot image *why.*"

"What if he was getting paid by them?"

"Ezra . . . *paid* by the Denver & Rio Grande? He was imprudent . . . but he's no Judas. That's a preposterous theory."

"It's not a theory," Cole said.

"What do you mean?"

"Miss de la Gravière was here yesterday," Cole began.

"Oh, the girl from the Mexican cafe?" Ames said dismissively. "She has been coming around a great deal of late. I believe that Ezra was trying to court her."

"Yesterday, she was here when Waldron was not," Cole explained.

"That was probably when he was at the Plaza thanking that man for killing the robbers."

"In any event, she was here and found a letter from the Denver & Rio Grande on Waldron's desk."

"What sort of letter?" Ames asked, showing a level of interest he had not previously exhibited.

"A letter confirming a payment of five grand for doing that which you're writing off merely as 'imprudent.' "

"Are you saying that he was *paid* to reveal the robbery?"

"That's what it said in the letter which Miss de la Gravière saw," Cole explained. "There was also a broker's statement pinned to the letter that showed your friend Ezra was making a lot of money from investing in Denver & Rio Grande stock."

"This is beyond belief," Ames gasped. "You say that the girl *saw* this letter? Are you sure?"

"I suspect that her seeing it damned near got her killed last night," Cole said.

"What?"

"That man Muriday, the one who you railroad men hired to help bring in the robbers, pointed his .45 at her head on the street last night."

"What? What happened?"

"He's now a patient over at Doc Richardson's. Before he gave up the ghost, he said somebody paid him three hundred bucks to 'kill the girl.' "

"Who?"

"Didn't say. His talkin' time ran out."

"You cannot think it was Ezra!"

"I do," Cole said. "I reckon that he found his papers had been gone through and that she had been here. I reckon that he promised Muriday three hundred bucks."

"The girl from the Refugio del Viajero *was* here," said the clerk who had just arrived at work in the middle of the conversation. "Mr. Waldron was shouting about somebody going through things on his desk. I took the account ledger but nothing else. She *was* at his desk. Was something taken? I see that he cleaned out his desk last night."

"I came here today willing to accept Ezra's being guilty of stupidity," Ames said sadly. "Even if I were to accept Ezra's guilt for theft and fraud, I cannot imagine him guilty of murder . . . or of *hiring* anyone to commit murder."

"Then you had better let me enlighten you."

The three men turned their heads at the sound of a determined, female voice.

"Miss de la Gravière," Ames said in surprised greeting, as Nicolette entered the front door. "What are you . . . ?"

"I'm here to have a word with Mr. Waldron," she said sternly. "Where is he?"

"He's gone," Cole explained, getting to his feet. "I came here with the same idea, but our friend Waldron has got himself 'relieved,' and he's long gone. I was just filling Mr. Ames in on his getting paid off by the rival road . . ."

"And the investments in that rival road?" Nicolette said angrily.

"Mr. Cole was explaining . . ." Ames said.

"Did *you* have any idea?" Nicolette asked Ames pointedly. Where once she had been intimidated by this man, her fury had now relieved her of this dread.

"Absolutely none," Ames replied indignantly. "You know as well as anyone that I was infuriated at his actions in trumpeting this revelation so publicly."

"And he was willing to kill people to cover it up," Cole interjected.

"I can't believe it," Ames insisted.

"Did Mr. Cole tell you that the letter contained a promise of further payment for disposing of 'two loose ends'?" she asked. "Sounds to me like the two robbers who are now deceased."

"*And* a woman who knew too much," Cole added, nodding toward Nicolette.

"Do you *really* think so?" she said, looking at the man who had saved her.

"I can tell by the look in your eyes that *you* believe it," Cole said.

"I don't *want* to," she admitted. "The idea that the man with whom I had sat through a theater production all night was the man who had ordered my death . . . it's so . . . I can't find the words . . . *horrible*? No, worse than that."

"You couldn't have picked a play that was more to the point," Cole said, almost grinning.

"You know *Macbeth*?" Nicolette asked, surprised that the drifting cowboy had even *heard* of Shakespeare.

"I'm not *entirely* illiterate," he said, feigning indignity. "Read it in school when I was a kid. That fellow was hiring people to kill everybody he knew."

"And *this* fellow hired Muriday to kill *me,*" Nicolette said sadly. "I suppose I realized this as soon as I found myself staring at that ugly man and Ezra ran away."

"Just like he hired Muriday to kill Stanton and Gardner," Cole added.

"Muriday killed them in a gun battle," Ames insisted.

"Doc Richardson can tell you that Gabe Stanton never held a gun and he was shot point-blank," Cole replied. "Why don't we stroll over there right now and you can ask him . . ."

"I cannot possibly walk all the way over *there,*" Ames said, almost desperately.

"I could go fetch him," the young clerk offered.

"Sure, go," Ames said with a toss of his fleshy hand.

CHAPTER 42

"It's gone," Nicolette de la Gravière said grimly.

"I would be surprised if it was *not* gone," Amos Richardson said. "If there was a document that implicated *me* in grand theft and a succession of killings, I would not leave it lying around to be discovered *twice.*"

Amos Richardson had reached the offices of the Atchison, Topeka & Santa Fe to find Nicolette practically ripping apart the desk that once belonged to Ezra Waldron, as Bladen Cole and Joseph Ames looked on.

Most of the paperwork that had been there yesterday was gone, but she was thrashing the remnants. Then she pulled the contents from a bottom drawer and almost idly thumbed through the contents. It was mostly very routine looking paperwork. Angrily, she turned the stack upside down and began repeating the process.

"What's *this*?" she exclaimed.

"What *is* it?" Cole asked, maintaining his place, seated atop another desk.

"It's a statement from the same brokerage firm," Nicolette said excitedly. "I recognize the letterhead."

"What does it show?" Ames asked. "Let me see it."

"It's from the same firm, Ripley, Storey & Bledsoe, dated from two months ago," she said. "It looks like he missed it when he was cleaning his desk because it was upside down. It shows him buying the Denver & Rio Grande shares."

"That's unmistakable," Richardson said, looking over her shoulder.

"Indeed," Ames said when he was handed the paper. His tone reflected a hint, almost, of sadness. "It does show that he owned their shares. Of course, we all know that their share price has risen to more that double that at which he purchased these shares. I know of Ripley, Storey & Bledsoe. They're one of the largest firms dealing in railroad shares."

"Is this what you fellows call a 'killing in the stock market'?" Cole asked ironically.

Richardson stifled a chuckle. Nicolette merely shook her head in disgust.

"To think that I was working just two desks away from the man," Ames said, staring at Waldron's name on the statement.

"At least you don't have to live with the realization that you were holding his hand in a darkened theater," Nicolette said, wiping her hand on her dress.

"Out, damned spot," Cole said with a wry expression on his face.

Nicolette responded only with a sputter of disgust.

"About the killings of the bandits," Ames said, addressing his remarks to the coroner, "Mr. Cole tells me that you found some evidence . . ."

"Only that one of the men was unarmed when he was killed at point-blank range," Richardson said. "Given the nature and occupation of the victim, it's not the kind of thing that would get a man on trial for murder, but it *does* show that Muriday made a deliberate decision to kill him rather than bring him in alive."

"What is it that I'm supposed to hear, Doctor?"

Everyone now turned to see Sheriff Reuben Sandoval come through the door with Richardson's assistant.

"I took the liberty of sending Domingo to fetch the sheriff," the coroner explained. "I think we should start at the beginning . . . with what Mademoiselle de la Gravière told

400

me yesterday."

Nicolette repeated the story of her discovery once again, for the benefit of the sheriff and the coroner, and Cole added the story of the attempt that had been made on Nicolette's life.

"Where is Waldron now?" Sandoval asked.

"He's been summoned to the home office," Ames explained. "Called to explain himself, and almost certainly be fired."

"That's not much of a penalty for a man who has done what he's done," Richardson said. "Of course they don't know the half of what he has done."

"It's not much of a penalty for a man who has made himself rich through his double-crossing ways," Nicolette added.

"They'll know," Ames interjected. "They will know before he arrives, because they'll be receiving a telegram *from me.*"

"There's the matter of an attempted murder," Cole interjected.

"With no witnesses, *that's* a hard one to prove," Sandoval cautioned.

"Can't you bring him in and *make* him confess?" Nicolette asked.

"Where is he?" Sandoval asked. "You said that he's been called back East?"

"The morning train," Ames said. "There's an eastbound train from Lamy that's leaving . . . just about now. He's probably on it."

"Can't you telegraph them and ask them to hold the train?" Cole asked.

"It's too late," Ames said, looking distressed that he had not thought of this sooner. "However, I *can* telegraph Cibola Station and tell *them* to hold the train."

"I'll go get him," Cole said, getting to his feet. "If I ride hard, I can be out there in probably three hours."

"Good," Ames said. "That's around the time that the afternoon train from Lamy will pass through Cibola. I'd hate to have *two* trains delayed."

"Of course," Cole said cynically.

As his name was being taken in vain in the offices of the railroad in Santa Fe, Ezra Waldron was climbing aboard the morning train, bound for points east, accompanied by the loyal Nathaniel Siward. Waldron knew that he could not leave behind the man who had ordered Ben Muriday to murder Nicolette de la Gravière on his behalf.

All night long, as he hurriedly cleaned out his desk and packed his bags, Waldron had thought about that terrible moment when Muriday had stepped out of the shadows.

"While night's black agents to their preys do rouse," Macbeth had said. "Thou marvell'st at my words: but hold thee still; things bad begun make strong themselves by ill."

Every time Waldron closed his eyes, he saw that terrible face and recalled the thoughts that had gone through his mind at that moment. Whenever he closed his eyes, he saw the beautiful woman with lips the color of chilies lying dead in a pool of blood.

He knew that he had been falling in love with Nicolette de la Gravière, and he knew that he would be haunted for the rest of his life by the image of her smile and nagged by the question of "what if."

"Avaunt! and quit my sight!" Macbeth told the ghost of Banquo. "Let the earth hide thee! Thy bones are marrowless, thy blood is cold; thou hast no speculation in those eyes which thou dost glare with!"

"Avaunt . . . quit my sight," Ezra Waldron murmured as the train rumbled, about to begin its journey.

"What?" Siward asked.

"Oh," Waldron said, opening his eyes. "I was just thinking about the theater production that I saw last night."

Through that entire production, Waldron had glanced from time to time at Nicolette and been puzzled by her relaxed smile. She had certainly seen the letter, but he gradually became convinced that she did not know what it all meant.

She was bright and intuitive, but was he reading too much into this? Was he a fool for thinking that a *woman* could understand the nuances of share prices?

At one point during Act IV, as he looked over at her beautiful face and her soft features, pleasantly smiling at the production, he had considered standing up and rushing out to call off the assassination.

He had not, of course, done that.

He decided that with a plan in motion, nothing should be done to jeopardize its momentum, or its outcome, or the money that was accumulating in his accounts.

Nicolette de la Gravière would have to die — beautiful, young Nicolette de la Gravière would have to die — in the service of sheltering Ezra Waldron's accounts.

It made him sad that this was the way things had to be, but it *was* the way things had to be.

"We're moving," Siward observed.

Waldron opened his eyes. He had dozed off, which was no wonder, given that he had not slept at all the night before.

His nightmares faded in the light of the

day. Night's black agents retreated to their caves deep in his subconscious.

"I'm glad to be done with Santa Fe," Siward said. "Guess we're getting out in the nick of time."

"Don't worry," Waldron assured him. "With Muriday dead, there's nothing to connect us . . . *either* of us . . . to the shooting last night."

"She's going to be telling everything she knows," Siward reminded him.

"Let her," he said, subconsciously patting the jacket pocket that contained the letter. He could have burned it, but he would need it when he walked into a certain office in Denver.

"She has not a single shred of evidence, nor is there anyone who can corroborate anything that she might have seen," he continued. "I doubt very much that she understood half of what she saw."

"Then why did you want her . . . ?" Siward started to ask.

"Just to make sure . . . to tie up all the loose ends."

"Doesn't it matter that this is a loose end that didn't get tied off?"

"By sundown, we'll be nearing Raton, and then we'll be across the Colorado line, and rid of New Mexico for good," Waldron assured him. "Nobody is going to bring anyone back across state lines on the flimsy word of a girl . . . are they?"

"I guess not," Siward said, relaxing.

"That is if they can find us." Waldron smiled as he closed his eyes. There would be an assumption that they were traveling all the way to the end of the line to answer Waldron's summons to the home office, but they were traveling on passes, so there were no tickets confirming this.

Waldron knew that he would step off the train in La Junta. Working through the mail, he had purchased a horse that would be stabled there. From there, he would ride this horse to Denver, where his accounts resided.

He supposed that Nathaniel Siward would probably also detrain in La Junta. Assuming that Siward was asleep as the train reached that station, Waldron entertained thoughts of just leaving him on the train, but he would not do that.

Siward did not realize that he too was a loose end, but he was. Last night, Waldron had failed to take care of a loose end — partly, at least, because he hadn't taken care of it personally. At La Junta, he would not fail.

Despite assurances to the contrary, Nathaniel Siward would not share in the harvest that Waldron planned to reap. Waldron wanted it *all.*

CHAPTER 43

"I'm sorry to be doing this to you," Cole said. "It's just gotta be done."

The roan just whinnied disgustedly and shook his neck. Cole had been riding him hard, with five minutes of galloping alternating with ten minutes at a walk. The heat of the day was upon them, and the roan was quite fed up with this urgent routine.

"It won't be long now," Cole assured him, not knowing himself how soon Cibola would come into their view.

Bladen Cole had ridden out of Santa Fe three hours before, armed with a written authorization on Atchison, Topeka & Santa Fe letterhead to remove Ezra Waldron from the train, signed by Joseph Ames. If there should be any doubt, he also carried a note signed by Sheriff Reuben Sandoval, which deputized him to bring the fugitive finance man back to Santa Fe.

"How much do you want as a fee?"

When Ames had opened negotiations for this bounty hunt, several figures had entered Cole's mind, but in light of the circumstances, he said that it was on the house.

Rarely had the bounty hunter engaged in a manhunt that was as time-critical as this one. He was anxious to reach Cibola as soon as possible, not because of Joseph Ames's concern about the railroad's schedule, but out of knowing that Waldron would grow suspicious if the train was stopped for no apparent reason. Cole didn't imagine there was much that Waldron could do out here in the middle of nowhere, but he did not want to take any chances.

Reluctantly, he kicked the roan into a gallop once again, and with even greater reluctance, the loyal horse began to run.

Coming over a low rise, Cole looked out into the distance and saw a small cluster of clapboard buildings. Because they had all been constructed of wood, rather than adobe, Cole knew immediately that they were railroad company buildings. This was confirmed by the line of telegraph poles stretching into infinity in ether direction from the buildings. As he came closer, he could see the rails, paralleling the telegraph poles into those two infinities.

What Cole did *not* see was the morning

train — nor indeed a train of any kind. Nor could he hear the chugging or whistling of a train in the distance.

Having decided that he must have made a wrong turn, he hoped that there would be someone at the buildings who could point out the direction to Cibola.

It was not until he read that place name on a sign at the end of one of the buildings that Cole knew that this *was* the place where the train was supposed to have been stopped.

"Howdy," he shouted to a man who emerged from the building to watch his approach.

The man waved back, acknowledging his arrival.

"Reckon this must be the Cibola Station," Cole said as he dismounted.

He was thankful for a hitchrail with a watering trough that was positioned in the shade.

The roan was ecstatic.

"Yep," the man confirmed. "If you was to be a-lookin' for Cibola, then I'd be telling you that you had found us."

"I was wondering about the train," Cole said.

"Then you'd be about twenty minutes early," the man said. "But I hate to tell you that you'd be about twenty minutes out of luck."

"How does that work?"

"On the morning train, we'd be a flag stop," he explained. "We put up a flag and she'll stop for ya. Afternoon train's a through train. Don't stop for hell nor high water . . . not that there's ever gonna be much in the way of high water in these parts."

"I take it that the morning train's already passed through?" Cole asked, fearing the inevitable.

"You missed that one by near three hours," the man said. "But you don't have to worry none."

"Why's that?"

"Because there's another one coming through tomorrow," the man said with a broad smile. "You're welcome to camp overnight right here."

"I had been told that the office in Santa Fe was going to telegraph you to stop the morning train here in Cibola," Cole said, finally getting around to finding out what had happened with Joseph Ames's promise of holding up the train.

"How come?"

"Some big problem."

"Didn't get no such telegram," the man

411

said. "There's no telegrams today."

"Why is that?"

"Well, you know that storm that came through last night?"

"Yeah."

"We lost the lines sometime in that. The country's so flat in places that the lightning likes to jump onto the telegraph wires. The lightning burns 'em clean though. I've seen it happen. There'd be a big *pop* and a lot of sparks."

"How long does it take to fix?"

"Depends. It depends on where it happened and how long it takes to find. Also depends on whether it got broke in more than one place. There's two hundred miles of telegraph along this railroad in New Mexico Territory . . . and the break *might've* happened up in Colorado."

"I understand," Cole said with a nod.

"You're welcome to go ahead and wait for the train tomorrow," the man said, ending the conversation to go back inside the station.

"Much obliged," Cole said, studying the timetable as he followed the man inside. "Looks here like these two trains get into La Junta, Colorado, at the same time. Is that right?"

"Five minutes apart," the man nodded.

"Like I said, the afternoon train out of Lamy is a through train. They both have scheduled stops in Las Vegas and up at Raton, but the morning train makes more flag stops and whistle-stops so it takes longer. The afternoon train has pretty well caught up with the morning trail by La Junta. It's at La Junta that they become the same train. Both sets of cars are pulled by the same motive power across the rest of Colorado and Kansas because there's no more mountains. It's as flat as the palm of your hand all the way to Kansas City."

"I see," Cole said thoughtfully.

Cole walked around to the other side of the station, where there was a short platform and a small bench for waiting passengers.

He stepped to the track and looked in both directions as the parallel steel rails converged far in both distances.

He pondered.

He thought.

He decided that he had come too far to turn back.

Returning to his horse, he removed the saddle and carried it into the station.

"I was wondering if I might stash my saddle in your baggage room for a couple of days?" Cole asked the station attendant, dropping several coins on the counter of the ticket booth.

"Sure," the man said. "You're welcome to board your horse out it the corral yonder too."

"Much obliged," Cole said sincerely, placing a gold eagle on the counter. "I'll pay in advance."

"You reckon to be back in two days?"

"Round about," Cole said. "No more than four, I reckon."

"Okeydokey," the man said, reaching into a drawer. "Lemme get you set up with a ticket on tomorrow morning's train."

"Actually, I'm planning on bein' on *today's* train," Cole said.

"Like I was saying before," the man explained, saying the words slowly, as though he were talking to someone who forgot things as soon as they were told. "The train's already been through here three hours back."

"I'm not talkin' abound *that* train," Cole replied. "I'm talkin' about the one comin' in round about ten minutes."

"But, mister, I done 'splained that the afternoon train don't *stop* in Cibola. Can't flag it down."

"I'm betting another eagle that you can make it *slow* down, though," Cole said, rolling another gold coin around between his fingers.

Cole crouched near an especially large bush of mesquite, which screened him from the view of any train approaching from the west. Some distance away, the station man was reluctantly burning brush, and glancing at him periodically.

The air was still, and the smoke rose mainly straight up, but from time to time, a little whiff of wind, a harbinger of the unsettled air that moved in with the afternoon cumulus clouds, would stir the black column and a bit of it drifted briefly over the tracks.

The bounty hunter shifted his eyes to the western distance.

The sound began as a barely perceptible hum in the steel rail ten feet from his right ear.

Next, there was a smudge of smoky grayness in the western distance, perched above the vanishing point of the converging rails like a dot on a letter "i."

He heard the distant clatter of pistons and push rods grow steadily louder as the smoke from the locomotive's firebox grew more prominent.

The shriek of the locomotive's whistle spoke of an engineer who had seen another source of wood smoke. The rapid chugging became slower. There was the hiss of air brakes and the squeal of metal on metal as the locomotive slowed.

A wave from the station man was answered by toots from the whistle.

The rumble of the train grew to thunder as the locomotive closed in.

Suddenly, it was right there.

It moved much more slowly than it had been traveling, but its speed was still considerable when judged by a man crouching still.

Cole watched a passenger car slip by, and then another.

Realizing that he was out of his mind, he rose and began to run as fast as he could along the gravel ballast next to the track.

He cursed at having weighted himself down with his rifle scabbard strapped across his back.

A baggage car, really just a glorified boxcar, came next.

It seemed studded with handles, but Cole's attempts to grab one failed.

He ran closer, so close that he could smell the grease and grit on the second baggage car.

He reached out, grabbed, and caught the metal in his hands.

The speed of the car, slightly greater than that of a man on a dead run, jerked suddenly. He felt as though his arm had been pulled out of its socket, but it had not.

Cole lunged upward, grabbing the next higher handle.

He felt his boots bounce on the gravel, then lift into open air.

Kicking and scrambling, he found a lower rung with his feet and hung on for dear life.

Now firmly attached, he finally exhaled and took a deep breath. Despite the smoke, this sigh of relief felt exhilarating. It also felt good to know that he had survived, and the nightmare scenario of being sucked beneath the car and sliced in half by the wheels had not transpired.

He could now take stock of his situation.

He was aboard and whole. Had he not tethered his hat with a chin strap, it would have been gone. He had not dropped the rifle scabbard strapped over his shoulder and was now glad to have it.

Meanwhile, the train was picking up speed again.

He looked down at the ground rushing past at a mile a minute. He had never experienced anything quite like this. Looking at the ground started to make him sick, so he turned, looked up, and began to ascend toward the roof.

This climb, while being buffeted by the continuous blast of air, seemed to take forever, but at last he was on top of the car. From here, he was able to climb back down between the cars, where he was out of the wind and could sit down and rest.

Ezra Waldron had not been stopped at Cibola, and he was better than three hours ahead, but at least the bounty hunter now knew that he was following him in a vehicle that was traveling at the same rate of speed, and slowly gaining on him as his conveyance stopped more often. Tomorrow in La Junta, Cole would be only five minutes behind Waldron.

CHAPTER 44

"How about a cold beer, Mr. Waldron?" Siward said as the train shivered to a stop in
Las Vegas, New Mexico. It was the last
scheduled stop before they neared the state
line at Raton.

"That is an appealing suggestion, sir," Waldron said, leaning back in the upholstered
seat. He watched as Siward crossed the
platform toward the man with a galvanized
wash pan filled with melting ice and beer
bottles, and thought about New Mexico,
the two years he had spent here, and how
he had never really felt at home.

He thought about how he missed his old
life in the hubs of the financial world, and
about how, given the present circumstances,
he really should not go back to the East. He
needed a new start, preferably in a place
where he wasn't known, and this is what he
planned.

"How were things in Las Vegas?" Waldron

said, more than asked, as Siward returned with two bottles, still damp and slippery to the touch from the tub.

"Didn't see more than the platform," Siward said. "Talked to the agent for a minute. He said the telegraph line is down somewhere between here and Santa Fe."

"How'd that happen?"

"He reckons the storm last night. There was a lot of lightning."

"Are they getting it fixed?" Waldron asked, realizing as he did so that telegraph lines and railroad lines were no longer subjects that should concern him.

"He said they found the break and they're gonna get it patched up."

"Good," Waldron said, without really caring.

He held the pleasingly cool bottle in his hand and studied Probst and Kirchner's maker's mark on the label.

"Without the railroad, this wouldn't be possible," he told his companion. After a professional lifetime in the railroad business, he was unable to distance himself from the notion of taking pride in that mode of transportation. "Without the railroad, it would simply not be possible to walk across a platform in Las Vegas and buy cold beer made in Santa Fe."

"Here's to railroads and cold beer, Mr. Waldron," Siward said, touching his bottle to that of the man whom he still considered to be his boss. "Without the railroad, there wouldn't be any civilization *at all* in places like this."

"To new beginnings," Waldron said, closing his eyes to savor the frothy, amber liquid rolling across his tongue.

As the contents of the bottle gradually slipped away, Waldron gradually slipped into that condition of half slumber that is the nearest facsimile of sleep available to most patrons riding a rhythmically jostling railcar.

In that condition of semi-siesta, gauzy curtains parted and the marvelous Nicolette de la Gravière appeared, her lips the color of chilies and her smile more radiant than ever.

He watched her face turn and her jaw go slack in terror as it had last night.

Was it only just last night?

It seemed like days, at least a week, since the trembling revolver of the grotesque Ben Muriday had turned the flawless face of Nicolette de la Gravière into a mask of horror.

Waldron awoke with a start.

There were beads of sweat trickling down

421

his cheeks, and the skin beneath his collar felt unbearably clammy.

"What did we do?" Waldron said.

"What do you mean?" Siward asked.

"Did we really almost kill a woman?"

Siward looked around. Fortunately, the adjacent seats were empty, and in the clatter of the train, voices did not carry far.

"Not so loud," he cautioned Waldron nevertheless.

"I'm not that kind of person," Waldron insisted, loosening his collar. *Am I?*

"What's done is done, Mr. Waldron. Nobody will ever know."

"I suppose," Waldron said, not articulating his fear that *he* would always know.

"I don't like knowing my own part in it, but what's done is done," Siward said. "I don't like it any more than you do, but you said it was necessary. You kept saying that all the loose ends kept getting in the way of the plan . . . so I reckon we did what had to be done."

"But, a *woman* . . ."

"Not so loud," Siward whispered. "But she ain't dead, so you just have to get over it."

"I keep seeing her face in my mind," Waldron complained.

"You'll never see her again. You're near

two hundred miles away from her now, and getting farther every minute . . . and you're never going back."

"You're right. I'm just exhausted from lack of sleep."

Waldron was just about to doze off again when the train suddenly jerked, shimmied, and quickly wheezed to a stop.

"What the hell is going on?" he sputtered, the hissing of his voice mimicking that of the air brakes

"May I have your attention, please," the conductor said as he came into the car. "We are making a flag stop in Wagon Mound. We anticipate a layover of about thirty minutes while we take on passengers and water. Feel free to step outside, but don't wander too far."

"How far is it to Raton?" Siward asked.

"We are exactly sixty-five and seven-tenths miles from Raton," the conductor replied, proud to know the distance down to the nearest tenth of a mile. "I anticipate our arrival in one hour and forty-eight minutes."

"Reckon it wouldn't hurt to stretch my legs," Siward said, standing up.

Waldron took out his pocket watch, as though handling and winding it would make time move more quickly.

He looked out the window, at Siward

wandering about the platform, and at the rocky cliff in the near distance that was the landmark and namesake of this desolate outpost.

He thought about Siward's choice of words, when he had said that without the railroad, there wouldn't be any civilization in places such as Las Vegas.

To this, Waldron added that in places such as Wagon Mound, and other whistle-stops through which they had just passed — such as Watrous, Shoemaker, Optimo, Bond, and Cibola — the railroad constituted the *only* civilization.

The man with the pan filled with beer had refreshed his ice by the time the second eastbound train of the day arrived in Las Vegas, but Bladen Cole was not buying. It was not that he wasn't thirsty, but that he was a stowaway without a ticket.

His letter from Joseph Ames authorized him to come aboard an Atchison, Topeka & Santa Fe train to remove one Ezra Waldron, but it did not authorize him to stay aboard for a ride. Depending on the agent or the conductor, he might be able to make the argument that it did, and he could always offer to buy a ticket now that he was already aboard, but he did not want to take a chance on being tossed off *this* train.

He knew that he should have gotten Ames to issue one of those railroad passes that allowed you to ride comfortably in a passenger car — but that would have applied only if the train stopped to let him aboard.

Between the cars, Cole rode anonymously. No one noticed him, and for the moment, no one would bother him. However, as he well knew, a man sitting between cars would stand out like the trespasser he was the moment the cars came to a stop at the station in Las Vegas.

Where could he hide?

Would he be noticed on the roof?

What about beneath the car? He could slide under there and hang on when the train was in the station. No, he would not. He could imagine no more terrifying place in the world than hanging beneath the train, and becoming trapped there as it picked up speed. He'd take a chance on his powers of persuasion and the letter from Ames before he'd do *that*.

As he pondered this dilemma, sitting in the space between the two baggage cars, with the cacophonous din reverberating all around him, he stared at the baggage car rattling along, six feet opposite where he was seated, and studied the door. It would be nice to get inside, but a locked door was as useful as the solid wall on the car where he was sitting.

He could probably force the door, but not without doing noticeable damage, and he did not want his presence to be noticed. Thinking that he might try to pick the lock, he began looking around for a suitable tool. The best he found was a piece of stiff wire wrapped around one of the railings.

Having unwound it, he stepped carefully across the chasm where the two cars were coupled and grabbed the handle nearest the door. This handhold wobbled slightly as though it was coming loose, but it held.

Taking a deep breath, he began exploring the inside of the lock with the wire. He felt the tumblers. They were old-fashioned ones, large and sturdy, which reminded him of the old locks that he and Will used to pick for kicks when they were boys.

Will.

It had been less than twenty-four hours since the ten-year road to the avenging of Will's death had come to its end, but Cole had been too obsessed with the avenging of the near-murder of Nicolette de la Gravière to pause for reflection.

Picking a lock was a matter of the subtleties of sound and touch, and in the clamor and lurch of the train, neither of these senses was available to him.

The tumblers were stubborn and resisted his efforts.

Finally, one desperate twist and he could feel with the wire that they had moved.

Stepping inside the musty interior of the car, Cole closed the door and relished the relative quiet. The noise was still deafening, but no longer did it threaten to rattle the teeth from his skull.

The way that the baggage and freight were positioned gave indication of the order in which they were intended to be removed, so Cole fashioned himself a place of concealment that was likely to be disturbed last, possibly as far down the road as La Junta.

It was here that the two trains would be joined as one, and Cole could step out of this car and simply walk up to the passenger car where he would astonish Waldron with an unexpected surprise — or at least that was his plan.

Chapter 45

"What . . . where . . . ?" Ezra Waldron said, waking up suddenly. He felt the jerking and hissing of the braking train as the demons that had haunted his catnap fluttered away on leathery wings, back to their hiding places in the recesses of his subliminal mind.

"Must be Raton . . . *at last,*" he said, opening his eyes.

"My recollection was of a town that was a lot bigger," Siward observed, looking out the window at a handful of dismal little shacks, which cast long shadows in the late afternoon sun.

"This is probably just the edge of town," Waldron said, leaning back. "Maybe there's another train in the station. The engineer is letting it clear before we pull forward. We'll be moving in just a minute."

A minute came and went, and then another. Soon, these two were joined by several more.

"We *aren't* moving," Siward observed.

His was not the only such observation. Several other passengers in the car were grumbling and remarking. One man pushed down a window and leaned out.

"Hebron," he said.

"Hebron?" someone asked incredulously.

For some, the first thought was of the ancient city of Israelite refuge, which was mentioned in the Book of Joshua. Waldron knew it as the Atchison, Topeka & Santa Fe whistle-stop a dozen miles south of Raton.

"How long are we going to be stuck here?" someone shouted as the conductor came into the car.

"All I can tell you is that the station agent received a telegraph message requesting that the train be stopped and held here," the conductor explained.

"Why?" another man shouted.

"I don't know that," the conductor admitted, clearly chagrined not to have the answer.

"How long?" Waldron asked.

"That I don't know either."

"I'll see about this," Waldron said, standing to detrain.

Followed by Nathaniel Siward, he stepped onto the platform and strode purposefully to the stationmaster's office inside the small depot building.

"I'm Ezra Waldron," he announced. "I'm an executive of this road with important business at the home office. I insist on knowing the reason for this delay. Is there something wrong with the tracks ahead?"

"Not that I'm aware of, sir," the man said, rising in the presence of a superior.

"Then why are we stopping?"

"I received a wire from Santa Fe, sir. Orders to have this train stopped until further notice."

"I thought the telegraph wires were down," Siward said.

"They were. All night and until about an hour ago. They've gotten them repaired."

"Who ordered the train to stop?"

The man put on his spectacles and picked up the telegram.

"Mr. Joseph Ames, sir."

"Ames?" Waldron said angrily. "What is that damned fool playing at?"

Waldron cursed under his breath and paced the stationmaster's office, making the other men nervous.

"I herewith countermand that order," Waldron said at last. "Get this train running."

"I can't do that, sir," the man said.

"Why the hell *not*?" Waldron demanded.

"The rules state that no order issued by

any main office can be countermanded in the field except in cases of imminent loss of life . . . I'm very sorry, sir."

"Damn you, man," Waldron shouted. "Get that train running!"

"Can't do it," the man said firmly. "I'd lose my job."

"Then I'll send a wire to Ames and tell him to order you to do it," Waldron said, stomping out of the office with Siward at his heels.

They went to the telegraph desk, where Waldron scratched out a message and exhorted the agent that it be sent to Santa Fe without delay. Waldron had no idea that *he* was the reason for Ames ordering the train to be stopped. He assumed that Ames still wanted him on his way to the home office as expeditiously as possible.

"Wish they had beer for sale here," Siward observed after having watched Waldron pace the platform for nearly half an hour.

His boss simply glowered.

In the distance, they heard a train whistle and looked down the track behind the stationary train on which they had arrived in Hebron. There was a tiny smudge of smoke on the horizon. With the earlier train having been delayed by lengthy whistle-stops, the later train was finally catching up.

"That's the through train," Waldron observed with a sense of relief. "They can't stop the through train. We'll just transfer our baggage to the through train and be on our way."

"That's easier said than done," Siward said cautiously. "There's no siding here in Hebron. Our train is in the way. It would be impossible for another train to pass ours. If *we're* stopped . . . they have to stop."

"Damn it," Waldron muttered, launching into a tirade of curses as the second train came into view.

"Now you have the through train stopped," he said to the agent as he appeared in the depot doorway. "Surely you'll have to move this train forward to a siding to let the through train pass by."

"Sir, my orders are to let no trains proceed past this point on the line," he replied as they heard the hiss of the through train's air brakes.

"I've already wired Ames, telling him to rescind this damned fool order," Waldron said.

"Sir, when I hear from him, I'll waste no time in releasing *both* trains," the man promised.

He then turned to go back to his office, leaving Waldron and Siward on the platform with the smattering of travelers from their train who were also pacing in frustration as they watched the through train pull into the station, its brakes hissing loudly.

"You left Santa Fe without saying good-bye."

Ezra Waldron turned quickly at the unexpected sound of a familiar voice.

It was Nicolette de la Gravière.

"You left so *quickly* last night," she continued.

"How did you get here?" he asked. "Why are you here?"

"When I learned that you had left on the morning train without saying good-bye, I knew I must catch up to you. There are so many things that were left unsaid between us. Mr. Ames was so kind to give me a pass . . . and to arrange for me to be driven to Lamy to catch the through train."

He blinked his eyes in speechless disbelief.

"You left so quickly last night that I did not have a chance to ask you why the man's gun was pointed at *me*," she said, her tone more stern than angry. "Do you know why, Ezra? Did this have something to do with a certain letter that you left on your desk . . . a certain letter from the Denver & Rio Grande?"

"You had no call disturbing my papers," Waldron said as the small woman in the dark blue traveling dress walked steadily toward him on the platform.

"Had *you* a call to scheme a robbery against your emloyer for your own personal gain?"

"You can't understand . . ."

"Your letter was quite clear," she said.

"What letter?" Waldron retorted with a nervous chuckle. "You said you saw a letter, but can you *produce* such a letter?"

"There was also the matter of a certain brokerage statement," Nicolette said pointedly. "Do you find the names Ripley, Storey & Bledsoe familiar?"

"Many people have accounts with them."

"How many people working for the Atchison, Topeka & Santa Fe purchased shares of the Denver & Rio Grande a month before a robbery on the former caused the shares of the latter to nearly triple in value?"

"Where's the statement that shows this?"

"You left *last month's* statement behind," Nicolette said. "Everyone knows what happened to the value of the shares, and with *that* statement, everyone knows that *you* own shares in the other railroad."

"I don't believe you."

"If you don't believe me," she said slowly,

"you may ask Sheriff Sandoval in Santa Fe. He's keeping the statement safe for you in his office."

"You've made your point," Waldron said quietly. She had now approached to a point just an arm's length away. "Let's just put this whole misunderstanding behind us. Come away with me. I have plenty of money. We could recapture some of the magic that we had . . . that you *know* we had."

"You still haven't answered my question," she said, ignoring his invitation. "But I think I *know* why that gun was pointed at *me* last night."

"I don't know what you're talking about," Waldron insisted.

"*He* does," Nicolette said, nodding to Siward. "I can see it in his eyes. As I remember, when that evil, ugly man lay dying, I demanded that he tell me who hired him. He started to say something that started with the letter 'S.' I thought he was just hissing, but he was saying 'Siward,' wasn't he? You're part of this too, *aren't you*?"

Siward blinked and looked away.

"What do you want?" Waldron asked, almost pleading. "Come with me. Come away with me. I have money, lots of it. If you came, we could have a . . ."

435

"I'm not going anywhere with you but *back* to Santa Fe," she said. "I want *you* to tell Sheriff Sandoval why that gun was pointed at me . . . I want you to tell him the *truth.*"

"Did *you* bring a gun, Nicolette?" Waldron said, continuing to back away. "Are you going to *force* me to go back?"

"I have no gun," she said, matching each of his backward steps with a forward one of her own. "I only came to ask that one question, and to tell you that you can never escape the *truth* . . . no matter how far you go . . . no matter how much money you have."

By now they had passed from the platform and away from the station to the threshold of the wilderness that had been cleaved by the steel rails.

He looked down at her beautiful face, bathed in the deep light of the sunset, and thought of their happy moments together. He looked down at her lovely features, exaggerated by the deep shadows of the edge of night, and thought of his haunting dreams.

He turned and walked away.

"I'll never let you forget me, and I'll never let you forget the gun that was pointed at my head," she promised, deliberately walking after him.

"Get away from me," he shouted. "Just leave me alone, you harpy."

"I've been called worse," Nicolette said with a taunting chuckle.

In the gathering darkness her voice came to him with the same texture of his nightmares. Maybe it was the exhaustion of having gone so long without sleep, or perhaps it was the weight of thinking of all his gold, languishing in accounts that lay waiting for him, but which were still just outside his reach.

If only Muriday had succeeded in killing this damned wench, she would not be here pointing her accusing finger at me, Waldron thought.

As he stared into the evening that was closing in on this desolate whistle-stop, an idea swam out of the darkening shadows of his mind.

After Siward had said that the railroad had brought civilization to Las Vegas, Waldron had the thought that in these whistle-stops, the railroad was the *only* civilization.

If a killing took place *here,* there would be no Sheriff Sandoval to investigate it. The railroad was the *only* civilization, and Waldron was, for the time being at least, *still* the railroad.

They were now well away from the sta-

437

tion, and the people back there had more pressing concerns to preoccupy them. Nobody was watching. It was getting dark, and nobody was looking their way.

What if *Siward* tried again to kill the girl?

What if he succeeded *despite* Ezra Waldron's attempts to save her?

What if Waldron succeeded in killing Siward in the tussle for the gun, this being Waldron's own desperate struggle for his own life?

Two loose ends, two last loose ends, would be loose no more.

"Just shoot her, damn it," Waldron demanded of Siward in a low voice. "Finish her off."

The hotter the fire burns, the more likely it is to consume the finer qualities of rational thought, and to tip the greedy toward the cauldron of madness.

"No, sir," Nathaniel Siward said. "I can't. We've done enough. We just have to stop. I can't . . . *We* can't . . ."

Ezra Waldron lunged angrily, grabbing the gun from Siward and wheeling around to point it directly at the beautiful face of Nicolette de la Gravière, the exquisite Nicolette de la Gravière, the enchantress, with her deep, dark eyes and her lips the crimson of chilies.

Bladen Cole's finger squeezed the trigger of his Winchester.

EPILOGUE

Autumn had come to the Mogollons in the fullness of its glory. The leaves on the aspens, painted deep gold by the season, fluttered across the foothills like an infinite treasury of golden eagles.

In the meadows, the sun was still warm on the back of the neck, but in among the ponderosa, the air was cool with the promise of winter. When the two riders paused to let their horses graze, the only sound above the level of the satisfied crunching was the light breeze whispering though the highest branches and the occasional racket of a woodpecker.

The higher they rode into the mountains, the deeper the blue of the sky became, until it was the most luminous cobalt imaginable, a color which invited the eye to drift aloft to linger, or to follow the progress of an eagle of the feathered species.

There were dangers deep in the Mogollons, the stronghold of the Chiricahua, but knowledge of saving the life of the son of a certain Chiricahua leader had spread though the mountains like shafts of light, and that light shone on these two riders.

The nights were cold, the sort of cold that invited a closeness to the campfire, popping and spitting as the flames licked the pine sap. As the fire turned to embers, the stars were bright, so vivid indeed that the Milky Way seemed to conceal the infinitely deep and distant blackness of the sky the way a warm buffalo robe enclosed those who paused to marvel at the infinite.

The sunrises of the clear mountain mornings were vivid and deep with color. The first thing the rays touched was the tops of the not-so-distant snowcapped peaks, and the palette was the deep rich color of butterscotch, or of the best Kentucky whiskey, depending on who was crafting the metaphor.

The mornings dawned so bright and so magnificently clear that one was tempted to marvel that the ends of the earth could be seen, if only one could climb to the top of yonder ponderosa.

They rode, not toward the points of any compass, but toward tomorrow, with yesterdays resolved and situated in permanent and settled places on the distant shelves of worldly endeavors. They rode onward, charting the course of a journey they dreamed would never end.

"Look," she said, reaching across to gently touch his wrist. "Look over there, through the trees. I can see red sandstone cliffs."